Praise for *Scissors, Paper, Rock*

"I finished *Scissors, Paper, Rock* in an unstoppable burst of enthralled reading last night. It is a wonderful book."
—Richard Howard, poet and professor of creative writing, Columbia University

"A wise and compassionate novel. . . . Johnson movingly conveys the senselessness of death, the inevitability of loss and the failure of families to shield us from either."
—*Publishers Weekly*

"Fenton Johnson has made Kentucky and the family the theme of what is perhaps the first novel to bring AIDS to the heartland. . . . Like all great storytellers, Johnson worries repeatedly a handful of narrative threads, confident of the old wisdom that no two tellings are alike, that each rendering brings a story along, uncovers its further essence. . . . Graceful . . . UNIQUE."—*San Francisco Examiner*

"I am amazed by the strength of these characters (so many!), by how sharply and unforgivingly they are drawn, and by the way the reader is compelled to love and forgive them. Raphael, the gay son, is a hero for our time or any time. I wish everybody who has a family or ever had one (chosen or inherited) would read this."
—Shirley Abbot, author of *Womenfolk*

"A deeply affecting novel about families and loss."
—*Philadelphia Inquirer*

"*Scissors, Paper, Rock* is a book about family, a book about memory, a book about depicting love and family and community as a continuum. . . . *Scissors, Paper, Rock* may be the best novel to date encompassing the themes of homosexuality and AIDS. It is beautifully written."
—*Lexington Herald-Leader*

"Fenton Johnson's novel is a journey into America; destination Kentucky, the family, the human heart. *Scissors, Paper, Rock* is an eloquent discourse on the wilderness of the human heart, and a profound meditation on what it is to endure."—Tom Spanbauer, author of *I Loved You More*

"A tender, haunting account of a rural Southern family's demise . . . *Scissors, Paper, Rock* manages to be both intimate and panoramic. . . . The book is especially strong in its exploration of the varieties of grief that accompany death and losses."—*Kirkus Reviews*

"*Scissors, Paper, Rock* teems with stubborn life. . . . Writing of endurance, memory, and of love, Johnson has created a traditional story about a new kind of death, where the young die in the arms of the old."—*Montreal Gazette*

"Strong and self-assured. . . . *Scissors, Paper, Rock* evoke[s] all the complexities of family and community both past and present. With its treatment of homosexuality and AIDS at its core, it could possibly be found to be indispensable."
—*West Coast Review of Books*

Scissors, Paper, Rock

Scissors, Paper, Rock

A Novel

FENTON JOHNSON

 UNIVERSITY PRESS OF KENTUCKY

"High Bridge" was published in a different form in the *Chicago Tribune*'s 1986 Nelson Algren Fiction Competition. It was later revised and republished in the *San Francisco Sentinel* and in the Winter 1988–89 issue of *Turnstile* and is included in *Henfield Prize Winning Stories* (Warner Books, 1992). "Back Where She Came From" was published in a different form in the *Sewanee Review*, Vol. 97, No. 4, Fall 1989. "Little Deaths" was published in the *Los Angeles Times Magazine*'s annual fiction issue, June 28, 1992. "Cowboys" was first published in a different form in the *Greensboro Review*, No. 43, Winter 1987–88, and later included in *Best of the West, Vol. 2: New Short Stories from the Wide Side of the Missouri* (Peregrine Smith Books, 1989).

A verse from the song "Fox on the Run" (lyrics by Tony Hazzard) is used by kind permission of Tony Hazzard and Mann Music Publishers Ltd.

Published by The University Press of Kentucky

Scholarly publisher for the Commonwealth,
serving Bellarmine University, Berea College, Centre College of Kentucky, Eastern Kentucky University, The Filson Historical Society, Georgetown College, Kentucky Historical Society, Kentucky State University, Morehead State University, Murray State University, Northern Kentucky University, Transylvania University, University of Kentucky, University of Louisville, and Western Kentucky University.
All rights reserved.

Editorial and Sales Offices: The University Press of Kentucky
663 South Limestone Street, Lexington, Kentucky 40508-4008
www.kentuckypress.com

The Library of Congress has cataloged the hardcover edition as follows:

Johnson, Fenton.
    Scissors, paper, rock / Fenton Johnson.
       p. cm.
    ISBN 0-671-79542-2
    I. Title
PS3560.03766S35   1993
813'.52—dc20

ISBN 978-0-8131-6656-8 (pbk : alk. paper)
ISBN 978-0-8131-6657-5 (pdf)
ISBN 978-0-8131-6658-2 (epub)

This book is printed on acid-free paper meeting
the requirements of the American National Standard
for Permanence in Paper for Printed Library Materials.

Manufactured in the United States of America.

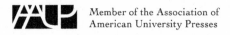 Member of the Association of
American University Presses

for
Lawrence Thomas Rose
and
Margaret Melanie Beene

Contents

Foreword

Fenton Johnson and I met in 1992 at the Bay Area Book Awards ceremony. We were both nominated for awards, and neither of us won. Adrienne Rich was there (surely she won something), and Fenton and I were giddy with the opportunity to pay our respects—two young writers invited to kneel (and we did kneel, literally) at the feet of a master.

Fenton and I recognized each other instantly and thoroughly, creating the kind of jolt to the system that gets a person believing in reincarnation, destiny, and soul mates—all those things the cynical side of one's heart tries to keep at bay. We were part of several of the same tribes, some of them obvious, some of them not so. The first words he said to me were "Cowboys are *my* weakness too." I had read *Scissors, Paper, Rock* before we met; read it again, starting when I got home that night; and a few more times over the last twenty-three years, when I taught it to various groups of creative writing students; and again, after perhaps a decade of *not* having read it, in preparation for writing this introduction.

To say that I had forgotten how good the novel is would be disingenuous. Living, loving, and dying as they do, in the deep ravines of Strang Knob, Kentucky, the Hardin family is, in my opinion, one of the most memorable families in all of literature, evoking shades of Faulkner's Compsons, Welty's Fairchilds, and Harper Lee's Finches. Tom Hardin, the family's patriarch, is every bit as enigmatic, as complex, as *multiple* as Jane Smiley's Larry Cook in *A Thousand Acres* or Flannery O'Connor's Hazel Motes in *Wise Blood*.

In 1992 many reviewers called *Scissors, Paper, Rock* the best novel to date encompassing the AIDS crisis, and I believe it remains worthy of that assessment. And there is no denying the novel's power to evoke, through the chapters narrated by the baby of the family, Raphael, the experience of a young gay man as he leaves his home in rural Kentucky in the late '70s, bound for San Francisco, and subsequently lives through the epidemic of the early '80s, only to return home to Kentucky in the midst of succumbing to the disease himself.

Also unforgettable is the elegant and efficient form Fenton has chosen for the novel: chapters that work like stand-alone short stories, narrated by various members of the Hardin clan—some who have stayed in Strang Knob, some who have fled. Chapter by chapter we witness each character's most dangerous hopes and problematic desires, their daily predicaments as well as the events that caused them life-shattering grief. We learn of Tom's stubborn pride, Bette's hidden shame, Raphael's silent rage, and Rose Ella's impossible reserves of strength that always show up at the unlikeliest times and places.

It's hard to forget that the time line of the book is not organized chronologically, or even according to any simplified version of narrative logic; instead, chapters are placed in sequence according to how they will ignite associative sparks among them, on the level of metaphor as well as on the level of plot. The book comes together less like a traditional novel and more like a quilt, handmade in an attic sewing room and thrown over a four-poster bed. Family secrets are often revealed later rather than sooner, and always at the exact moment they will pack the most punch.

Nor had I forgotten that *Scissors, Paper, Rock* is written with Fenton's rare blend of fearlessness and sensitivity, that it defies easy classification (novel versus collection, family saga versus gay coming-of-age story), and that it is deeply honest, well crafted, and full of generosity and heart.

But what I *had* forgotten since my last reading—perhaps because I was not quite old enough a decade ago to fully recognize it—was the wisdom, compassion, and grace with which Fenton renders this extended family (the Hardins, their cousins and neighbors, the brothers at the local Trappist monastery, and especially Miss Camilla, the spinster who lives next door), these locations (San Francisco and rural Kentucky), and this very particular period in time (1942–1992).

During my most recent reading, I was amazed (noting the youthful author photo) at how comprehensively Fenton understood, even then, that we carry our families—their love and their burden—with us wherever we go and that their disapproval lives inside us like an autoimmune disease forever, making us susceptible to specific kinds of trouble for the rest of our lives. But Fenton also knew that a piece of good ground—if we inhabit it fully and with an open heart—can live inside us too and can even, in the hardest times, rescue us from ourselves, can show us—if we sit still there long enough—how to turn what we thought of as weakness into a way to rise.

In perhaps the novel's most powerful scene, in a chapter called "All Fall Down," Tom and Rose Ella Hardin, whose marriage is fraught in the best of times ("they bound themselves to each other," Miss Camilla says of them, "and it was a hurtful binding"), try to reckon with the death of their eldest son, Clark, in Vietnam and wind up attacking each other physically, raising bruises and drawing blood. After the fight and the sex that follows, after Rose Ella understands that Tom is "daunted by the largeness of her heart—by the completeness and certainty of its demands," after she reflects that "I am the one who forgives . . . this is the source of my pain and power," she thinks: "Grief is like any wound—some terrible pleasure resides in it. Better to knead that pain, that terrible pleasure than to have nothing at all. If love fulfills itself in companionship, grief fulfills itself in solitude, for we grieve finally and necessarily less for the dead than for our living selves, our aloneness in our survival, our inescapable invitation to the dance" (76).

In Miss Camilla, the novel finds not only an axis around which the Hardin family spins, not only a receptacle for all the Hardin family secrets, but also a way to speak in its own voice. In the book's final chapter, Miss Camilla confesses, and gossips and philosophizes—one is inclined to say *testifies*—about *Scissors, Paper, Rock*'s ultimate subject: "What is love but the intersection of memory and desire, past and future? . . . In love something miraculous happens. In loving someone we give them an ideal against which to measure themselves. Living in the presence of that ideal, the beloved strives to fulfill the lover's expectations. In this way love makes of us the bravest and best persons that we are capable of being" (228).

Since that night long ago at the Bay Area Book Awards, I have come to know Fenton Johnson as a gifted teacher, a brave and exacting writer, a deeply thoughtful philosopher, a loyal friend, an entirely reliable colleague, an accomplished two-stepper, and one of the last of the great Southern gentlemen around. When I think of our time together, I think of long investigative conversations about art and literature, faith and hope, love and God and death, in a car driving over Colorado passes, at a four-hour breakfast in the East Village, around a chrome and Formica kitchen table in a rented house in Provincetown, Massachusetts, or on a hiking trail surrounded by the Martian green of the spring palo verde in the Superstition Mountains.

In an introduction to the collected works of the Canadian short story writer Clark Blaise, Fenton writes, "Across a lifetime a writer's words, diligently and honestly compiled, allow his essential character to emerge, and as it emerges to shape what comes behind, a symbiosis between art and nature in which the writer shapes the clay that shapes himself." And in *Keeping Faith*, the book that followed *Scissors, Paper, Rock*, Fenton wrote, "The greatest philosophers so completely and seamlessly inhabited their lives that death was of no consequence, since to betray one's principles would be to betray oneself—a living suicide worse than any that might come from the poisoned cup or on the cross."

These two quotes, taken together, have always seemed to me to comprise Fenton's life project: to compile words diligently and honestly, so that he might feel that he is completely and seamlessly inhabiting his life, to the extent that it is possible for anyone to do so. *Scissors, Paper, Rock* is a book that is "all in" on this project in every regard, and for that reason it is a net that catches all of us—male, female, gay, straight, urban, rural, devout, atheist—all of us engaged in the process of loving, of being loved in this difficult world. I'm excited for you, if this is the first time you are coming to it. I predict it will not be the last.

Pam Houston
Author of *Cowboys Are My Weakness*
and *Contents May Have Shifted*
Founder and Director, Writing by Writers

High Bridge

[1990]

On his workshop bench Tom Hardin lines up the woods he has chosen, his favorites: chocolate-brown walnut; ruddy cedar he has cut and cured himself; bleached white cypress, salvaged from mash tubs at the old distillery and smelling faintly of young whiskey. To these he adds newcomers: gingko, buttery smooth and yellow; wild cherry, pale rose, from a tree he'd planted himself, forty years before.

Rose Ella, his wife, is dead. Before him—who would have thought it? A year and a half ago she'd helped shovel him into an ambulance, to take him to a Louisville hospital where they'd removed most of his cancerous gut. He'd recovered, to stand half-hollowed out and hear the doctor give him a year to live. Across the next months he and Rose Ella talked very little and thought a great deal about what was to come of her after his death.

Now she has been dead for almost six months, while he stands among the antique tools and stacked woods and power saws of his woodshop, assembling wood for a lamp for Miss Camilla Perkins, his next-door neighbor and in forty-seven years of marriage the only woman he has kissed besides his wife. "Forty-seven years and one other woman," he says to himself. "And that just a kiss." He is astonished by his loyalty. If on his wedding day someone had predicted this, he would have laughed out loud.

When he turns his back to the woodshop window he

hears his children's voices, chanting the naming poem they'd made up themselves—what Rose Ella called the litany of the stars:

> JOE Ray, BARbara, LES and CLARK,
> GET ready, GET set, ON YOUR MARK,
> BET-te, ROBert, then there's RAFE,
> WHICH one OF us GETS—HOME—SAFE !

The first time Tom Hardin heard these voices he turned around, expecting to see the hot, bright green of the yard filled with the menagerie of neighborhood children *his* children always attracted, especially after he built them a swing set from scrap iron. But when he turned around, it was midwinter gray, the swing set long since dismantled and given to one of his sets of grandchildren. Nothing filled the yard but ghosts.

It was the cancer, he decided, or more likely the chemo they gave him for it, that was making him crazy, or (worse yet) sentimental. Today when he hears the voices he turns on his shortwave weather radio and hunches more closely over his work.

Since Rose Ella's death he has kept all but one of his children at bay. In various ways they have asked to come; through muleheaded stubbornness he has kept them to weekend visits. Not by words—he avoids talking of his illness—but by his plain refusal to be cared for. They have their own lives and he is careful to remind them of this: jobs, families, community responsibilities.

Only Raphael, his youngest, has come back. At thirty-six, he is not married, has never had so much as a girlfriend. Instead he brings home men from San Francisco, where he lives—a different man every summer. With those visitors,

Rose Ella was civil, even flirtatious. Tom Hardin stayed in the shop.

This time Raphael has come home alone. Out of the blue he showed up one day, looking thin and anxious—he'd quit his job, a decision of which Tom Hardin disapproves. Whatever the job, to his way of thinking a man didn't up and quit without good reasons, and if Raphael has good reasons he has yet to set them forth.

With his foot Raphael pushes open the door. He carries two mugs of coffee, which he sets on the workbench. "I brought your coffee."

"I can see that." Tom Hardin points with his plane, the old-fashioned kind with the knob and the crossblade, that requires muscle and a good eye. "Set it over there."

"So how are you feeling?"

"Not bad." How good can a dying man feel? Tom Hardin holds his tongue.

"Mind if I look on?"

"No, not at all." All through his childhood Raphael never set foot in the shop except under threat of a whipping. Now he wants to look on. It is this, the changing of things, that angers Tom Hardin. For all their lives he and Raphael have hardly spoken to each other except to snap and back off. When circumstance forced them to speak on any subject of consequence, they found themselves brought to some cliff, over whose edge lay a fact of Raphael's life for which Tom Hardin had no words and about which Raphael seemed eager to keep silence. How was it possible to talk about something when no speakable words existed to name it? Snap and back off—that was safest, even if afterwards Tom Hardin felt some kind of guilt that was itself unnamable.

But now Tom Hardin is dying and they are supposed to

get along, here is Raphael asking to be taught in a month what it took Tom Hardin himself a lifetime to learn. "What kind of wood is that?" Raphael asks, pointing.

"Gingko. Came from the monastery walk. You remember those big trees where you used to park for midnight mass."

Raphael shakes his head. "I guess that was before my time."

Tom Hardin puts on his glasses and holds the wood to the window. Raphael flips on the overhead fluorescent. With the board Tom Hardin swats the switch off. "I need the sun to look at this." He turns it back and forth in the window's square of light.

"Well." Raphael stands and brushes his jeans of wood shavings. "Time for my session with Miss Camilla. You want your coffee? It's cold."

"Leave it. I'll drink it."

Raphael shuts the door behind him with a careful click.

The last time Tom Hardin drank coffee his stomach seized up in knots, but he has not told this to anyone. When he sees that Raphael is inside Miss Camilla's house he takes the coffee, opens the door, and pours it on the ground.

In 1953, when Camilla Perkins was forty years old, she moved to Strang Knob and applied to the parish board to teach penmanship and English in the Catholic grade school. Hiring her would be a radical step: she'd be their first lay teacher. Tom Hardin, who was on the parish board, knew they decided to hire her because they believed her safely into spinsterhood, no temptation for the high school boys or the men of the parish.

She was tall, thin, *arch;* curlicues of dyed black hair dangled over her arching forehead, penciled eyebrows arched over deep-socketed, protruding eyes. When she moved in next door

Rose Ella had dismissed her as plain—Tom Hardin himself had agreed.

But she'd been in Strang Knob only a few months before this became clear: She was a city woman, come from Chicago, who had about her if nothing else the allure of contrast. Here in Strang Knob the women of Tom Hardin's generation were lined and sagging from childbearing. Weighed down by babies, groceries, laundry, gravity, they'd grown thick in the hips; they'd slowed their steps and words and thoughts.

At forty Miss Camilla was plain, but with her years her blanched skin stretched tight. She'd come to speak and walk with a forward-moving intensity that commanded attention: she was a teacher.

At forty-one Tom Hardin had too many children and a life that was slipping through his hands. Raphael, number seven, was due that December. Tom Hardin felt trapped. When that November friends asked him to go deer hunting in upstate Wisconsin he fled, leaving Rose Ella a three-word note: "I'll be back." In it he folded two crisp one-hundred-dollar bills.

"Guilt money," Miss Camilla told him later on their first drive to High Bridge. She was blunt about this, like everything else; it was another reason Tom Hardin liked her. Women under Strang Knob were not raised to be blunt. Daughter of a Strang Knob woman, Camilla Perkins had not been raised to be blunt, but she was plain and came to understand this early on. "What have I to lose," she'd said to Tom Hardin.

Rose Ella, who was married and not plain, could not bring herself to voice her anger. She took the two hundred dollars that Tom Hardin left to buy food and Christmas presents for the children and bought herself a new coat. In 1953 two hundred dollars bought a very nice coat indeed—a scarlet wool knee-length affair with a real mink collar. Miss

Camilla learned all this because five days after Tom Hardin left to hunt deer, Rose Ella came to her backdoor, the scarlet knee-length fur-collared coat flapping about her swollen belly, to beg for money to buy groceries until Tom Hardin returned. Miss Camilla had just bought a new car and was none too well off herself, and so for the next two weeks the six Hardin children ate supper crammed around Miss Camilla's walnut gateleg table, with Bette C., the youngest, perched on a stack of *Compton's Pictorials.*

Tom Hardin looks up from his workbench to see Miss Camilla hobbling across the yard. She has had two heart attacks; she has been told she will not survive the third, and that it may come at any time. Weather permitting she comes over daily to his shop. On this cold January day, weather most certainly should not be permitting, but she is coming. Tom Hardin likes her for that.

He pulls up stools by the stove, pours them both a finger of whiskey in plastic cups. Miss Camilla raises hers to the rafters. "The meeting of the Mostly Alive is called to order," she says gaily. He raises his cup, touches it to his lips, sets it down with a grimace. "Forty years of making this stuff and all of a sudden I can't stand the taste of it."

"I saw Raphael leave," Miss Camilla says. "I saw you pour out your coffee. You really think it's important to hide that from him? He's a grown man, you know. He's no stranger to trouble. He left a job to be with you."

"Any job that he can just up and quit can't be much of a job," Tom Hardin says. "In my day you knew a man by his work. Furniture, or tobacco, or plumbing—things you could call a name."

"Like whiskey." Miss Camilla raises her cup.

"Like whiskey. Now all they turn out is paper. And to me one piece of paper looks pretty much like the next."

"Raphael worked at a library in San Francisco. A *big* library, which you know perfectly well. A fine job, I might add, that he must have good reasons for leaving, which you don't know and which you've never asked after."

"How do you know what I know," Tom Hardin says, but he grins at her impertinence.

"Between teaching your children, knowing you for almost forty years, and listening to Rose Ella complain about your faults, I think I have a good idea of what you know. A better idea, I think, than you, sometimes." She touches her whiskey to her lips.

Tom Hardin takes up his glue bottle and finds it clogged. He tries to squeeze it open by force of strength, but he can't squeeze hard enough to clear the spout. He takes out a knife and carves away the dried glue. "Everything is so goddamn slow," he says.

Miss Camilla drains her cup.

Live dangerously: he scrabbles among the litter on the workbench until he finds the prime block of his best walnut. To its four sides he glues thin planks of pale gingko. He clamps this work in a vise, then sits heavily, breathing hard. "You watched through all that. Rafe would have asked five questions, not one of them worth the time it took to spit out."

"And he would know more than I do."

"He would know the names of things, but he wouldn't know how to *do* them. I'll bet you could come back here tomorrow and do what I just did, do it in the same amount of time and do it good."

"*Well,*" Miss Camilla says. "Do it well, and I would do it well, I will be happy to do it well." She stands and picks up her cane. "It was *good* to talk to you. Try to remember: you work *well;* you do *good* work."

Tom Hardin returned from that upper Midwest hunting trip with a magnificent ten-point rack. Raphael was born a week later. In that week Rose Ella lay around the house, swollen and waiting, while he went to the shop to mount the antlers on a plaque of worm-eaten chestnut he'd saved for a special occasion.

Tom Hardin required of his sons that they earn the right to enter his shop. Excepting his oldest friends, the men of the town stood outside until invited in. On his second night back from Wisconsin, Miss Camilla strode in, refusing him so much as a knock. She planted her squat black pumps on the poplar planks. Burned by the heat of her arching gaze, Tom Hardin saw her for the first time as something other than plain. "You have abused your wife," she said. "You must apologize."

"Apologize, hell. She's got her coat." Fresh from a hunt, ten-point rack on the bench before him, Tom Hardin was feeling rambunctious. He was sanding the chestnut plank. He shook it at her, not meaning to threaten, only wanting to make clear who here was boss.

She jerked the wood from his hands and slammed it to the floor. It split along the grain. "I have no desire to lecture you on things you already know. You know what is good and what is evil. One way to know evil is that those who commit it hide from what they have done. You are hiding, here, from what you have done." She left, walking sweaterless into the December night. Standing in the light from the doorway, Tom Hardin watched her cross the yard, her pumps leaving dark circles in the frozen grass.

He was at the distillery when Rose Ella went into labor.

She did not call him but drove herself to the hospital. When after work he found the house empty, he asked Miss Camilla to drive him over. At the hospital he had her wait, while he bought roses for Rose Ella from the florist in the lobby. As he left the florist's shop he held them extravagantly high: December roses! Miss Camilla gave him not so much as a nod.

Raphael was a difficult birth. Tom Hardin and Miss Camilla waited together long into the night. In the stuffy hospital heat the roses wilted. When the next morning the nurse called his name, Tom Hardin took Miss Camilla's hand, pulled her along; he wanted her to witness this gift.

Rose Ella lay spent, black circles under her eyes, hollow-cheeked. Raphael lay in a crook of her arm, unmoving. The last two or three babies had come so easy, Tom Hardin had forgotten that birth could be this hard. He lay the roses on the bed. "Dead flowers," Rose Ella said, turning her face to the wall.

These nights Tom Hardin sleeps not at all. How can he sleep, with no guts to anchor his body to its bed? If his problem were only the pain he would have no problem. But each day he leaves a little more of his life behind. In the mornings, crossing the flagstone patio (stones he had hoisted and cursed into place) he is sapped of a half-hour's strength. He sits in the shop, breathing heavy and shallow, until he hears Raphael open the back door to bring coffee. Then he stands and picks up a piece of wood, or an awl, or an oil can, anything to look busy. "It's not like Rafe would know what goes with wood and what doesn't," he grumbles to Miss Camilla, one morning after Raphael has come and gone.

"*As if*, please, introduces a dependent clause. It's not *as if* Raphael would know the difference."

"Besides, you'd think he was on vacation."

"Is that so terrible, that he would spend vacation time with his father?"

"He drags out here at ten o'clock with coffee, like I ever drank coffee in the middle of the day. Then he mopes around all day taking naps and hits the sack before I do. You'd think he was the old man."

"Maybe he's not feeling well," Miss Camilla says. "Maybe you should ask after his health."

"Health, hell. Until this little liver problem came along I'd never been to a doctor in my life except to get sewn up from when I'd cut myself doing something I should have been smart enough not to do in the first place. And even then I had Rose Ella take out the stitches. He's thirty years old, for Christ's sake."

"Thirty-six," Miss Camilla says wearily. "I take it you've scared him away from asking questions."

"He hangs around. He's persistent, I'll give him that much."

"What he has to say is important. Otherwise he could bring himself to speak." She takes up the glue. "How many more layers are you planning to have me stick on this thing?"

"It's nearly done. The hard part comes next, the turning on the lathe." He hands over the planks of sweet-scented cedar. "You still drive," he says. "I see you take your car out."

Miss Camilla glues a plank in place and sets and clamps the block. "Just for trips to the store, or to church."

"How about going for a drive, some sunny afternoon?" From his perch near the stove he tosses her a rag to wipe the glue from the bottle spout. He can see her hesitating; probably she knows where he will want to go. "A dying man's last request," he says. "That's a joke."

"I suppose I owe you something for all this woodworking education," she says. "What do we have but time?"

By February things come to the point where Tom Hardin cannot work at his bench. Something new is happening here— he feels the cancer spreading. At night he places his hand on his side, feeling the cancer pulse with a life of its own, its beat a half-beat behind the beat of his own heart. He cannot escape the notion that he is doing this to himself—the cancer is a part of himself, after all, that is killing him, and taking its time in getting around to it.

As he has lost the will to ward off the voices and visions, they have grown more persistent. As a young man he needed to forget—he was too much immersed in life to spend time in memory. But he is old now, and the landscape of memory is vast and varied. His children are wrong in thinking he is growing forgetful. What they mistake for forgetfulness is its opposite: too much memory rather than too little.

On sunny days he does nothing but sit and remember, he who has worked every waking minute of his life. Rose Ella learning to set bank poles, until she was a better fisher than any man in town; his son Clark riding shotgun when they delivered Christmas baskets; Bette C. in cheerleader skirts, boys swarming after her like bees; Raphael, pulling from the drive in the old Rambler, on his way farther west than any of them had ever imagined he might go. The bad times recall themselves too—Bette C.'s screaming insistence that he allow her to go away to college; Joe Ray's accident; the impenetrable silence that always surrounded Raphael. But memory has done its job, beveling the pain's sharpest edges. Tom Hardin remembers less his hollow grief at Clark's funeral than the soft nap of the flag folded fresh from his coffin, the snap and crack of the guns' salute, the bugler's embarrassment at bungling "Taps."

These voices and spirits are growing more real than the planks of wood covering his workbench or Raphael's living presence. Dwelling in memory, Tom Hardin considers the measure in which, for a strong-willed person like himself or Camilla Perkins, how much of death is a matter of choice, a decision at some point to give up and yield to others the carrying on of things.

He wills himself awake. He is not yet ready to sink into memory—he has too many tasks left to finish. The block of laminated wood sits before him. The gluing has not been done well, but he is pleased to find that he faults neither himself nor Camilla—finally, this late in life, is he beyond fault and faulting? He hopes only that the block will hold for the lathe, and that when the time comes he will be able to uncover the living form concealed in its multiple woods.

In the mornings Raphael still brings coffee, but he cuts short his hanging around to imply questions. Instead he crosses the yard to Miss Camilla's, where he stays for two or three hours. This delays her arrival at the shop. Tom Hardin finds himself getting irritated with Raphael, though he knows he has no reason; it's not as if Raphael is holding something up. Miss Camilla will work her way across the yard in her own good time. What concerns Tom Hardin more is the thought that she may be revealing to his son a life that she would never show to him. "What do you *do* over there anyway," Tom Hardin says to Raphael one snowy morning, when it is clear that Miss Camilla will not make it across the yard.

"Nothing much."

"So you sit around like lumps on a log."

"We talk about books. Miss Camilla taught English, you know. She doesn't get much chance to talk about that kind of thing."

"Do you talk about her heart? How is her heart?"

Raphael grins. "You know Miss Camilla. She'd no more talk about her heart than"—he pauses a small second, searching for the comparison—"you'd talk about your liver."

"You talk about me?"

Against the window's glare Tom Hardin sees the outline of his son's chin, identical to his own: cut with a T square, nicked at its corners. Identical yet not identical—something of Rose Ella's chinlessness sneaked in here; or maybe it's that Raphael does not set his chin exactly like Tom Hardin. "You talk about me," he repeats, no question this time.

"She talks about you, yes. She's eager to talk about you. Always has been."

"You're hogging her time." Tom Hardin speaks sharply, then regrets his words; not their sharpness, but the showing forth.

Raphael picks up both mugs, still full. "I'm here now, dammit. What more do you want." He kicks open the door and dumps the coffee in the snow. He crosses the yard to Miss Camilla's, leaving the shop door open. From his seat Tom Hardin watches the coffee's brown stain, until the falling snow covers it over.

The snow has not completely melted when Miss Camilla next crosses the yard. Tom Hardin opens the door, but she does not come in. "Why can't you acknowledge that he is here?" she asks. "And what he is here for?"

Tom Hardin turns away to pick up the laminated wood, still clamped. His fingers test its seams. "It's trying to warp. That could be a problem."

"Is it because he used to avoid your shop? He'd be happy to learn, if that's what you want. He wants to learn."

"In three months. Four months."

"Do you think he gave up a job and came back only for that?"

He turns to her then. "Rafe hasn't said a word to me. If he wants to tell me something, let him say it. He knows how to talk."

"He is too much like you to speak first."

"He is *not* like me," Tom Hardin growls. "Let him get a woman. He's never had a woman. He's never even mentioned a girlfriend. He's not married. He has no family."

Miss Camilla's face tightens, bitter and narrow. "Neither have I, old man." She turns and stumps across the snow-puddled yard.

A month after Raphael was born, Tom Hardin drove Miss Camilla in her brand-new DeSoto on their first trip to High Bridge. By then Rose Ella was speaking to him, to ask him to chop more wood or to see to the leaky faucet in the outbuilding where they'd rigged up a bathroom. That was all she was saying; no gossip, no jokes, no flirting.

One February day snow closed the schools, but by noon the sun emerged and the main roads were clear. Tom Hardin left the distillery to visit Miss Camilla.

He asked her to go for a drive, asked if he could drive the brand-new DeSoto. She must have wondered when he drove on and on but she did not ask to turn back. He was on the parish board, after all. He had voted to hire her—Rose Ella had seen fit to remind Miss Camilla of as much, across those days when Tom Hardin was hunting in upstate Wisconsin.

The sun was low by the time they reached High Bridge. Built over the Kentucky River gorge, it was Andrew Carnegie's proof that the impossible could be done. At the time he built it, High Bridge was the world's highest railroad bridge, carrying the Cincinnati Southern south from Lexington to the coal mines of Kentucky and Tennessee. Three years later someone built a higher bridge, and someone else built still higher bridges after that.

Tom Hardin and Miss Camilla walked on the pedestrian catwalk to the middle of the bridge. Words crowded his heart, jammed against each other in his throat—he stole sips from a half pint tucked in his pocket. Far below in the long winter shadows, the cornstalk-stubbled bottomland was dusted with white. From a tiny farmhouse a single trail of smoke rose to spread flat, a thin gray tablecloth of haze covering the bottoms.

"Wait," Miss Camilla said, touching his arm. "I can feel the bridge shaking. A train must be coming."

In a moment they heard its whistle, in another moment they saw it round the bend. The engineer blew his horn in short, angry blasts. They were close enough to see him shake his fist. The bridge vibrated and hummed, its webbing of girders swaying in harmony with the train's speeding mass. Miss Camilla's eyes narrowed with alarm. Tom Hardin cupped his hand to her ear. "It's OK!" he shouted. "It's built to do that!"

It seemed natural then to slip his arm around her shoulder and press his mouth against hers. For the long minute of the train's passing he kissed her. She neither resisted nor kissed him back. Then the caboose passed, sucking up the train's roar and leaving behind only the jeering shouts of the brakemen.

She pulled away. They stood until the last echoes tangled themselves in the trees' bare limbs. Then she spoke, still looking out over the valley. "Is this a bribe?" She plunged on, not waiting for his answer. "I know your kind. You think any flat-chested woman should faint in your arms and be grateful for the chance. I've known your kind for years. I've fought them for years. Don't think you're any different, just because you gave me a job." She turned away, to step smartly along the catwalk in her neat black pumps. In shame and anger Tom Hardin trailed behind.

On an indifferently sunny day in late March, Miss Camilla and Tom Hardin take their last drive, with Miss Camilla peering through the steering wheel of her 1953 DeSoto. Raphael waves them off. "Have a safe trip," he says. Tom Hardin feels like giving him the finger, but out of deference to Miss Camilla he keeps his hands in his lap.

They are hardly out of the drive before Tom Hardin turns to Miss Camilla. "How about driving to High Bridge?"

"I knew you would ask that. That's more than an hour, and I've seen better roads."

"We'll go slow. 'What have we got but time?'"

She ignores his small mimicry. "Why do you want to go back there, of all places?"

"You know why I want to go back there."

She does not answer, but she turns in the right direction. Tom Hardin settles back in his seat.

It takes two winding hours. They pass landmarks: My Old Kentucky Home, where Stephen Foster never set foot; Perryville Battlefield, where on a hot, drought-ridden September day, eight thousand Union and Confederate soldiers died in a fight for a drink from the only running spring.

They reach High Bridge at noon. Spring is early—on the south-facing side of the river, redbud and white and pink dogwoods bloom against the limestone palisades. Miss Camilla parks in the gravel lot, under the historical marker. Hers is the only car.

Tom Hardin climbs the small stoop to the bridge catwalk. At the top of the steps he stops, wheezing and panting. Under his shirt his right side hangs heavy, his swollen liver pressing against his belt.

He takes Miss Camilla's arm. "I was going to make a lamp from that block of wood." He chooses his words carefully. He does not want to misspeak now.

"I know."

"I was going to give it to you."

"I thought as much."

"I'll never finish it. Turning it takes a good eye and a steady hand. I've lost that. But I thought you would want to know. I was making it for you."

"You're very kind." With her cane she points to the blooming redbud. "It's greener now than it was then. Really, this is a better time of year to come."

"Miss Camilla." He is afraid to form the question, his words come out flat and hard. "Can I kiss you?"

She laughs, short and harsh, "*May*," she says. "*May* I kiss you. No, you may not."

His disappointment and humiliation are too great not to give them voice. "My God, Camilla, why are you saying no now? What difference does it make?"

"Before, Rose Ella lived, and you took what you wanted. Now she is dead, and suddenly you ask."

"I couldn't ask, then." He forces himself to find and say the words. "I didn't know how, then. Things are different now. I'm older."

"Old enough that even I look good."

"You looked good to me then."

"Anyone would have looked good to you then. Any*thing* would have looked good to you then. I was available, with a new car and a school holiday." She plants her cane, covers one mottled hand with another, stares over the valley. "Tom Hardin. You seem to think I have never known love." She speaks in a voice determined to convince. She might be lecturing herself. "I have known love. I have been lucky in love."

"Tell me who has loved you."

For a long moment she says nothing. Then, "Those of us not so fortunate as to be born to family must make it for ourselves, if we are to have it at all. I have made my family, and it has sufficed."

"And who are they."

"My neighbors." Her voice falters. "My students. Your son."

Tom Hardin drops her elbow. "I should tell that boy to leave." He walks to the car. Along the way he listens for her voice. He hears only the rush of the wind through the bridge girders and the chatterings of the swallows.

When finally she reaches the car he holds the door for her, but does not shut it once she has climbed in.

"Tom Hardin," Miss Camilla says gently. "You have been looking in the wrong places."

He does not move. "Do you think she ever forgave me?"

She says nothing. He knows she is turning her answer over in her head, an answer she is sure of but uncertain whether to present. "No," she says finally. "No, I don't think she ever did."

They arrive home as it is getting dark. Raphael bounds across the yard, full of noise and concern. Miss Camilla leans across the seat to plant a kiss, her lips cool and paper dry on Tom Hardin's cheek. "You're persistent," she says. "I'll give you that much." She climbs from the car and shuts the door.

That night is a bad one, brought on, Tom Hardin knows, by the sitting and riding and by Miss Camilla's words. The next morning he is in the shop before Raphael is out of bed. He can do no more than sit, now, but he prefers sitting here, among his tools, to sitting in the house, where Rose Ella reigned.

Though Raphael no longer brings coffee, he still comes and sits on the stool near the woodshop stove. Some mornings he has sat for half an hour and they have said nothing.

This morning Tom Hardin waves Raphael away from the stool. "I want you to do me a favor."

"Sure."

"I want you to take this package over to your friend next door." He has wrapped the block in brown paper grocery sacks. He waves Raphael at it. "Tell her I thought she might use it to fuel her stove." Raphael lifts the sack, feels its weight, hesitates. "Go on!" Tom Hardin says.

He watches his son cross the yard. In Raphael's walk he sees his own walk, that bow-legged strut peculiar to the Hardin men.

Tom Hardin sits for a few minutes, then Raphael returns. He comes in without knocking and places the unwrapped block of wood on Tom Hardin's workbench. "She thanks you," Raphael says, "but she insists that it be finished, and says to tell you that she does not want to see it otherwise. She tells me that I am to finish it. You are to show me how, she says."

"She does." Tom Hardin takes the block of wood and holds it to the unforgiving light, which shows forth its warped seams and unsealed gaps. "It can't be done," he says. "It won't hold up to the lathe."

Raphael moves to the doorway, looking out at the newly greened lawn.

From across the yard Tom Hardin hears Miss Camilla's door open, and he lifts his head. Raphael steps out and crosses to offer his arm, which she accepts. For a second they talk, then they turn away, to return to Miss Camilla's house.

Tom Hardin studies her three-legged walk, as she pulls herself to the door with the help of her cane. *I am too old,* he thinks. *I have too little time left to change. If that is stupid and narrow, so be it. I have earned that privilege.*

Yet he watches Miss Camilla poling away from him, his son at her side. He hefts the wood in his hands, turning it over in the window's light, his unthinking fingers testing its strength against the turning on the lathe.

Back Where She Came From

[1991]

Elizabeth Hardin props her feet on the dashboard, to wedge a bottle of nail polish between her big and second toes. She unscrews the brush from the bottle and touches its maroon tip to the cuticle of her big toe. Dennis pushes the floor stick through its shift pattern. "The first time I kissed you, you were painting your nails." He sniffs. "Twenty years since we've kissed and that smell still makes me think of making love."

"Not with *me*. I never once let you past second base."

"That's not to say I wasn't thinking about it."

Elizabeth waves her glistening toe in the hot air rising from the sunbaked dash.

They are driving a 1961 International Harvester farm truck from Philadelphia to their childhood home in Kentucky, where Elizabeth's parents and two of her brothers are buried, where her remaining family still lives, where Dennis sells automobiles, has a wife, three kids, a suburban tract home. Elizabeth shares a Hollywood Hills apartment with her lover Andrew, an artist specializing in high-concept, postmodern, postminimalist sculptures—such as the Hardin family tombstone, which Andrew designed and ordered from Italy, and which Elizabeth and Dennis have just retrieved from a Philadelphia dockyard.

Dennis points at Elizabeth's feet. "Springtime. 1968. You were sitting on the glider in your folks' backyard, painting your nails. I looked the length of that long leg and got up the nerve to kiss you, in broad daylight. Twelve years in Catholic school couldn't keep me from it. The first time I'd ever kissed anybody. The first time you'd ever been kissed."

Elizabeth remembers the incident another way: She'd been sitting in the front yard, her nails stripped and ready for polishing, when Dennis walked up. Worried that he would think her blanched nails ugly and cracked, she reached up and pulled his face down to hers and kissed him before he could look any closer.

At seventeen, vice-captain of the cheerleading squad, could she have been so brazen as to tell him she'd never been kissed? At eighteen, captain of the basketball team, could Dennis never have kissed anyone else? "Totally," she says aloud.

"So it's more than twenty years and here I am, still ogling Bette C. Hardin painting her nails. But in a borrowed farm truck this time, with a mountain of pink rock from Italy riding the flatbed."

"It's not pink," Elizabeth says. "Anyway, don't look at me—I didn't order it. Andrew insisted that my family deserves the finest marble in the world, which to a sculptor means Italian marble." Elizabeth pulls a package of violet tissues from her purse and busies herself wadding them between the toes of her finished foot. "Besides, there's a plaque that Andrew designed and that *he* says could only be cast by this one Italian firm."

"So Andrew orders the stone and designs a plaque, and you call your high school boyfriend for the first time in years and ask him to dig up a truck and meet you in Philadelphia."

"I didn't ask. You volunteered."

"You're right. After discovering somehow that you needed a volunteer."

She props the finished foot on the overnight bag that

Dennis has stuffed beneath the dash, then raises her remaining foot for critical inspection. "So how are Crystal and the kids? Last time I saw you, you two were on the verge of breaking up."

Dennis holds out his right hand, palm up, then flips it over to show the flat, square back of his hand, branching into fingers as square and ordinary as the International's hood.

"I'm surprised she let you come, myself," Elizabeth says. "Crystal never impressed me as your New Age kind of woman."

"New Age?"

"But pretty. She was always the one to get asked out by the guys on the other team."

"And ready to get married. Unlike somebody else I could name, who was hot to trot to get herself off to Hollywood." Dennis stretches his arms overhead, first his left, then his right, which he drapes across the back of the seat in an awkward arc.

Elizabeth touches the brush to her last naked toenail, stuffs Kleenex between her toes, leans back to study the effect: maroon nails spaced out with crumpled violet tissue. "It's been years since I painted my nails. Andrew calls it tacky."

"So what does Andrew know? You're the actress."

"Andrew grew up in Los Angeles. He's an *artist*—he really has a better sense of what impresses people. I mean, I'd still be dressing out of Sears catalogues except for him."

"You dressed out of Sears catalogues in high school and looked pretty damn good, if you ask me."

"But now we're talking L.A. Where, thank God, I'm not." She scrunches down in the seat to study Dennis, silhouetted against the window's glare. His hair is thinning, his shirt creases at the bulge over his belt, but he still tends toward blond, he looks boyish in a way that probably sells lots of cars. The square cut of his chin, the broad slope of his forehead are strong as ever . . . She points her foot, tipping the truck's rearview mirror with a maroon toe.

Abruptly she sits upright. "Sorry," she says, reaching to straighten the mirror. Her hand collides with his.

"Cute. Very cute." He squeezes her shoulder, then replaces his hand behind her back, resting it lightly on her neck.

Elizabeth pulls maps from the glove compartment. "Where do you suppose is Pittsburgh?"

An awkward moment, then Dennis removes his hand from her neck. "Sorry. An actress must have guys putting the move on her all the time. I didn't mean anything by it. Honest."

She winces at the hurt in his voice. "Dennis. Why would guys put the move on me? In acting it's in one day and out the next, and I'm out. Boy, am I out." She busies herself in the folds and flaps of Rand McNally's Eastern Seaboard. "But so what? The same thing could happen to anybody. Look at you. People in Louisville stop buying Fords and all of a sudden you're selling Hondas."

"Well, now, I don't know about that," Dennis says carefully. "I'd have a hard time putting my heart behind a Japanese car."

The International hits a pothole. The draft from the rotting floorboards catches the map from Elizabeth's knee, to flap it across the cab and into Dennis's face. Dennis swerves, swatting the map to one side. A passing BMW lets loose an angry bleat. Dennis gives the driver the finger, then resettles his arm behind her back.

Elizabeth wrestles with Rand McNally. "There is no Pittsburgh. This map stops at Lancaster." She crumples its panels in her lap.

Only last night Elizabeth had taken the red-eye from her home in Los Angeles to meet Dennis and, at a Philadelphia dockyard, the well-traveled tombstone. Now she closes her eyes against the relentless striping of the road and the hot, late-morning sun of August to drift into a place between waking and sleep, to a conversation she had with her mother, when Elizabeth first announced she was thinking of breaking up with Dennis and moving to California to be an actress.

"Move to California," Rose Ella said.

"*Mo*—ther," Elizabeth said. "How can you be so certain about such a tough decision?"

Rose Ella shrugged. "Dennis will provide. This much we know already. But you don't need a provider. You can provide for yourself."

"You talk about it like you know the future."

Her mother sighed and took Elizabeth's hand in her own. "Bette C. Let me tell you about Dennis. He'll be . . . a salesman. They love sports stars in sales, everybody remembers their names. He could sell anything. It's good money. He won't much like the job but he'll take it because of his family, and he'll be right to do that. People will respect him for it.

"But you don't want a family. You want a man with ambition. He's going somewhere. You're going somewhere. You meet and love each other along the way."

Elizabeth pulled her hand free. "So I should give up a sure thing for a complete unknown quantity."

"I want you to have the sure thing, honey, but first I want you to find yourself. A girl needs to find herself. Then even if things end up in divorce she still has that."

"Mother, I *have* found myself!" Elizabeth cries.

Her eyes fly open, to take in the broad slope of the International's fat hood and the crumbling shoulders and rusting guardrails of the Pennsylvania Turnpike. Had she actually cried out loud? Had Dennis heard? She feigns sleep, slumping against the door so as to crack one eye at Dennis. His eyes are steady on the road. Elizabeth opens her eyes slowly, yawning and stretching. "Did you hear anything?"

"Um, no, not especially."

"Well, I mean, did I say anything? I mean, in my sleep."

"Were you asleep?"

Elizabeth huffs in irritation and flops over to face her window.

"If the guy's playing around, you've got every right to leave him."

Elizabeth bolts upright. "You were listening!"

Dennis shrugs. "I got ears."

"Andrew loves me too much to play around."

"Then how come you're not married?"

His right arm is still draped across the seat back. He massages her neck with his hand. She leans back, into the pillow of his hand . . . she sits upright, shrugging her neck free of his fingers.

Dennis grips the wheel with both hands, fixing his eyes on the road. "I'll bet he introduces you as his wife. I'll bet that whenever there's somebody he wants to impress—"

"Dennis. He's *asked* me to marry him. I said no." She pulls the tissues from between her toes, wadding them into a ball in her purse, as the International climbs west, rising into the Pennsylvania mountains.

They stop for lunch at a Howard Johnson's. Engulfed in pink and turquoise leatherette, they look out over the parked International and its heavenward-pointing monument. Shaped like the Matterhorn, wrapped in Hefty bags, the tombstone defines the space around it—in this case, the HoJo parking lot. Its black plastic sheath is beginning to shred from the battering of the wind, revealing a nubbled tit of flesh-colored stone.

The waitress leans against their table in a tired slouch, resting her pad on one hip. "Order?"

"Double cheeseburger, fries. A Coke. No, make that a vanilla shake."

"Dinner salad. Thousand Island, low-calorie."

The waitress brings their food. Dennis starts into his salad. "You were a distraction. Standing on the sidelines, in those cute skirts . . ."

"That was the first year the nuns let the cheerleaders wear pleats. Sister Angelina made us kneel before every game to make sure our hems were long enough to touch the ground. As soon as she turned around we rolled the tops of our skirts up over our belts."

"You had them hiked up far enough at the district championship."

"Dennis of the perfect memory."

"I wouldn't forget a second. It was a great game."

"We lost. Danny Burnham missed that crazy jump shot from the corner baseline that he should never have taken and we lost."

"I don't care. It was still a great game. And you came up to me at the end and put your arm around me and told me it didn't matter, that I was a star."

"You *were* a star. You should have tried out for pro. Really! At those regional tryouts the pro teams give. You *averaged* eighteen points."

"Nineteen-point-six."

State flowers decorate the sugar packets. Dennis dumps them out on the table, then picks each up by a single corner and flicks it, with a snap of his forefinger, at the empty sugar bowl. "Bette C. I couldn't have made pro."

"You could have tried. You never know."

Dennis stacks and replaces the packets.

"I'm sure you're a great father," Elizabeth says. "I'm sure you're a great husband."

"Even if I've run out on Crystal."

"Wait a second. I thought Crystal gave you the OK to come on this trip."

He flips the last sugar packet at the bowl and misses. "You played what . . . Barbara Allen, in *Dark of the Moon*. You were great. Every time you came out it was like the whole cast got serious. Same for the audience."

"Dennis. What about Crystal?"

Dennis picks up the packet and begins fluting its edges between his thumb and forefinger. "You called and I wanted to come, I was obsessed, I couldn't sleep, I thought about it that much, and I couldn't ask Crystal—I mean, what if she said no? Which she'd have every right to say and surely would have said. And I would have gone ahead and done what I wanted to do and so what the hell, why not blow the top off of all this and just up and leave."

"Dennis. You're babbling."

"She's sweet and she's still pretty and I could say or do anything, the worst thing I could think of, and she would never, not ever leave me. So yesterday came and I picked up and left." The packet breaks, spilling sugar over Dennis's salad.

"She has no idea where you are at all?"

He spreads his square hands flat against the table top, fingers splayed. "I was nuts about you that last year."

Once fine as a piano player's, his hands are swollen and lined now, and not just at the knuckles. His skin has coarsened, veins branch across the bones. She lays her hand next to his—finer-boned, smoother-fleshed, better cared for but still unmistakably the hand of a woman who has seen something of the world.

"So how are things with Andrew?" he asks.

"I took off and left Andrew."

"I figured as much."

"We'd been fighting a month, and all the time this damned tombstone was sitting in Philadelphia piling up storage fees. So a week goes by and we've hardly talked, I mean, you know what I mean? And then over the breakfast table he asks me to marry him. Not for the first time, either, but the other time I was kind of expecting it, you know, it was up at Big Bear or some romantic place. But this time it was like totally whammo, out of the blue he asked and I said no, again, and then I had to get out. I can't do this to him, you know? I can't even let him do it to himself."

"So you called me up."

"And you, thank God, said yes. My brothers and sisters don't even know I'm showing up with this—*rock*. I mean, they're expecting it to arrive on the back of a freight truck or something, with Andrew, if anybody, in tow."

"So are you going back to him?"

She takes up her fork to toy with her fries.

He reaches across the table then, to take the fork from her hand and take her fingers in his own. "We'd been married about two years when I started thinking about leaving Crystal and following you to California. I even thought about it the day I got married, except I was a twenty-year-old hound in heat and there were all these presents and all these people and so what do you do? You get married. And then just about the time I got really antsy the kids came along, they're great, and I settled into it, I made a deal with myself: You just make yourself be satisfied, you just count your blessings. Everybody wants to be a star when they're a kid, that's what I told myself, and then you get older and you aim a little lower, when those feelings come along you just put them aside, until finally you figure out that you're being a star just by managing to get through the world in one piece and that's all anybody has any right to ask for and so you shut up and don't ask for anything else. But Jean Marie—she's the youngest—she's almost in high school, she's all the way to seventh grade, they're growing up, almost grown up, and all that wanting, it's all come back, you know? You know?"

"It's OK, Dennis. Really, you're lucky. You've got your kids. You've got health insurance. You've got a retirement plan."

"You've really put yourself out there. Hell, you were right to say no to Andrew. You were right to say no to me. You're really out there, in Hollywood. Making it happen."

She squeezes his hand. "Dennis. I quit acting a couple of years back."

Dennis leans back. "You quit acting?"

"I'm handling real estate. It's what you do in L.A." She avoids his eyes. "My God, Dennis, it was the eighties, you could make a bundle on nothing but fluff and turn. A little paint, a few potted plants, and bingo—twenty, thirty thousand profit in six months. I'd have been a fool to pass that by. My mistake was in not doing it sooner."

The waitress, who has been hovering at some distance, closes in. "Eat up, folks, if you don't mind, it's getting on time to change shifts, and if I could, if you could . . ."

"Sure, ma'am, no problem," Dennis says. He drops Elizabeth's hand to pick up his fork.

❊   ❊   ❊

Dennis walks to a nearby Drug Town to buy some gum. Sitting in the truck's cab, Elizabeth studies her toes. Ten little piglets daubed with maroon, they look fiercely tacky, spread against the floorboard, wedged among the farm junk that litters the truck—jumper cables, a tobacco knife, hog rings.

She takes the tobacco knife and climbs out of the truck and onto the flatbed. She feels the stone through its layers of black plastic, searching for the plaque, whose design she has never seen. "A surprise," Andrew said, when she asked to see his sketches. "A melding of elements from old and new concepts of death, designed for a family on the cusp between the two."

She locates the plaque under the plastic cover and uses the tobacco knife to hack a hole in its protective covering. She bends to peer inside.

All those weeks of The Judds and Windham Hill on Andrew's CD player—really, she ought to have suspected.

The plaque is mounted in one side of the rough-hewn stone. Elizabeth's mother and father lead off its list of names, followed by the names of their seven children, their spouses, and their grandchildren:

HARDIN

ROSE ELLA PERLITE 1920–1989

m.

THOMAS HARDIN 1912–1990

Joseph Raymond 1945–   m. Catherine Ellison 1945–
   Michael Leslie 1970–
   Sean Thomas 1974–
   Thomas Hardin, Jr. 1982–

Barbara Marie 1947–   m. Brady Wexelford 1941–
    Mary Michael 1983–
    Christopher Samuel 1985–
    Matthew Curtis 1987–

Leslie William 1948–   m. Helen Jackson 1950–
    Theresa Jane 1981–
    Paul Benjamin 1982–
    Helena Marie 1984–

Robert Crosby 1949–   m. Louise Gray 1948–
    Sarah Marie 1977–
    Margaret Erhart 1979–

Clark Andrew 1950–1970

Elizabeth Christine 1951–   m.

Raphael Cary 1953–1990

Around the plaque's edges are engravings: a rosary, a leaping fish, crossed shotguns, a pair of books (one open, one
closed), deer antlers, the Great Seal of the Honorable Order
of Kentucky Colonels, ranged in a semicircle below an ancient
Egyptian ankh—symbol (she has learned this from Andrew)
of eternal life.

"Can I look?"

Elizabeth jumps, startled. Without waiting for her answer Dennis climbs to the flatbed. He holds back the plastic
between pinched fingers and peers over her shoulder at the
plaque. "These are supposed to be like—symbols? Of your
parents?"

"It's lovely," she says.

Dennis drops the plastic veil. "So why are you defending the jerk, if you left him in L.A.?"

"So why aren't you with your wife?"

Dennis jumps from the flatbed and climbs into the truck.

Elizabeth crouches to Andrew's plaque. She lifts the plastic, her fingers read the raised bronze letters: her parents, then one by one her six brothers and sisters and their spouses, she among them: once the penultimate child, now youngest, now that Raphael is dead. The daughter whose name is followed by "m." (she'll wring Andrew's neck for that), and following that "m." nothing, *nada*, the void, the long, unnerving blank—spinsterhood's hieroglyph, graphic proof for generations to follow that she has never found herself, or anyone else.

She climbs from the truck and walks to a nearby liquor outlet, where she buys a couple of tallboys, then crosses to a drugstore, where she searches for condoms. She yearns for this to happen, for those few seconds when desire triumphs over time and she lies unthinking, unaware of all she once wanted, where she is now, where she is going . . . She buys condoms.

Back in the International she takes the wheel, to drive deep into the Pennsylvania mountains.

Now that her mother is dead, Elizabeth understands why Rose Ella so much wanted her last daughter to leave Kentucky, to move to California, to try her hand at acting. And Elizabeth went, to learn in California what Rose Ella could not have known. By leaving home and family, Elizabeth now knows what she has lost: a landscape more familiar to her even now than any part of Los Angeles; an understanding of blood history and her place in it; the unquestioning womb of family, in whose comfort and security she might have enfolded herself after her mistakes and tragedies; an openness to the world, which in Los Angeles was no more than an invitation to be exploited. These things and more she has given up, in exchange for—herself. Her self.

Would she have been wiser to have stayed in Kentucky? In the end she suspected it all came out to the same. The first, or second, or third law of thermodynamics—she remembers this from a college physics professor on whom she had a crush. Conservation of energy. If anything was to be gained, something must be given up. If she was to find herself, she had to leave her family, her home.

"Life is the little that is left over from dying," she mutters to herself, something she'd learned from some English teacher somewhere long ago. When both her parents died, she understood a little better what her teacher had been getting at. Then Raphael died—little brother, fellow Californian, closest of her siblings, fellow seeker of emotional asylum; and his death enforced understanding.

And now not much more than a few months later she is somewhere along the Pennsylvania Turnpike traveling with the dead, carting across America the only certain, indisputable facts of life, cast in bronze ("lasts way longer than any granite," Andrew is speaking at her ear), and at her side is her traveling companion Dennis. She is struck by how alone she feels with him here—more alone than if she were alone. He cannot know or share her grief, she thinks, and she knows no words that might do it justice. The only thing she *knows*, that she can put a finger to, is desire—for Dennis, who so clearly wants her in return. What can this mean, love and lust in the face of all that death? Surely two people who so nearly want the same thing may find their ways to it, she thinks, if only for the space of a single hour on a single afternoon.

She leans over and plants a kiss on Dennis's stubbled cheek.

She exits onto a dead-end country road, the most deserted she can spot. She hands Dennis a beer, leaving the condoms in the bag. As she drives he drinks wordlessly, first his beer, then hers.

She turns into a lane, two ruts leading through a broken-down gate and dead-ending in a waist-high field of wheat. The culvert is decrepit, she narrowly misses lurching into the ditch. The truck bounces. The tires scrape the wheel wells. With a tug of the emergency brake she stops.

Dennis clears his throat.

In her vision they would not need words. Dennis must know what she is up to and would lean across the crinkly plastic bag and kiss her and save her the embarrassment of telling him what the bag contains.

The silence lengthens. The sun sinks. Dennis sits staring out at the gently waving wheat, his hands long against his lap.

She lifts the beer from Dennis's hand, opens the plastic bag, lays a condom in his still-opened palm.

The sun is low in the sky, the light flat and clear and sharp as memory. Behind the seat there is a blanket, a little greasy, flecked with hay and horsehair, but they spread it on the ground next to the wheels. Elizabeth lies back. As Dennis brushes his lips against hers she looks up, watching as the line of the truck's shadow creeps up the tombstone until the sun strikes only the tip of the rock, pointing to the sky, an admonishing, rose-tipped finger.

Years of monogamy and she has forgotten how laborious sex can be. Dennis is gentle and this is not what she wants, at the end of this dirt lane where she has brought them. She who has never married wants adultery, desire without conditions, hot and steamy, all-consuming and above all fast; and here is Dennis, twenty-one years a husband, a father three times over, brutally tender, wanting love. The weight of his loneliness crushes her more thoroughly than Dennis himself, who has filled out considerably since his basketball days.

He is making clumsy love, and she is somewhere else, and finally he turns away. "I can't do this."

Elizabeth pulls his head to her breast. "The ground is too cold." She stares up, past his thinning brown hair with the gold highlights—how she remembers that gold, at the end of a summer of outdoor practice his hair was almost blond . . . She stares up, trying to forget, to abandon her dreams to the dreamless blue bowl of the sky, while Dennis clambers to his feet and buttons his shirt and mumbles an apology, and all the while a corner of her mind that will not shut up rehearses lies for those survivors who are waiting for the tombstone, back home in Kentucky.

Discreetly diplomatic, she hands the keys to Dennis. She walks behind the truck, guiding him with hand signals onto the narrow culvert, but the right rear wheel slips into the ditch. With a delicate crunch the muffler snaps, while the rock tilts, slips, catches, holds; barely.

Dennis leaps from the truck. "This is *your* fault! Every bit of it! You told me to go to the right. Look at that ditch! Any bozo can see you're supposed to cut to the left."

Elizabeth leans coolly against the International's concave grille. "I signaled you to cut left. You forgot you were looking in the mirror."

"You think I can see through that goddamned rock?"

She heaves herself away from the truck to shout in his face. "You think you can yell at me like some goddamned mule?"

They glare at each other in the evening light, until Elizabeth breaks away to pace the length of the truck. "First let's get this truck out of the ditch. Then we'll worry about who got us here in the first place."

They search out rocks to wedge beneath the back tire. Elizabeth takes the wheel, working the truck back and forth: gas, brake, gas, brake. Dennis shoves rocks under the tire, until Elizabeth feels traction and floors the gas. Belching blue smoke and spitting rocks, the International crawls from the ditch. Startled crows rise from nearby trees, circling over wheat fields in the evening's blue light, their caws punctuating the explosions from the broken tailpipe.

Elizabeth backs the truck out the gate and onto the pavement. She slides from the driver's seat to gather up the blanket. She climbs into the cab, leans over to open the driver's door. Dennis climbs in. They sit and sit, until Elizabeth spreads her hands.

"Dennis. I'm sorry. I don't know—"

"It's OK." He raises one hand, to silence her, she thinks; he slaps his own cheek lightly, a bishop's confirming tap. "I thought I was waiting for you. Come to find out I've just been . . . I don't know. Waiting." He guns the truck to life and roars down the road.

Down the western slope of the Appalachians, into undulant Ohio. The wind tears at the tombstone's black wrappings. The whip and pop of the plastic and the engine's unmuffled grind make it easy to avoid talking.

They are floating down a long grade when Elizabeth turns around to look through the cab window at the tombstone. Streaming ribbons of black plastic, almost naked, it glows an opalescent rose, its edges softened by the setting sun's light, except for the plaque, whose hard right angles and sharp edges and glittering letters and numbers stand out—and following her own name that long blank, the black hole into which so much of her life has been sucked. "A poor country girl, with no more to sustain her than native wit and a fast-fading beauty, must take care to marry well"—this pearl of wisdom pops into her head and she cannot locate where she first heard it. In some college course in English Lit—maybe Jane Austen? Or maybe she'd heard it from the ditzy drag queen who lived below Raphael's apartment, whom she'd met when she'd taken her brother's ashes to San Francisco to scatter on the bay.

Dennis pulls off to get gas. Elizabeth leaves him at the truck while she pays the bill. In the restroom she cleans her purse of the crumpled tissues, dropping them into the overflowing trash can: a moist bunch of violets, redolent with acetone.

She is inside only a few minutes, but when she returns Dennis is gone. The International sits pulled off to one side, empty. She peers around the corners of the gas station. Then she crosses to the truck, trying to look as if she might have forgotten something—in case anyone is looking, in case Dennis should catch her in the act. Maybe he is crouched under the dash, pulling her leg? Unlikely, but she opens the door just in case. No Dennis. Even his overnight bag is gone. She searches for the men's room. She pauses outside its door, then she knocks. "Dennis?" She rattles the door handle. "Dennis!" No answer. She leans against the cinder-block wall, whitewash rubs off on her hair and her blouse but she does not care, she raises pleading hands to the sky.

Then she hears what he must have heard—the reverberant thud of a basketball against asphalt. She follows the sound through a straggling mass of black-eyed Susans, stepping over a trampled chain-link fence and past Dennis's overnight bag onto a playground.

Dennis has joined a kids' pickup game, changing his loafers for a pair of high-top lace-ups. He is older and taller and rounder than the skinny kids he plays with, but he dances and feints, the kids wave their hands. In the dusky light the scene has no depth, she might be watching a movie: Dennis and the kids are cutouts moving against the flat plane of the court's asphalt and the blank brick walls of the school it abuts. The basketball is not a sphere but a round circle, a flat dull leather dot traveling from hands to slap the pavement and back to hands.

He knows she is there and he shows it, not by any call or signal but in the tone of the shuck-and-jive he patters with the kids, in the fancy moves he makes. In the flair of his ducks and glides, in his fakes and dribbles she sees only their failures (athlete, father, husband; actress, lover, sister), until she brings herself up short with this necessary truth: how much larger are her eyes than her stomach; how much greater what she dreams than what she can ever do.

Then in one smooth motion he turns and hooks the ball up and back and over his shoulder. In his turning he cuts a full figure. The ball arches up from below his hip, following the perfect arc of his arm and the curl of his fingers, flying up and out of shadow and into the sun's last light. Suddenly bright orange and very round, it arches to the goal and drops through the hoop without a glance off the backboard or a touch of the hoop's metal ring. It drops through with that cleanest and most invisible of sounds, broken in its fall and cupped for the shortest second by the net's narrowed bottom, and in this second, unthinking, Elizabeth fits her fingers to her teeth and jumps into the air, splitting the dusk with the pierce of her whistle.

Little Deaths

[1942]

The sky was paling in the east but it was still dark on the porch of the Perlite farmhouse. Ragged limestone cliffs rose to either side, blocking the winter light from the bottomland, pinched in a fold between two steep ridges. It was cold—Rose Ella Perlite was cold—she'd waited outside for half an hour, rather than sit near the stove with her mother implying "I told you so" with every thrust and jerk of her darning needle. "You said be ready before dawn," Rose Ella told Tom Hardin when finally he pulled up in his truck.

"So what's time to a hog." He leaned across the seat, opened her door from the inside.

Not a promising beginning for a first date, but then she couldn't say she hadn't been warned—her mother had done nothing but warn these past few days. Without all that warning Rose Ella would most likely have stood him up.

"Patch," he said, jerking his head to the rear. She thought this was a command, some obscure man-talk, until she turned around and saw in the truck bed a wire-haired mongrel, somewhat bigger than a breadbox, dirty white except for a black eyespot that gave him the air of a canine pirate. He shot her a look of lascivious familiarity. "That dog knows me from somewhere," she said.

Tom Hardin started the truck. "He gets around."

He was trapping furs for the high-toned buyers from New York and he'd asked right out on the courthouse square if she wanted to help him run traps. They'd known each other exactly five minutes when he'd asked, she with all of her girlfriends standing right there knowing perfectly well that she was already promised to Camp Junior. Who was more dumbfounded—she when he asked, he when she said yes? Either way here they were, speeding down the winding road, Tom Hardin with one hand on the wheel, the other rooting under the seat.

He was the first man she'd met who hadn't fallen all over her. That was partly why she was here; she'd said as much to her mother. Rose Ella was mystified by this phenomenon—these great lunks pursuing her with offers for dates—but she'd come to accept this as her gift, the way some people came by rhythm or perfect pitch or (in the case of Tom Hardin) a smart mouth. It was a gift that until now she'd taken for granted—she'd realized that for the first time this morning, as she'd stood in the cold waiting for this stone, this Tom Hardin.

Bouncing and jostling over the uneven pavement, Rose Ella considered this: that men fell all over her because unlike most girls she was smart enough not to fall all over them. Certainly it wasn't because she was flawlessly beautiful. She had these Betty Grable legs, it's true, tapering to the most delicate of ankles, that last summer had scandalized the town when she'd worn a skirtless bathing suit to the river. But her chin was a little weak, and she had the kind of impressively full bust that in small women runs to pudge at the sight of ice cream.

She'd not much given a damn about men one way or another, so that when one came along who didn't fall all over her it gave her a chance to prove she was above all this whoop and holler. Anybody with any spirit would rise to *that* bait—she'd make the same choice tomorrow. For Rose Ella it was the challenge of outwitting herself—Tom Hardin was just the means to that end.

He pulled a pint from under the seat, pulled the cork from the bottle with his teeth. He raised the bottle. "Us against them. Want a sip?"

"I don't drink in the mornings." She didn't much drink at all but that was the sort of revelation that might jeopardize a boy's coming back, and she had been raised not at any costs to jeopardize the boy's coming back. She was not in this game to jeopardize Tom Hardin's coming back—she wanted him to come back (already this was her plan) so as then to be able to turn him down.

"Suit yourself." He took a long pull. "You spend enough time running traps, you'll change your mind."

"This is the first and last time you'll catch me running traps," she said, staring out the window. "And I'm not much given to changing my mind."

Tom Hardin recorked the bottle and tossed it in her lap. "I bet you ain't."

On all sides the river was in winter flood. Three days of rain, then the rain had turned to falling ice before giving way to this morning's gray dawn. The sun was not yet above the knobs but already the half-light caught the ice-rimed branches, filling the trees with light until the meanest of them sparkled.

They turned into a graveled lane strewn with potholes, the headlights picking out barns and houses, dark gray against the silvering sheet of the sky. "This road goes to Perlite Ford," Rose Ella said. "My father's family used to run a mill out there."

"That's right. Best trapping in the county. Never been out there that I hadn't seen a fox. There's a whole crew of 'em, practically, as social as foxes ever get, that live near the old mill. 'Course, seeing one and trapping one's a different matter. But still." Tom Hardin slammed on the brakes at a culvert, causing the truck's tail end to sashay a little over the gravel.

"County says they're paving this road, putting in a bridge. That'll wreck hell with the trapping."

They climbed from the truck. Tom Hardin pulled a trap from a large knapsack and set it on the truck's tailgate. "This," he said, "is a trap."

Rose Ella was still a little shaken from the skid and more than a little angry at waiting a half hour in the cold—she was a Perlite, after all, even if they didn't have a dime to their name. "Do tell," she said. "I could have sworn it was a fishing pole."

"Good to know you're not above swearing. You'll need it before this morning is out."

I'll be damned if I'll give you the pleasure, Rose Ella thought. A Perlite woman was above that kind of blue-streak swearing, at least in front of a man. Already she was remonstrating with herself for having said yes to this craziness. It was a small town, a small state, and she could tell anyone who bothered asking right now that news of her taking this trip, what she was wearing, what time she'd left, what time she got back—all this, embellished for the sake of dramatic effect, would make its way to Camp Junior at the university.

And now she was in it—she was here, five miles from home and probably one of her girlfriends was already telegraphing the word to Camp Junior, who stood to inherit money and who was headed for law school and who anybody, most especially her girlfriends, could see was a catch. There was no help for it now but to be as unpleasant as she could be to Tom Hardin—at least then nobody could accuse her of leading him on.

She ignored the trap to kneel in front of Patch, who had jumped from the truck bed. "Oh, you're a sweetie," she said. "Look at those big brown eyes—and that spot around your eye, makes you look dangerous. I'll bet you're a knockout with the girls."

Tom Hardin made a noise of disgust. "No more than I can help. I want a dog, not a pet." He laid the trap against the truck bed's wooden planks and pried open its jaws. "Stick in your thumb. Go on. I just want you to feel the tension. It won't cut your finger off. I hear that kind of thing all the time. 'Oh, the poor animals,' they say. Think about it. If a trap'd cut your finger off it'd cut the mink's leg off, and if it cut the mink's leg off it'd run away, and if the mink got away what good would that do? Hmm?"

"No good at all," Rose Ella said. "For the mink."

Tom Hardin gave her a sharp glance. "If you're going to get all soapy about cute furry animals, just say so now and you can take the truck back. I'll run 'em by myself."

"Two days ago I had a flock of hens that I'd raised from when they were fuzzy little chicks. Last night we had fried chicken. Does that answer your question?" She took the trap by its chain and struck out down the path, swinging it like a yo-yo.

She was a good fifty yards from the truck before she realized Tom Hardin and Patch had crossed the road to the other side of the culvert. She retraced her steps and stood above him as he climbed down the bank and onto the creekbed slate. "Culverts are best for trapping mink," he said patiently, as if she'd been following attentively all along. "They stick to the water and when they get to a culvert you can bet they ain't going to go up and over it. Animals do things by habit, they'll always do it the same way, you just size up the situation and figure out what that way is and then set your trap to take advantage of it." He picked up a fallen branch the thickness of her wrist and snapped off one end. "This could come in handy." He swung the stick like a baseball bat. "You get something you want that's still kicking, you come up behind him, whack him over the head, that's it, he's dead. Never knows what hit him. You carry a gun in your pack in case you need it, but this is better—this way you get a clean pelt, no bullet holes, no cuts or blood."

She watched Tom Hardin and Patch nosing about the culvert. *Men,* she thought. Arrogant sons of bitches, full of nothing but themselves and the only reason to choose one over another was if he had good looks, or money, or a way to get her where she wanted to go, which was as far away from this burg as the high road ran—preferably west, preferably to California, preferably to Hollywood. Camp Junior qualified for two out of three of these male requirements, and if he weren't much in the looks department she shared her mother's opinion that a law degree went far toward improving a man's appearance. As for Tom Hardin, he wasn't bad-looking, she granted him that—his thick hair bristled as if maybe he and Patch shared some blood inheritance, but at least it wasn't going to thin out and disappear like Camp Junior's. Tom Hardin had a sureness of foot and a strength—the memory came, unbidden and unwanted, of the ease with which he broke that stick, and some buried part of her swelled and turned over like a lake. "Nothing but trouble down that road," her mother had told her only yesterday. "'A poor girl from the country, with only her wits and a fast-fading beauty to sustain her, must watch out to marry well.' That's my grandmother talking," Rose Ella's mother had said, "not thirty years off an English boat and bad enough married to know what she was talking about."

Not that Rose Ella's mother had married well—she'd married a Perlite, and however they might be the oldest family in the county and honest as dirt they'd lost most of their money just in time to put what little was left into stocks right before the big crash. Marrying poor was not in the cards for her; this Rose Ella had sworn to herself before and she repeated it now.

Tom Hardin bent to the blue-black slate. His boots cracked the thin ice around the water's edge and squelched in the mud. He held up a sprung trap. "Something could've sprung it. Or it could've sprung itself. That happens." He reset the trap and climbed the bank.

They moved down the trail until Patch leapt ahead, splashed through the creek, dashed up the far bank. He ran back and forth on the other side, barking to raise the dead. Tom Hardin disappeared over the creek bank's edge.

From the lip of the bank Rose Ella peered down. In the creek's center a thin, dark shape floated under the surface. Tom Hardin gave a low, sharp whistle—Patch bounded over the slate, broke the crust of ice with his paws to seize the mink in his mouth and drag it to within Tom Hardin's reach. "Hot damn!" Tom Hardin cried. He took the mink from Patch, pried open the trap jaws and waved the stiff body in the air. "Easy money come home! Here, hold this while I reset the trap." He tossed the mink at her.

He lectured as he went about the task. "This is a drowning set. A mink'll go straight for the water once he's in trouble. He'll do it every time. So you figure out the most direct path to the water. Maybe you find a little trough." With the toe of his boot he scraped a groove in the creekbed. "Or if you're real smart maybe you make a little trough. You set your trap at the trough's end, then tie it to a wire that's weighted down in the creek. When the mink gets caught in the trap he'll drag it to the water, but then he gets tangled in the wire and the weight of the trap drowns him. A few minutes and you got the cleanest pelt there is, not so much as a scratch."

She hefted the mink in her hand. She nearly dropped it, it

was so light. Her thumb and forefinger fit around the thickest parts of its slick, black body. Its sharp teeth were bared in a frozen snarl and its dark eyes stared wide.

In her imagination she had connected somehow Tom Hardin's invitation to run traps with dropping a hint about what a nice present something made of fur would make for a girl. That was stupid, she was smarter than that, but then it wasn't as if this was the first time she'd done things she'd been smart enough to know not to do. "What makes you think I want to hear all this about trapping?" she demanded, irritated with her own weakness.

"You come along, didn't you?" He reset the trap, weighted it in the water, climbed the bank, took the mink from her, and clipped its rear paw to his belt.

They walked in silence, Tom Hardin stopping every few yards to inspect the brush or the path, Rose Ella lost in the landscape. She loved this country in flood: the wide flat expanse of muddy water, spreading almost to the feet of the knobby hills, filling sloughs and hollows, giving places she knew as well as she knew this countryside a look of foreignness, as if this were another country that she was wandering through, she a traveling woman from some foreign land instead of plain old Rose Ella Perlite, who had picked blackberries in every one of these hollows and who knew the exact location of every generous-limbed hickory or black walnut in this end of the county.

And here she was with Tom Hardin, who dealt regularly with travelers from the most exotic places, which she could only imagine from her Saturday matinees at the Mary Anderson. Her curiosity got the better of the silent treatment—it was her weakness and she knew it, but if a girl was to go into the world she needed some idea of what she was getting into.

"You have much truck with those buyers from New York?" she asked.

"As little as I can get away with."

"Tell me what they look like."

"Well, they're short—"

"No, I don't mean that. I mean, what kind of clothes they wear."

"They wear minks," Tom Hardin said. "Lots of minks. Think about how many minks it takes to make a knee-length coat. And then multiply that by a hundred, by a thousand, by ten thousand. That's how many minks they wear. And two-tone shoes, look like they ran out of the right color halfway through." He scratched his head. "That's what sticks in my mind."

"They come down here, they must think they're visiting the back side of the moon."

"They come down here to screw us over and we turn up our tails and ask where. You come into the warehouse with a pile of fur, they cut the price by a third, what are you going to do? Throw it back in the creek? 'Oh, Mr. Hardin, but look at this bald patch.' 'Oh, Mr. Hardin, fox is out this year, we can't use that fox.' It's city folks against country folks and the deck stacked as usual. If fur was the only thing they wanted out of us, we'd be up shit creek without a paddle."

"So what else do they want?"

"I'll give you two guesses and the first two don't count." When she didn't answer he pulled the whiskey from his knapsack and held it out to her. "How 'bout a hint."

"I told you I don't drink in the morning."

Tom Hardin squinted at the overcast sky. "Could be high noon, for all I can tell." He took a long pull, recorked the bottle and tucked it away, moved on down the path.

"I'd love to go to New York," she said, mostly to irritate him; judging from the movies she'd seen, California was more her kind of place.

"You'd last about as long as one of them would out here."

"I'd last longer than you."

"That I do not doubt." He dropped to his knees. "I should have a fox set about here." He peered around in the brush. "You're damned lucky to get a fox, especially a red fox. They're loners, and smart as they come. You save some piss from a fox you've killed and sprinkle that around to cover up your smell and attract the others." He held up the trap. "Sprung, dammit. With a red fox you have to set a whole new trap—they mark the ones they've sprung and won't be a fox near it for a month."

She handed him the trap she'd been carrying since leaving the truck. He took it, wrapped it in a rag, tucked it in his knapsack. "Covered with your smell. A fox'll figure out that scent and follow it from one trap to the next. He'll spring ever' last one of 'em and then piss on 'em to rub your face in it. He's a gambler, he's got to do it—it's in his blood. He's probably running ahead of us right now, springing them one by one and laughing at us while he does it." He took a fresh trap from the knapsack, set it in place, patted dirt around its edges, sprayed it from a bottle he carried in the sack.

The wind picked up, scraping tree limbs together and rattling the red-orange bittersweet and dried brown milkweed pods. Above the wind's sigh, from across the swollen river, she heard a moan—something between the scream of a locomotive and the bellowing of cattle. Patch froze, hackles rising on his back, hind legs trembling. Rose Ella knew that sound, but Tom Hardin knew it faster. Already he had whipped a choke chain from his knapsack and fastened it around Patch's neck. "At least this time I come prepared," he said. He tossed her one end of the chain. "Hang on tight. Some city folks have moved in across the river with a whole pack of bitches, all of 'em in heat so far as I can tell. Last time I was down here I had to use a chain from one of my traps to tie Patch to a tree just so I could finish my rounds, and even then by the time I got back he'd all but chewed through the damn trunk."

"So what's wrong with letting him run loose?" She waved at the churning brown stripe of water. "It's not like he can jump across."

"For a girl that claims she just shot a whole flock of chickens you're pretty damned ignorant."

"Axed," Rose Ella said.

"What's that?"

"I didn't shoot them, stupid. That's for cowards. I chopped off their heads. Besides," she said, mocking him, "if you shot them you'd fill all the meat with buckshot, and if you filled all the meat with buckshot what good would that do? Hmm?" She tilted her head and pouted her lips in a half grin of triumph. He turned away, but not before she caught the ripple of anger that tightened his jawline.

Tom Hardin walked down the path (*retreat*, was how Rose Ella thought of it). "You don't mess around with a river in flood," Tom Hardin said. "You don't mess around with love. Love is a flood," he said. "It's got to have its way. The weak and foolish it bowls over, the strong and smart hold out longer but it grabs you by your roots and in the end it all comes to the same."

"That's not love."

"Well, pardon me." He turned around to face her. "You got a better name for it?" She blushed. "Go on, I'm interested."

Anger triumphed over modesty. "That's sex. Like two dogs rutting in the road."

"And have you ever had sex, like two dogs rutting in the road?"

"I can't believe I'm standing here listening to this."

Now it was his turn to grin. "So keep walking, Miss Priss." He moved down the path, thrashing at the broomsage and blackberry canes with his stick. "Your time will come."

"What makes you so sure?"

"Because you're a pretty woman and you want it to happen, and pretty women usually get what they want. Or hadn't you noticed."

"What a talker."

"That's OK. You just hold on to that dog."

The clouds began to spit snow, and before they reached the next trap a fine white powder covered the path. Across the river the mournful howling rose and fell—Rose Ella thought of the coal freight that came through the valley, whose moaning whistle you could hear now more, now less distinctly as it passed across the wide open flatness of a trestle or through a dense clump of trees. Patch strained at the leash, whining through clenched teeth. "If that wouldn't drive you crazy," she had to say aloud. "You'd think they'd breed them or spay them, one."

"They're from Louisville, they ain't got the sense," Tom Hardin said. "They spend as much time yelling at each other as at the dogs. You stop for a second when the wind is blowing right and you'll hear the old man after his wife, or her after him, or both of 'em after the son, and all of 'em after the dogs in between. I'll be sorry to see that bridge come through, and not just for what it'll do to the trapping. We get along just fine with a river in between, and the wider the better."

They were near the river itself now—she smelled its cold wetness and the mud. The path descended a steep, wooded limestone cliff to snake along the curves and oxbows of the flooded banks. They passed landmarks—two massive white oaks, all that remained of the farm where Rose Ella's father had grown up; a creek that her father spoke of fording on his brother's back, and that Rose Ella and Tom Hardin and Patch crossed using a log that the flood had lodged in place.

Another quarter-mile and they came to a carcass of a town. A vast grist mill stood at the river's edge; the river funneled one turbulent arm through the remains of a sluice. But the millstone was gone, and thick water slid past and over the windowsills of the mill store and post office and church, all tilting drunkenly toward the water as if anticipating the flood's carrying them away.

"My father talks about when his folks ran a whole town here," Rose Ella said. "Well. A little town."

The river rolled brownly by.

"All that work," she said.

She hung back, letting Tom Hardin gain ground. With sunrise the sky was clearing and the wind was picking up, blowing now from the northwest, from across the river, and she wanted to listen. She cocked her head—she heard only the dogs' howling and the slipping and sliding gurgle of the water—unless those punctuating sounds were people yelling. She wouldn't believe it. Nobody she knew argued like that—at least, no man and woman, and not practically at dawn. She would sooner believe in ghosts. A chill seized up her shoulders—someone walking over her grave, she told herself, though it could just as easily have been the yelp and yowl from the far riverbank or the brass-bra cold. She tugged at the leash—Patch was still straining toward the river—she looped the chain around her hand and dragged him along, to catch up with Tom Hardin.

They crested a small rise, to hear above the wind's whistling a thrashing in the brush. Patch froze. His ears pricked up, he focused his eyes and nose on the path ahead. Tom Hardin quickened his step. Patch lunged the length of the chain, pulling her along.

The fox was almost invisible against the golden broomsage. He saw them and lay back, baring his teeth, not moving until they were almost upon him. Then he lunged with a high-pitched growl. In midair he reached the length of the trap's tether. He jerked and fell to the ground.

Patch was feinting, dancing, barking at the end of his chain. Tom Hardin spoke a sharp word. Patch looked doubtful. "Sit, dammit!" Tom Hardin said. Patch lowered his haunches to the frozen earth. Tom Hardin waved Rose Ella forward. "Move around to the other side. Give the dog just enough slack to get the fox's attention."

She edged around. The fox leapt at her; she jumped back, scraping her pants on the thorns of last summer's blackberry briars and teasel. "What if he bites?"

Tom Hardin set his lips in a tight line. "I'll call a doctor. You don't *let* him bite. Stay on your toes and out of his reach, and that goes for Patch too. Make the fox come at you. I'll take care of the rest."

She stepped forward, paying out the choke chain that held Patch from tangling with the fox. The dog stood on his hind legs, straining at the chain and barking furiously, a deep bass bark counterbalanced by the high-pitched screams of the fox and underscored by the moaning from the hounds across the river, rising now in intensity and pitch.

The fox lunged again. She held her ground. Tom Hardin raised his walking stick. Stepping in, he struck from behind, a solid blow just behind the fox's jaw. The fox slumped at her feet. Tom Hardin placed his boot behind the fox's skull and stepped forward. Over Patch's barks, over the howling from across the river she heard the sharp crunch of the fox's delicate neck.

For a moment they stood silent while the snow fell, dusting the fox's thick ruddy coat. From its mouth a thin trickle of bright scarlet stained the snow. In the dull daylight its eyes glittered, still hot with rage.

Then Tom Hardin pulled out his flask. "Shit fire!" he cried. "That's no mean job, trapping a fox. Look at that coat." He took a long pull from his pint, threw his arms around her, kissed her hard on the mouth. "You done good, pistol. Here, take a drink." He held out the pint to her.

Later she would convince herself (it would be very much later before she and Tom Hardin spoke to each other of this day) that she just forgot she was holding Patch. In a way it had been Tom Hardin's fault—he offered her the pint; she loosened her grip on the chain to take it; Patch pulled free.

A simple enough excuse except that she wasn't really a drinker and had no intention of drinking at what was practically the break of dawn. Rose Ella never saw much need to remind Tom Hardin of that particular fact, nor did she see much need for herself to recall it, though in the way of such things it returned across the years of its own accord, as clearly as the image of the frozen mink suspended under the water or of Patch's broken body.

And now Patch was gone, a white-and-black half-breed bullet across the snow-flecked field, and Tom Hardin after him just as quick, his whiskey dropped in the snow. Rose Ella had no idea such a big man could move so fast. He leapt bushes, scrambled over a small ravine, plunged through briars, stumbled across the frozen ridges of last fall's plowing, but

Patch got to the river first, and then he was in it. Tom Hardin dropped his pack and splashed in after him—Rose Ella winced when he hit that cold, brown water—up to his knees, and only the tangle of driftwood and briars kept him from going farther. He stood there, muddy water swirling around his legs, crying as if his heart would break. "Patch! Patch!"

She watched the dog's piebald head; she saw him caught up—not pulled under. Then his head jerked back—the choke chain, probably, wrapped around some underwater stump. She saw bearing down on him the floating sycamore trunk, saw it push him along, his paws flailing at its speckled girth; pushing him closer to the shore, into an eddy where maybe Tom Hardin could reach him, until she saw it crush him against the gate of a half-submerged fence. In the stillness of this morning (what happened to the howling from the dogs across the river? this is where her mind went, not wanting to think about what she had done and why she'd done it, this is where her thoughts were as she was watching Patch go under), in the stillness she heard for the second time that morning the crunch of breaking bone, and the dog's single sharp cry. The log rolled past Patch, around and over his head, a lazy, unconcerned, indifferent rolling, and then it was drifting downstream, leaving Patch hung against the gate, unmoving.

By the time Rose Ella reached the river's edge Tom Hardin was splashing through the water—up to his waist now, he was not so much walking as wafted along by eddies in the current. He caught Patch, slipped the chain from his neck, half-floated, half-carried him to the shore and into the field, where he fell to his knees and laid him out in the frozen mud. His hands passed over the dog—big, callused, competent hands, and to her everlasting humbleness Rose Ella Perlite felt rising within her that same hot swell that she'd felt earlier that morning when Tom Hardin had snapped off his walking stick. What would it mean, to have hands like those pass over her body in exactly that way?

"He's still living," she said, to say something.

"You could say that." Tom Hardin did not look up.

"I didn't let him go." The falseness in her voice prodded her to spill some small part of the truth. "I mean, I might have wanted to, but I didn't."

"And why the hell did you want that."

"Because I didn't believe he would go for the river. I thought he was smarter than that."

"Like smartness has anything to do with it." He stumbled to his feet, scrabbled in his knapsack, stuck a pistol in her hand. "Shoot him. Go ahead, dammit. He's no good for a hunter anymore and pet dogs are a dime a dozen. Or you can carry him home and play nurse. He's yours and I hope he lives to enjoy it. It's up to you." He clipped the fox to his belt and stalked away.

Alone with Patch. She studied the gun, studied the dog—his glazed eyes, the jerky rise and fall of his chest—broken ribs, probably, and a broken leg for certain, a compound break, the bone's ragged edge cutting into his chest, striated layerings of muscle visible through the torn flesh. But not much blood, not yet. With help she might get him back to the truck alive. If he lived through that (not likely), then with a lot of help and a lot more luck she might nurse him back to some kind of three-legged health. Or she could leave him lying—something would get him within the hour. Turkey vultures at least, or bobcats, or just plain shock and cold.

She knelt, checked the magazine, put the pistol to his head, closed her eyes, pulled the trigger, felt the pistol's recoil in her arm and somewhere deeper.

Among the debris cast up by the flood she found some

rags and waterlogged cardboard, not much but enough to wrap around the dog's body. On her way back she tripped over the pint, which still held a slug of whiskey. She lay Patch on the ground, raised the pint to the sky, made a wordless wish, downed it in a gulp. Then she gathered the dog into her arms and carried him to the truck.

Almost there and she met Tom Hardin. "I'll be damned," he said. He turned back. At the truck he opened the tailgate.

"Get out of my way." She heaved the dog, heedless of her clothes—she was covered with blood—into the truck. Where had she found such strength? She slammed the tailgate shut, tossed him the gun—she hoped it went off in his face. "Get me home, you goddamn son of a bitch."

Tom Hardin climbed into the cab, gunning the accelerator and shoving the truck into gear before she had her door closed.

They climbed a steep grade to sail wordlessly along the stony spine of an ancient ridge. Below and to either side fog filled the hollows, pillowing white; overhead the sun pierced the clouds in patches of blinding blue. Caught and refracted in every ice-rimed branch and twig, a million brilliant suns dazzled their silence, and in that silence, in the avalanching memory of Tom Hardin's careless, heedless, headlong run and the sure touch of his oversized hands, Rose Ella Perlite understood that here was a man with whom she had been called upon to reckon.

All Fall Down

[1969–1972]

These were the tense years. The city, once so distant, moved closer—on hot, still summer days they could see the gray pall of its fumes rising over the northern hills; its nighttime glow erased Polaris from their lives. Through television the city entered the Hardins' living room, and in the absence of any pictures of their rural world they came to understand how different they were, what a sheltered life they led, how no one in the great, sprawling mass of their countrymen much cared about the fate of their hinterland village, which for generations they had considered the center of the known universe.

Then the cities exploded. Demonstrations and riots in Watts and Harlem, then Detroit, where they had relatives, then Louisville, growing always closer, or so it seemed to the white men of Strang Knob. Tom Hardin was not the first to keep a loaded pistol in his nightstand drawer. Meanwhile men were going straight from high school to boot camp to Fort Knox to Saigon to Khe Sanh, Cam Ranh Bay, Da Nang; and some from there to the cemetery at Our Lady of the Hills.

While Clark Hardin was still in high school he served as acolyte for the burials of any number of local men. Then he graduated, to attend the local community college for one semester and wait to be drafted. When he was called, he went. A fleet of buses picked him and some other nineteen-year-olds up at the county courthouse to drive them to a Louisville induction center for their mental and physical exams.

Clark was assigned to a group of five boys he'd never met, all of them so green he was the only one ever to have ridden an elevator. Throughout the day Clark guided them through the process—assured them they'd all pass. They were country boys—already they knew how to handle a gun; they were familiar enough with death (all those squirrels and doves and deer) to appreciate the power and pleasure of bloodied hands. When one of their number was rejected (heart murmur), they raged as a group. At Clark's suggestion all five gathered around the officer who sported the most bars and stars, who looked to be running the show. Why, they'd known their friend since he was a kid, they protested; they'd seen him throw hay and strip tobacco! The officer agreed to forward the case to Washington. Touched by their earnestness, he suggested they consider enlisting as a group. They left his office tinged with no small excitement—Washington! It was as close to glory as they'd known.

The night before he left for boot camp, Clark stopped in Our Lady of the Hills, lit a votive candle, and knelt. He intended to say his usual memorized prayers—a rosary or even the Litany of the Saints. Their singsong monotony of call and response elevated him into a kind of meditative trance, the most peaceful state he knew (long after Vatican II he still delivered his responses in mysterious, extraterrestrial Latin: House of Gold, *miserere nobis*; Mystical Rose, *ora pro nobis*).

But this night his heart broke inside him. Out poured feelings he'd not even suspected: fear, anger, resentment (*why me?*), guilt (*I should be proud to serve my country*), and swarming throughout all a remnant of his thinking, rational self, figuring the odds, attempting to stanch the torrent with reason: *You'll come back. You'll survive.*

He had come to the church for peace and he found none,

and finally he decided he would be better off amid the noise and bustle and farewell drinks of his family. He rose and turned to go, to be overtaken by this single, great fear, born of too many nights of watching the war play itself out on Walter Cronkite. He turned back to the altar, slipped a quarter into the slotted brass box, and lit a votive light before the statue of Saint Anthony.

He'd known since knowing that it was against the rules to wish for some specific benefit—it was demeaning to the whole notion of prayer to see it as some kind of tit-for-tat devotion, so much piety in exchange for a late-model Corvette. Besides, it stood to reason that God and the saints were above such manipulation. There was no more certain way to jinx a wish than to articulate it straightforwardly, to ask for something for yourself. The secret lay in subterfuge—if what you really wanted was a swing set, pray for a neighborhood playground.

But his religion was a mixture of Baltimore Catechism and childhood superstition, and Clark, lighting the votive candle before Saint Anthony, could not keep himself from wishing—just this once, even though he knew he was breaking the rules. So he struck the match and lit the candle and spoke aloud the worst fate his heart could enfold and comprehend. "Don't let me come back crippled."

1970—midway through Clark's tour of duty—two dress-uniformed soldiers appeared at the Hardins' door, one older (a chaplain, but not Catholic—the Catholic chaplain was already with another family in this Catholic neck of the woods with so many twenty-year-old soldiers). The younger soldier broke down and cried as he delivered the news, even as Rose Ella and Tom Hardin stayed dry-eyed. The chaplain was grateful for their composure, though he thought to himself that they'd suffer for it later.

❀   ❀   ❀

The soldiers are gone. From the window Rose Ella and Tom Hardin watch their black, government-issue Ford back slowly from the drive (it's a tricky dogleg, it's easy to ram the Chinese elm, Rose Ella finds herself worrying about such things). And then they are left alone with each other and their grief. They pass a few minutes in stunned silence, neither so much as weeping. Then in their way they separate, Tom Hardin to his woodshop, Rose Ella to her flowers.

Behind the locked door of his woodshop, Tom Hardin remembers the day when he and a team of white men pulled from the icy river a colored boy, surely no more than sixteen, who'd been knocked in the head, then thrown from the railroad bridge by an overzealous train watchman. A night and a day in the river and the boy looked like he'd just fallen in—the river had preserved him in its cold embrace. As they lifted the boy to shore, Leola Ferber, Rose Ella's laundrywoman and the boy's mother? grandmother? let forth an unearthly keening cry, the moan of a hundred lost souls. Here in his workshop Tom Hardin understands that in that moment all griefs had been enfolded into Leola's grief, all losses were her loss. He feels now welling from his gut that same woman cry and he chokes it down and back, he swallows it into rage at himself for all the chances he missed to be a better father to his son.

It was his son's duty, his father's duty, he tells himself this. They have been good citizens.

He kneels before his workbench and strikes his forehead against its sharp edge until blood mixes with his tears and the pain drowns the cry stuck in his throat. From under the shelf he pulls a bottle of whiskey. He drinks in long hot swigs until he passes out.

Sometime in the night he awakes covered with his own

vomit. He is savagely proud of this humiliation *(This is what I think of You and Your fucking life, God damn!)*. He feels taken, used, a fool—where is the honor that he thought would come with such a death? It isn't politics that has robbed this from his son and from himself—he knows what he thinks about the politics of it all and Clark's death has done nothing to change his opinion *(to hell with the protesters, they should be rounded up and stuck in the front lines as cannon fodder, a fate too good for them, if a dozen had been standing in front of Clark, who'd been doing his duty in fighting for them, he would still be alive now)*.

Something else has happened here. He has discovered that he is a father. He is bound to this distant corpse in ways stronger and larger than he can comprehend.

Later, when Clark's body is returned, Tom Hardin's grief will center itself on the slow and necessary labor of accepting what cannot be accepted—that this son, with Rose Ella's tapered legs and his own broad shoulders, will never return. They will not look up one day to see him loping up the drive. Miracles do not happen.

For now, his discovery of his father's place seeks its greatest pain in the understanding that like most revelations, this one has come too late. All he has now is knowledge of his loss. He can be no better or kinder to Clark than he once was, or wasn't. If a time might come when the pain of this knowledge might teach him something—he cannot and does not want to imagine that far in the future. Lying on his side on the workshop floor, knees drawn to his chest and arms crossed, he is nowhere but the here and now, where he is discovering that with Clark's death some living and essential part of himself has died.

Tom Hardin had chosen (yes, he'd had opportunities— he could have moved to the city, made more money, lived in a suburb in a tract house), he had chosen to live his life in one place because he wanted to remain loyal to that place, to pass a lifetime making love to it and then to be enfolded peacefully into its open earth at his death. Now his son is dead ten thousand miles from a home that no longer seems like home, that through Clark's death has lost its sacredness, has been transformed from a holy place into a plot of dirt indistinguishable from any other. It is Tom Hardin's first intimation of old age—his first understanding that the places and the life he has taken for granted are growing and changing into places where he will not be following. Places and faces more familiar to him than his own hands are leaving him behind; the day is coming when he will look upon his heart's landscape only to find it so changed that he is no longer part of it, no more than a pilgrim moving across its foreign face to journey's end.

His own father hadn't launched Tom Hardin into the world with any understanding of this—there'd been no need for it. The world was a known quantity, the ways a man might grow into his hands were fixed in number and entailed three considerations: learning how to do a given thing (carpentry, whiskey making, hunting, running a store); knowing somebody who would teach you to do it well; passing it on to someone in your turn. The learning and the knowing demanded hard work but both were easy enough come by—you just had to keep your eyes open and look around. As for the passing on—this was why a man had several sons, so that there would be at least one at hand to take up his proper place when that time arrived.

Where had Tom Hardin got the notion that this way was not good enough for his own sons? He couldn't say. All he knew was that from his earliest thought of having sons (not the daughters—sure, they'd been educated, but that was Rose Ella's doing), he understood that his boys were to learn books, they would go to be a soldier or get a scholarship or whatever and then use that as a way to get to college, to find their ways into safe jobs where they would wear coats and ties and make enough money to live in the kind of luxury that Tom Hardin himself had once turned down. That none of his sons would follow him into his work, that they would move far away, that he would have nothing in common with their new world, that one would die in some unheard-of foreign place—who could have told him this? How might he have learned this, except by living through it? For better and worse, Tom Hardin had known the world he was entering when he entered it. Now when he speaks to his sons it's as if he's talking across a river, that has grown wider and deeper with each passing year. Only Clark had shown any signs of wanting to stay nearby, to learn what his father had to teach—wood, and hunting, and the multiplicity of small things a man of Tom Hardin's generation needed to know to get by. And now the river separating him from Clark is never to be bridged.

He will be better to his remaining sons, Tom Hardin swears this as he hauls himself to his feet. He will try to enter their lives, rather than demand that they enter his.

How is it possible to comprehend fully the dimensions of love except through grief? Rose Ella seizes upon this terrible dilemma in the days following the chaplain's visit—this thought and nothing else keeps her from breaking apart. While Clark was alive she took him for granted. Now that he is dead she sees the scope and grandeur of her love. She spends her time trying to convince herself that this is only human, that this is the purpose of grief and death, that these exist to teach the heart its dimensions. Clark's memory and presence are now defined by the length, height, depth, and mass of her grief, which is exactly as tall, wide, deep, and heavy as she.

If she could see his body she would be able to cry—in the first days following the chaplain's visit she tells herself this: See him dead and she would be able to believe in his death. But in the absence of his corpse his death is nothing but loss, emptiness, nothingness, whose reality is as abstract as zero.

And then his body arrives. A week, two weeks since his death in a hot, tropical country—they cannot open the coffin. "He died in a war, ma'am," says the soldier when she asks; then, as if to make amends for his bluntness, "He was a hero."

Her heart has no room for Tom Hardin—that will come later. In the first months following the news, the arrival of Clark's body, the funeral, there is only the contradiction between the infinitude of her suffering and the neat black dimensions of her loss.

She cannot go out. The sight of people together—a girl and her boyfriend, a man and his wife, most especially a woman and her child—causes her physical pain. If they are affectionate or chatting her envy forms an acid hole in her stomach. If they are fighting she wants to fly at them, to remonstrate—don't they know the insignificance of their petty argument, the value of their time together, what they're frittering away?

She passes afternoons—the hardest times—digging in her flower beds, working to accept the burden of her grief. While Clark was alive she'd never acknowledged what she now admits—always she'd thought of him as the safe son, the son who never got into trouble, who seemed best adjusted to the world. He wasn't rambunctious (like Joe Ray) or bedeviled by some deep bone of solitude (like Raphael). With so many children it was a relief to have one who seemed to flourish on his own, about whom she didn't have to worry. She'd wondered some-times if he didn't need a little more personality—she'd thought a stint in the military might be good for him, might toughen him up and help him settle who he was and where he was go-ing. His death she sees now as her punishment for taking him for granted, a sentence that she has no choice but to serve out. Her penance is to keep his memory alive as long as she lives, and to pray for his soul.

But when she kneels before Our Lady of the Hills her heart is blank, a newly erased blackboard on which she is afraid to write because she knows what will come: rage, disbelief, bitterness. No prayers come to her, not even the memorized mantras (Hail Mary, Our Father, Glory Be) that she knows deep as love itself. Finally she asks forgiveness for her doubt, rises and crosses herself, promises to return tomorrow.

And she does return, for the better part of a year she kneels daily and waits for Clark's memory, his living face, some ghost to seize her heart and break it if need be, but she looks down into her heart and she sees no spark, no light, only a blank and even gray stillness.

Each evening Raphael and Tom Hardin watched Walter Cronkite alone—with Clark in Vietnam, Rose Ella couldn't bear the shots of bomb-strewn villages, mangled and decapi-tated bodies, crowded hospitals, and always the possibility (certainty?) that Clark was in there somewhere; and then the news of Clark's death.

The night after Clark's funeral Raphael and Tom Hardin found their separate ways to the television—Tom Hardin to prove to himself that nothing had changed, that the world was still the same; Raphael in the certainty that now, surely, Tom

Hardin would understand all that was different, the revolution that was upon them.

Across the next months they watched in silence—almost in silence. Villagers fleeing burning huts—Raphael shook his head and muttered, "Our tax dollars at work." Protesters rioting in the streets, tac squads wielding bullet-proof shields, tear gas, batons—Tom Hardin growled, "Too good for them."

Each night the air grew more charged, until no one else could bear to enter the room, and still Tom Hardin and Raphael made their father-and-son ways to sit before the television and watch.

Until barely a year after Clark's death, when Raphael was called for the draft, driven to the county seat by a tight-lipped Rose Ella, put on the bus, and taken to the Louisville induction center.

In little more than a year this much had changed: The stories Raphael heard on the bus involved how to stump the doctor, how to fool the system. Everyone in his group knew how to use an elevator. They'd all watched the war on television; everyone thought of himself as potential cannon fodder. Drinking six-packs of Cokes to raise the blood sugar, downing white crosses (plentifully available now, from returned GIs who had picked up the habit in the service and were selling them to make an easy buck) to screw up the blood pressure. There was discussion of how to fail the mental abilities test, but Raphael knew he'd not get far cheating on that—he a scholarship recipient.

But before the medical and mental exams Raphael came to this small moment of truth. *Do you have or have you had any of the following?* the induction form asked. *Heart disease, diabetes, rheumatic fever?* Raphael checked *No—No—No*, until he came to this casually planted time bomb: *Homosexual tendencies?* Raphael read the question with an electric shock, checked a hasty negative, moved down the page.

He filed as a C.O.—conscientious objector. The draft board secretary, a buxom childless woman, studied him with a worried glance. Did he realize—of course not, he was only a teenager—the implications of what he was doing? Forget about a career in politics! she said, and that's only the beginning.

But branded for life as a C.O. wasn't the worst fate one could suffer, Raphael thought; the Army itself acknowledged as much. It was better than confessing to wanting men.

And so Raphael went before the Jessup County draft board. He lied to Tom Hardin and Rose Ella—told them he had a date, asked Rose Ella to cut his hair, and borrowed the car from Tom Hardin. He drove to the county seat, to be grilled by seven old men (two farmers, one preacher, two shopkeepers, a teacher, a salesman). He knew five of them. They all knew his father.

"I want you to tell me why a son of Tom Hardin's would waste our time with such bullshit." That was the first question. "You know why they call it C.O.?" the salesman asked, and answered his own joke. "Short for C-O-W-A-R-D." The preacher, chairman of the board, spoke up. "We'll have none of that."

Across two hours Raphael cajoled, flattered, charmed, pleaded, argued. He quoted the Bible to the preacher, and though they argued the question back and forth the preacher acknowledged that there was a good deal in Scripture to support Raphael's choice.

In the end Raphael won on a 4–3 vote. The preacher voted for him and persuaded one of the farmers, who felt that with Clark's death the Hardins had suffered enough. The teacher and the salesman voted to support his application because they figured they'd be doing the armed forces a favor by keeping him out. The shopkeepers and the other farmer voted as a bloc: no, no, no.

Soon afterward the government announced the end of the draft.

But Raphael guarded in his heart this new knowledge, imparted to him by the military questionnaire. It was the first time he'd ever seen the word *homosexual* used in some ordinary public place, it was his first clue that there were others who were something like the something he feared he might be; enough of them (evidently) that the Army worried about keeping them out.

The same night of the draft board's confidential hearing, the preacher told his church secretary about the board's decision (they were secretly in love and shared all secrets). The next day she told the county judge—she could hardly keep it a secret; it was only the second such hearing in the history of the draft board and naturally the judge was curious. In turn he told a monk from a nearby monastery who was in traffic court for speeding (50 m.p.h. in a 25 m.p.h. zone). And the monk, Brother Hippolytus, told Rose Ella when they saw each other in the monastery vestibule after Sunday mass.

That afternoon she searched Raphael out—he was packing for college, for the trip west he was about to take. "I saw Brother Hippolytus," she said. "He tells me you—that you met with the draft board the other night."

Raphael kept packing.

"Why didn't you tell us about it?"

"It's not like one of us wasn't enough. You have to ship *me* off, too."

Thinking back, Rose Ella realized she'd never heard him

speak so openly such resentment and anger. But at the moment she was blinded by her own anger. He had never talked to her like this—none of her children had. "You don't know how I feel," she said. "He was my son."

He gave her a look of such contempt that she left the room.

That afternoon, for the first time in their marriage, Rose Ella asked Tom Hardin to meet her in his woodshop. She had to tell him about Raphael's hearing and the board's decision— better she than somebody Tom Hardin ran into on the street. She had a notion that she'd seat herself on Tom Hardin's high drafting chair—her feet barely reached its footrest—and tell him everything that Hippolytus had told her, everything she knew about the hearing and the vote (excepting Raphael's last look as he was packing—she'd leave that part out. Tom Hardin would cut a forsythia limb and whale into Raphael as if he were a child, and Lord knows what that would lead to). She sat in the kitchen marshaling her arguments: This war had damaged the family enough, she was not about to let it divide them further, Tom Hardin would support Raphael in this or at least hold his peace. Then she went to the shop.

She shut the door behind her—Raphael was somewhere around the house, and she had no wish to let him witness this conversation. She turned to face her husband, all his familiar lines and creases; she opened her mouth to plunge into her speech.

"Love is a flood," was what she said. She crossed her arms, clenching her fists into her armpits. "A creek coming down, is what you meant. One big wall of water and then nothing but a dried-up old slough." It was the first time either had spoken to each other of their first date.

He frowned for a moment, then picked up a block of pale cypress he'd been cutting into a hobbyhorse for Joe Ray's new baby. "To tell the truth, I never thought you'd shoot that dog. I thought you'd carry him back to the truck—make him into a pet. You could of done that. He wasn't hurt that bad."

She looked down at her hands—she saw them covered with blood. Patch's blood, after she'd carted him a mile and more from the river, to heave his corpse into Tom Hardin's truck? Or her own blood, the afterbirth of her children?

Afterward she could not remember what followed, except that she was screaming and throwing what was in reach— chisels, nails, a hammer—at Tom Hardin until he pinned her against the wall, clutching her doubled wrists in one hand while with the other he slapped her with silent, fury-filled blows that she watched happening as if from another world and time and place. And then she was punctuating the close air of the shop with her screams and he was on his knees sobbing at her feet.

She ran from the shop to escape, but where was there to go? This house was her only home—to enter it was no different from walking deliberately into a trap, a drowning set in which she herself was drowning. She ran past the house, down the dogleg drive until the stabbing pains in her side forced her to slow to a walk, but she walked on until she reached the fresh mound of Clark's grave, where she lay herself carefully down on the grass and turned her eyes to the sky and its silence. Here she lay for some long time.

Lying on the grass she removed her memory to the morning a few years into their marriage, when Tom Hardin taught her to set bank poles. They'd left Leola at the house, then crept past the room where the children slept four abreast in Rose Ella's grandmother's four-poster. They drove the old truck (held together with barbed wire and baling twine but still running) into an opalescent dawn. From the riverbank they ducked through a cut and into the river's green tunnel.

Life devouring life: mosquitoes sucked at Rose Ella, minnows snapped at mosquitoes, frogs snapped at minnows, turtles snapped at frogs; when Rose Ella waded into the water, crayfish nibbled at her toes. River, river, the place that she loved more than any other place. She waded toward the first bank pole, to be startled by a dead branch that plopped into the water, then swam away.

They pulled one pole, then another from the bank: no luck. Tom Hardin thrashed at the smartweed with a long wand of cane. "I know I stuck a pole in here somewhere."

"Father." These names, taught to their children and then learned back, they now used for each other.

"Won't you know it'll be the one with the five-pound bass." Oblivious to the stinging leaves, he waded into a jungle of smartweed. Rose Ella saw nothing of her husband, only the plants' thrashing tops.

"There!" Pole and man came flying out of the weeds. No fish.

She pointed at the next pole, dipping and bobbing. "Looks like we got *one* anyway."

And that was all they got. Rose Ella swam across a deep hole, pulled the pole from the bank: He was hooked good, a nice steel-blue channel cat.

Back at the house the kids were still in bed. Tom Hardin hooked his fingers under the cat's gills and handed it to her. "You catch it, you kill it."

She looked blank. "Well, it's not like it's a chicken."

He laid the fish on the carriage rock, a huge block of limestone from which his great-grandfather had mounted horses. "It's tough to do it quick with a knife. A cat has this thick skull—a knife just bounces off. What I do is pick it up by its tail and slam its head flat against the rock. That's fastest for the fish, seems to me." He stood behind her, wrapped his body around hers, ran his arms down her arms and his hands over her hands. As if clutching a baseball bat their hands entwined around the fish's tail—some smooth, prehistoric thing, less like a fish than some large worm that had crawled from the muck.

Supper, she thought, and together they swung, and the impact of the fish against the rock stunned her like sex.

Beside the newly planted sod of Clark's grave, Rose Ella remembers not so much the solid smack of life against rock but the pleasure of learning, and being taught, and—she is too honest with herself to deny it—the running of his arms down and along her own.

It was the learning that drew her to him, she understood it that morning at the carriage rock, she'd understood it without knowing as much when she'd first said yes to his invitation to run traps. From him she could learn something about the workings of another, different world. Camp Junior—he'd been at the university learning law, learning about the feint-and-dodge manipulations of men and women, but she was a woman, to whom an understanding of all that came with her particular territory. (In another, later era she might have been a lawyer—years later her youngest daughter told her as much.) What stirred her about Tom Hardin was his different knowledge, his place so foreign from her own; the lure of a lover as foreign as she was likely to find under Strang Knob. This he would never lose; this, and the plain old challenge of riding herd over her own desire for a man more bullheaded in desire than even she. This would last her lifetime.

But with Clark's death their stubbornness had reached a standoff; hardly for the first time, though this time the enormity of their pain intensified the moment. Once again it had come to this, where one or the other would have to yield and submit.

Always Rose Ella swore that this time she would be a bigger rock than he, a wall higher than his, a range of mountains to his high peak; and then the memory returned of those terrible days following Raphael's birth, when she had been a rock, a wall, an unmoving range until her stomach rebelled and every bite of any food tasted of her own bile and Tom Hardin had been—himself; unmoving, unmoved.

Now she was here again with seven children (no, *six*, now, *six*) all grown but still hers. She had things to do, a world to attend to, she was the wearing water, the river flowing to the sea and still he was the rain-washed stone, the unmoved and unmoving rock in the river, his wearing down was that slow.

Tomorrow she could reason all this out—she could see how exactly right she was, she would know exactly what she ought to have said and done. But at the moment itself she was always seized by—what? Some force larger than herself, that she did not want to name but that held in it all that time and children, Clark and now Raphael and even Patch, and the desire that could seize her still when that time came and the moon was right and it had been long enough since she'd had his chest under her hand.

And so she would break around him and move on. Did this make her a fool or a saint? That question she could not answer. She knew only that she was the ever-changing foundation, the fixed place that changes its shape to accommodate the needs of the hour, the day, the year. She was what this family must have if it was to endure.

She rose and walked home to fix supper, an ordinary supper of mashed potatoes and fried catfish and green beans.

Tom Hardin remained in the woodshop, too stunned by what he had done to follow his wife. He'd never before been seized and drawn out of himself in front of another human being, though looking back now he saw how and where this had been coming: the storing up of anguish, waiting for the opportunity of lashing out at the target closest at hand; and Rose Ella was always closest at hand.

He forced himself to sit at his bench, to take up the hobbyhorse on which he'd been working. It quivered in his hands as if alive—it was his hands that were trembling.

He took out his knife to bevel its edges. His fingers knew how to shape the wood without thought or volition on his head's part; the knife was an extension of his hand, a sharpened sixth finger. Watching the horse emerging from its sleep in the heart of this blond block of cypress, Tom Hardin resolved this: Rather than risk such violence he would retreat from himself. He would place enough distance between his heart and what he does that there can be no chance of his striking her again.

He would not speak of this decision, he decided, to Rose Ella—to speak of it would only be to invite this turmoil back into his life. He had struck her from some blind love—for his dead son, for her—and from some self-contempt too deepseated to risk examining: contempt for his wordlessness, his stubbornness, his inability to submit to the yoke, his shifting of its burden always to her. He understood this, at the same time that he feared more than pain the labor of putting it into words. He was too proud.

That night he turned to her, to rest his hand on her swollen cheek. She did not resist. He opened his mouth—he wanted to find some words with which to speak of love. He was daunted by the largeness of her heart—by the completeness and certainty of its demands.

She covered his lips with hers; she made love to him.

She is big enough to do this, he thought. *Of the two of us she is the stronger.*

I am the one who forgives, she thought this in her last thinking moments before desire consumed her thoughts. *This is the source of my pain and power.*

It was not what she had imagined when she was young, or what they'd had in the first years after they married, but it was more than sex—it was all that shared time and memory that had bound them together on this starry, pricking wheel, long after they'd settled into the ordinariness of their married lives. Clark's death was one more binding thing—even as it belonged to them separately it was another of those things that held them together. They both knew this, in some unchanging way; it was the only unchanging thing they knew.

He never raised his hand to her again. Raphael's military service vanished as a subject of conversation or argument. The war itself vanished: Raphael left to drive west to California for college; Tom Hardin stopped watching Walter Cronkite and went directly to his woodshop from supper. They had no more sons to give; they would not think or talk of the war again. It was as if Clark had died in a car wreck, or of some strange, unheard of, untalked about disease.

Grief is like any wound—some terrible pleasure resides in it. Better to knead that pain, that terrible pleasure than to have nothing at all. If love fulfills itself in companionship, grief fulfills itself in solitude, for we grieve finally and necessarily less for the dead than for our living selves, our aloneness in our survival, our inescapable invitation to the dance.

Rose Ella still takes flowers to Clark's grave—flowers that she cuts from her yard, mixed with wildflowers that she gathers along the roadside and from fields. She arranges these in containers that she herself designed to sidestep the new cemetery rules against flower arrangements. Spring: jonquils, sweet-scented hyacinth, daffodils, extravagant peonies. Summer: roses, sweet william, honeysuckle, day lilies, money plant, brilliant ironweed, and the recumbent obedient plant. Autumn: black-eyed Susans, joe-pye weed, purple loosestrife, chrysanthemums. Winter: cattail, crown of thorns, lustrous green magnolia leaves, pampas grass; tight-berried scarlet cones of staghorn sumac entwined with red-orange bittersweet.

The flowers on Clark's grave evoke for Rose Ella the progression of the seasons—she measures, for example, the end of summer by the day when she cuts the last violet inflorescence of ironweed from the fields. His grave comes for her to represent time passing, her own mortality, and she goes and stands before his plain white cross and grieves into the unbroken gray stillness of her heart.

The Way Things
Will Always Be

[1963]

Climbing the ravines that carve the sides of Strang Knob is the only way to reach the rock house. From above, an overhanging cliff forms a pouting, precipitous lip; to either side a dense undergrowth of briars blocks the way. The cliff forms the roof and ceiling for the house, whose floor is a flat, sandy ledge, always dry except in one corner, where a spring seeps from a crevice in the limestone. To find this place a newcomer must be guided by someone who knows the land, who in his turn has learned the way from someone before, on back to the Cherokee who camped here on their hunting forays into the valleys under Strang Knob.

During Tom Hardin's childhood, arrowheads had been plentiful—in the ravine that funneled down the cliffside from the rock house they'd all but crunched underfoot. By the time his son Clark walks these hills the arrowheads have almost disappeared, picked over by white men and children and lost to erosion. But on sunny afternoons in early spring, after winter rains wash the banks of dead leaves but before the concealing sprouts of ginseng and coltsfoot, Clark still turns up an arrowhead or two, their immigrant flint foreign against the calcified limestone.

Each summer and into the fall the rock house is home for Gaspard, the last Cherokee whom anyone in these parts knows of, who is possessed of the cheekbones and straight black hair to prove his lineage. He lives in the rock house until Christmas Eve, when he brings his few possessions down from the hills to Leola Ferber's house, to receive his Christmas basket from Tom Hardin and to spend his winter months living with the woman the town has decided to call his wife.

On this particular Christmas Eve, Clark is thirteen and readying himself to spend the afternoon at the house of some friends who (they claim) have sneaked a pint of whiskey from some suspecting adult's liquor cabinet. But Tom Hardin corrals his son at the door, to order him to come along on his Christmas rounds. Clark argues, but Tom Hardin is not much given to listening to argument, especially from his sons. "You're of an age," he says. "It's time you learned your responsibilities."

Rose Ella has prepared baskets, each with cheese, bread, store-bought Florida citrus, secondhand clothing, nuts, cupcakes, and some practical gift (for Leola, a hammer; for Gaspard, a wool cap). She searches her closets to put together a packet of ironing—paying work for Leola. To this Tom Hardin adds a gallon jar of white dog, gin-clear whiskey legally made and illegally tapped from the condenser before years in a charred oak barrel give it color and weaken its proof, and before the government men have gauged it for their tax. Clark loads the baskets in the car and he and his father set off.

Leola lives in a small house in what passes for the colored section under Strang Knob. Excepting her months with Gaspard she lives by herself, but until the past few years she has never been alone. First she had her own children, then grandchildren and great-grandchildren turned up on her doorstep, left by sons and daughters long gone to the city. Leola was not one to haggle over details of genealogy. So long as they were not the proper ward of some overzealous Christian charity she took them in. If they were old enough, able-bodied, and clear of mind, she put them to work ironing and chopping wood. The feeble and the maimed she shut inside a chicken-wire fence, where they were safe from the depredations of the pigs and where they more or less entertained themselves with whatever lay at hand.

Then the promise of some kind of freedom lured these children, grandchildren, great-grandchildren, and neighbors to the big-city ghettos. The government came and took away the maimed and infirm to what they promised was a better life. By Christmas Eve of Clark's thirteenth year Leola's house *is* the colored section—she is the only black person left under Strang Knob, her house the only house on Cornbread Alley where the census taker troubles to knock.

It is a tumbledown house, which white folks comfortably call a disgrace. An aluminum ladder missing most of its rungs angles across its gabled roof. In winter its windows trail tattered plastic that Leola staples to the frames for insulation. The yard is packed bare and strewn with other people's trash (the shell of a 1939 Ford, the mangle from a wringer washer), that white people bring and dump here under the assumption that the poorest poor are most adept at making silk from sow's ears. The house has weathered to the color of the limestone cliff against which it crouches. As Clark and Tom Hardin cross the yard a half-feral sow casts a malevolent eye from a hole in the planks that skirt the crawl space below the porch.

Inside, Leola is ironing. Great folds of flesh hang at her cheeks, her legs are two thick pilings supporting her bulk—later Rose Ella will tell Clark that she suffers from some disorder of the glands. She wears sheer nylons rolled at the knee and a shapeless dress of some coarse black fabric, with another nylon pulled over her grizzled hair as a cap. At her side she keeps a

Mason jar, holes punched in its tin lid, filled with water with which she sprinkles each shirt before its pressing. She smells frankly of winter weeks without hot water.

Gaspard sits at the table nearby, rail-thin, a dog-eared game of solitaire spread out before him. His face is as seamed and wrinkled as the shirts Leola pulls from the laundry basket. His cheeks are grizzled—"the white blood in him, that makes those whiskers," Tom Hardin told Clark this on the drive from the Hardin house—but above these his cheekbones slash forward sharp and chiseled as arrowheads. His eyes sit deep in their sockets, his forehead is a map of some broad and furrowed field. Clark has known Leola and Gaspard all his life, but always he has encountered them on *his* turf, as visitors in *his* life, and he has never before noticed who they are, which is to say who he himself is. Now he sees for the first time how his own features, his family's features, belong to his immigrant forebears—their broad, blank foreheads, their wide-spaced eyes, their strong chins of some Scottish Highland people squared and set for generations against any kind of revelation of what might lie underneath. Gaspard and Leola—they are homely, there is no denying this, but their faces are like mountain ranges, raised and folded and creased, the living manifestation of the forces at work within. It is all Clark can do not to stare. What would bring faces to look like these?

Tom Hardin places one basket on the table. Clark places the other at Gaspard's feet and hands Leola the packet of ironing from his mother. From deep in his hunting jacket Tom Hardin pulls a pint of white dog. Leola sets her iron aside—Clark recognizes it from its first life under Rose Ella's hands; she'd passed it on when she bought one of the newfangled kind that make their own steam.

Leola pulls up a chair for Tom Hardin, overturns a

wooden crate for Clark, circles these around the wood-burning stove, welded from an empty oil barrel and some excess stove pipe—Tom Hardin has been at work here. From a cabinet Leola produces three empty peanut butter jars scrubbed clean. "Your counting's falling off," Tom Hardin says, and Leola returns to the cabinet to scrabble around until she finds a fourth jar. Tom Hardin pours two fingers of dog in each glass. He hands these around, giving the last to Clark. It is the first time his father has offered him a drink.

Clark puts the glass to his nose. Underneath the pungent, sinus-clearing dog he smells a faint whiff of Skippy. Leola takes up her glass, then her iron. They wade into the winter afternoon as if it were a warm and shallow summer-comfort lake.

The past is what they talk about. Leola remembers some-one who is dead, or gone to the city—the same state of being to her, since the city, a place she has heard about but never been, is no more or less real to her than the realms of the dead—heaven, hell, purgatory; limbo, where so many of her babies now reside. Her surviving children are all gone, to the ghetto, to be soldiers (her oldest great-grandchild has just been shipped to some distant, war-struck place), to the pen (several of her sons are serving time at La Grange).

All these years of caretaking and now she is alone with her ironing. There is less work for her under Strang Knob—the white folks' children are growing up and leaving, too, and the younger mothers are buying fancy steam irons. But she has only her own mouth to feed now and she gets along. She is good at getting along.

Leola pours forth a story, a slow-flowing river of words that rolls and tumbles on, about a brother of hers killed in the thirties, the slim years, when he jumped from a cliff onto a moving coal car, so as to toss chunks of coal onto the railbed for people to gather. On this day something went wrong—he misjudged the speed of the car? Struck his head while jumping? Leola's neighbors claimed a train guard chased him down and threw him from the railroad bridge. However it happened, the next day they found the boy floating in the river, hung on a snag beneath the railroad trestle, hardly a mark on his body for all his trouble.

After a respectful pause Tom Hardin follows with his version of the same story, which includes some gentle correction of Leola—Tom Hardin having been during those same years an employee of the railroad.

The story is sensitive—Clark feels that sharpness about the edges of words that signals a forthcoming change in the topic of conversation. And after a while Leola begins to talk of the young pictureman who came to town long ago, Miss Camilla's father, who took Leola's mother's washing money and her picture and then left town, never to return with the pictures they'd paid for and he'd taken.

Tom Hardin laughs at this old story. "He probably never bothered to load the camera," he says.

As for Gaspard, he does not talk much but offers choral commentary. "He ought never have taken those pictures, if he had no intention of getting them back to their rightful owners." "She ought never have gone chasing after him, if she wasn't going to bring the baby back here and provide her a home."

Four fingers of dog and Tom Hardin will talk about his sons. "Education," he says.

"That boy goes to school."

"They's all his children gone to school. Even the girls."

"Every one of those boys you'll see in a cap and gown.

It'll happen. As for the girls—they're Rose Ella's affair. But I've gone along, I'll keep on going along. Up to the point where they start learning too much for their own good."

"What they don't teach in school it don't do them no good to learn." Leola shakes her iron. "You want they should learn how to use this?"

"Damn right."

"Huh. You won't find them *boys* working in a 'stillery."

"That's all right"—this from Gaspard—"'cept who's to bring us dog at Christmas?"

"They'll be somebody," Tom Hardin says. "They'll always be a Hardin. You listen to me: Some things never change. You think they'll ever come a time when people stop drinking whiskey? And as long as they're drinking it somebody will make it, and as long as somebody's making it they'll be a Hardin to tap into it and bring you some."

"Tain't nobody else got the heart to bother"—Leola, at the ironing board.

Tom Hardin laughs. "Ain't nobody else got the *key*. And I can take care of that." He slaps Clark on the shoulder. "You hear me say it now. One of my boys is always going to know the ins and outs—one of my boys will bring you dog, as long as you're here to drink it. One of my boys'll see to it that you're *buried* with your dog, if that's what you want."

"Then he'll be prizin' a empty bottle from my folded fingers," Leola says. "Gaspard'll have got to it before then."

A few more fingers of dog and they fall silent. The only sound is the low hum of the stove and the rasp of Leola's iron across cotton. Surely *now* they will take their leave, Clark thinks, but the light fades from the windows and no one talks and they sit and sit, except for Leola, who irons. They are lost in memory, but Clark has not yet accumulated a memory in which to get lost and so he squirms and then rises from his crate to pace the room looking for something to look at. There is nothing to look at except years of the county newspaper with which Leola has insulated the walls, and so he reads these. First to himself, then, as the silence and his impatience grow, aloud. "Flood," he reads.

"What flood?"

"March 27, 1953."

"That was no flood," Tom Hardin says with a reader's satisfaction at unearthing error in print. "They were just needing a headline. Now the flood when I met your mother—*that* was a flood."

"Mother told me you met her at a church social."

"When I met your mother she was on a date with the man she was already signed up to marry," Tom Hardin said. "They were at some fancy-dress party to raise money for the people who'd lost their houses in the flood. Some fool mistakenly provided me an invitation. I slipped a quarter to a colored boy to tell your mother's date some guy was outside working over his car. By the time he got back I had talked her into leaving with me." Tom Hardin closes his eyes. "You let that be a lesson to you when the time comes."

Clark reads on. Weddings, births, football championships, homecoming queens. Then he comes across a prominently displayed article. "Garfield Wilson Accused of Murder," he reads.

"I was the one what found Garfield Wilson sitting on his porch," Leola says. "'Morning, Leola,' he says, just like it was any old ordinary day and I was coming to get the ironing, which is what I was doing. 'How's your wife,' I ask. And he says, "Sdead.' And I says, *'Dead?'* And he says, 'Yep. Shot her.' And I says, 'With a *gun?*'—I knows with a gun, o' course, but all of a sudden I feels her own self looking over his shoulder and him talking to me like it was the courthouse steps, only me right there out on the farm with nobody but him and myself and what was left of Miz Wilson. And he says, 'Yep, I called the shurf and I's sitting here waiting for him to come and hope they put me in the pen which I deserve and worse.' And sure 'nough in a few minutes along come the shurf—they goes inside the house and gets her body—I never set foot inside that house, I couldn't no way make myself do it, she wasn't inside nohow but out there on the porch with him and me and I knows there was no way she could be outside with him and me and still be living in her own body and so I just wait for them to come and then stands there watching them take him and her away. And then the twelve-man jury goes and give him six year, and old man Judge Selkirk give him time off because they said his wife was a mean-hearted woman. My name is in that writing—people has told it to me as a fact. Read it to me," she says, a command, and Clark reads aloud: *Leola Ferber of Cornbread Alley told Sheriff Greenleaf she suspected trouble as she was approaching the house to take in laundry. 'There was some kind of wrongness about the place,'* Leola speaks the words aloud as Clark reads them. She spits on her iron. "He'll burn in hell if it comes to that," she says. "Justice is the Lord's."

"She put herself in his way, Leola, you know that," Tom Hardin says. "A man chooses his bed, or a woman, is what I say, and then it's his, or hers, to lie in, and however lumpy they might find the mattress they can always up and leave."

"Yes, sir, but Miz Wilson was long past choosing by the time I rolled up to that porch."

"She could have up and left herself."

"And you'll tell me where she would go? You know she had three childrens and not a provider in sight unless it was

Garfield Wilson, and him only when she could get him drunk enough to take right from his pocket."

"She couldn't have left that particular morning, maybe, but Garfield had been stone drunk for a month and not the first time he'd pulled that gun. You can't tell me he hadn't written out the handwriting on the wall. Plain as day for anybody that can read."

"Plain as all that." Leola takes up another shirt and spits on her iron again, biting her lips at its sizzle. "Reading the writing on the wall. Plain as all that."

Eight fingers of dog and Tom Hardin will talk about politics, though Leola is not keen on the subject and Gaspard takes on the countenance of a stone. Tom Hardin rails, he is performing and they are his necessary and captive audience. "You look at what happened to Jack Kennedy," he says. "You make your own bed, you lie in it." Once in a while Leola shakes her head and murmurs soothing noises, but at her side the stack of pressed and folded shirts grows more rapidly. As for Gaspard, he drifts off, and it is his snoring that finally reins in Tom Hardin's polemic horses. "Isn't that right, Leola," Tom Hardin says. Leola holds a shirt to the light and gives a little cluck of disgust. "No *way* I can send this back in this kind of shape."

Tom Hardin excuses himself to take a leak on the hard-packed earth of the backyard. There is a wave of cold air as he opens and shuts the door, then the thrumming of his unloosed stream against the porch's plank skirt. The warm, thick smell of urine seeps into the room. Clark shifts uncomfortably on his feet—this smell is so private, and from his *father*. The old man might at least step away from the house—he does this much at home, when he is working in his woodshop and can't be bothered with running the family gauntlet to get to the inside bathroom.

Then this thing happens. Leola sets her iron upright on its metal stand and steps away from her ironing board. Bending a little at the knees, she takes the hem of her black bag of a dress in either hand—she might be a ballerina, poised for a deep bow as flowers land at her feet and applause rises around her like a flood. She lowers herself on trembly legs, then raises her skirt to her hips, her waist, higher. Clark stares. She wears nothing underneath. She is nothing if not massive, and at the center of her massive brown hips the single, lidded eye. Clark stares, and surely he imagines this—for the remainder of his life he will tell himself and no one else that he imagined this well in the middle of the bush, this omniscient, scandalous secret, grave and silent until it delivers a slow and majestic wink.

Clark darts a glance at Gaspard. His head is bowed to his game, he licks one deliberate thumb, transfers a card from one pile to its neighbor. Clark's eyes will not rise to meet Leola's, his consternation and terror are too great, but his absolute need to know gets the better of his fear and he forces himself to look up.

Her face is a mask, but her eyes, jaundiced and bloodshot, meet his own. Her eyes are joking and angry, mocking and fierce, and in them he sees this: She knows things about him that he himself is only beginning to learn. She knows, for example, that he, a good white boy, can say nothing of this to his father. Beyond that she knows a great deal more, that he is too young to understand. She knows more about him than he knows about himself.

Cold air at his back. Clark turns around. Tom Hardin is coming in the door. Clark turns back. Leola is at her iron. Gaspard turns over another card. "Shut your mouth, boy, the flies will get in," Tom Hardin says.

By now the weak winter light has disappeared from the

windows, and Clark, searching for an excuse to leave, walks to the door. "Father, if we don't go we'll miss dinner and mass both."

"No great loss on either account," Tom Hardin says, but he picks up his coat.

"Good thing he's got a son to keep track," Leola says.

"What's a son for," Tom Hardin says. He throws Clark the keys. "You're getting us home."

"But I don't have a license."

"You got your father's permission. That'll do. Merry Christmas, Leola. Merry Christmas, Gaspard."

Leola sets her iron upright and waddles to the door. "Merry Christmas, Mister Hardin, and the same to Miz Hardin. Don't you worry the usher to save a place for us in church."

They are in the car, Clark has started the engine and put it in gear when Tom Hardin lays a hand on his arm. "So tell me what you learned."

Clark speaks from the two fingers of white dog, still warm in his blood. "I learned where my eyes come from." Silence after this, until Clark says, "I mean, that they're family eyes, come from the blood. From whoever we come from."

"What else?"

Clark speaks carefully. "I learned something about Leola and Gaspard. Who they are. Where they fit in with the family."

Tom Hardin sits back. "That's something. That's a place to begin."

Clark is not lying—these are things he has learned, from seeing instead of just looking at Gaspard and Leola for the first time. And he learned, or at least he heard Tom Hardin say, that a man chooses his own bed to lie in; this is something he will think about.

As for what Leola did, or what he imagined she did—the

thought of this is enough to bring forth in him the first swell of understanding that there are ways of being in this world for which no grownup will ever offer an explanation, things he will never be able to understand but can only accept. But this extraordinary knowledge is too huge and dangerous to be put into words and so he turns his thoughts to something safe, something he can put into words, and these are the words in his head, this is what he wonders as he drives his dozing father home: *Who will bring dog to Leola and Gaspard after Tom Hardin is gone?*

Cowboys

[1972]

Up and over Strang Knob, west from Kentucky, Raphael Hardin drives the family gift horse, a 1964 Rambler Rebel with cherry-red bucket seats, a black vinyl roof, Flash-o-matic floor shift, 115,000 miles on the odometer, and an affection for running hot. Riding in the passenger seat is Willy, a middle-aged German hitchhiker whom Raphael picked up west of St. Louis to help with driving and gas. Willy is too old to be hitchhiking, at the gas pump he claims an empty wallet, but Raphael is too exhilarated to care. He has never driven cross-country, he knows nothing of cars, but he is on his way to California to college, for the first time he is driving his own car, with a red-haired, radical European riding shotgun. Together they are crossing America, easy riders in the family sedan.

Across hours of Missouri Willy complains of the new morality. "In the sixties we took to the streets to fight for the right to express our love freely. Now you are becoming businessmen, spending money, getting married." Willy sniffs. "Was it for this that we fought the tear gas and the dogs?"

"Tear gas?" Raphael is puzzled. "Are you talking about Vietnam? Or getting married?"

"I am talking about the free expression of love," Willy says. "Between men and women, or women and women. Or men and men." He touches Raphael's shoulder lightly. "But perhaps I offend."

Raphael, taken aback, stays cool—cool is where he wants

to be; it is the state of being to which he aspires. "Jeez, man. I'm almost nineteen years old."

"Then perhaps you are married. Or engaged."

"No, no."

Raphael wonders at the drift of this conversation, and its progression from marriage to sex to himself. He pushes his uneasiness from his mind. He is on his way to California, where he will meet and fall in love with a California girl, preferably blonde. Elated at the thought, he grins, raising his fist to the roof. "To the new morality!" he cries. "In defeat of ourselves!"

Willy nods, a satisfied bob of his chin. "I will tell my friends of this. They visit New York, they see the Statue of Liberty and think they have seen America." He pats Raphael's shoulder. "*I* have set out to see the true America. And *you* are my first true American."

"I'm not much of a true American," Raphael says. "I'm volunteering for the McGovern campaign. I'm practically fleeing my county draft board, which would like nothing more than to stick a gun in my hands and ship me off to Vietnam. I'm driving an eight-year-old car made in Detroit."

"What could be more American?"

"Lots of things," Raphael retorts. "Jell-O. Soap operas. The flag. Racism. That's why I'm heading to California."

"Ah," Willy says. "You will escape all this in California."

"The East has better schools," Raphael says confidently, "but it's everything I want to get away from. Old. Stuck on itself. Hidebound."

"Hide-bund?"

"*Bound.*"

"Ah, *bound.* As with leather."

"No, that's different. *Leatherbound* is for books."

"Books? What have books to do with leather?"

Raphael, who has never spoken with a foreigner, feels as if he is being mocked. He raises his voice, as if he can convey comprehension through volume. "Never *mind*. The *point* is you go *west* to get away from all that background and *history*. What about you? Why are you going west? I mean, why that place over any other?"

"Cowboys," Willy says promptly. "I am interested in cowboys. Are there cowboys in Missouri?"

Raphael turns to the window to hide his smirk. "There aren't any cowboys at all. Not anymore."

"But I see them in movies. I learned English from them. 'Do not forsake me, oh, my darling,'" Willy sings, Gary Cooper with a German accent.

"That's in the movies," Raphael says witheringly. "Surely you don't think that's the real thing."

"All America is a movie. You are living in a movie."

"Oh, give me a break."

"I do not expect that you would think so. I am German. I am the audience. You are American. You are *in* the movie."

"I am *not*—"

"I saw cowboys, in Chicago. Wearing pointed boots and big white hats."

"People still wear cowboy *clothes*. I mean, people can wear anything they want to."

"In America."

"Anywhere. But they aren't real cowboys. First the railroads came," Raphael says, quoting some distant history book. "With the invention of barbed wire—"

"And Indians, with their beautiful hair, I saw them in the streets, like Sicilians or Turks. Dirty, poor, drunk at noon."

"Well, the Indians have been treated brutally."

"At the hands of the cowboys, yes. Whom we will meet.

Although"—here Willy's hand makes an end run around the Flash-o-matic, rising to stroke Raphael's hair—"*your* hair, it is as nice."

Raphael shifts in his seat. He jerks up his arm as if fending off a blow, but Willy's hand is gone, leaving Raphael waving his hand above his head and feeling foolish, while Willy plants a crescent fingernail on the map, tracing their route west.

They stop for the night at Wigwam Village, a bungalow motel outside Emporia, Kansas. The bungalows are built to resemble tepees, reinforced concrete over a tent of rusting I-beams. They range in a circle around a cracked and rusting swimming pool. The pop and click of a red neon sign (OTEL—OTEL—OTEL) is the only sound.

Willy emerges from the office, holding a key high. "We are in number nine," he says, and sets about scanning numbers over tepee doors.

The motel manager—big-busted, black-haired with pink curlers—props herself against the office doorjamb, holding a shoulder bag. "Kind of young to be traveling alone," she says to Raphael.

"I'm almost nineteen years old," Raphael says. "And I'm not alone."

She saunters to Raphael's side, runs a frank hand over his chest. Some visceral part of him grumbles and contracts. He stuffs his hands in the back pockets of his jeans and scuffs a toe at the rich Kansas loam, so different from the thin, stony soil of the Kentucky hills. "Relatives don't count," she says.

"Relatives?"

"Your brother."

"There must be some mistake," Raphael says. "He's not my brother."

The manager's eyes drift shut, then she opens them and steps back. "Figures. You run a motel, you see it all." She drops the bag. "Whatever he is, he left his purse." Raphael retrieves it from the dust.

"A picture!" Willy beckons from the wigwam door, waving an Instamatic. "We must have a picture. You must ask the manager if she will take it."

"No pictures with me. No way."

Willy points to the wigwams. "But this is America."

"*Your* America, maybe. Not mine." Raphael takes his shaving kit from the car and enters the room, dodging the camera in Willy's outstretched hand.

Number nine has only one bed, a small double. At the sight Raphael's gut ties itself in a small, terrified fist, but he quells his fears. After all, he is the driver, the native son, the English speaker. He is cool; he is in control. "I have a girl-friend," he says with studied casualness. "I'm meeting her in San Francisco."

"Of course," Willy says, tucking the camera in his bag. "You are an American, child of the seventies. You will meet your girlfriend in California, where you will marry by the ocean and go to the university in law." Willy laughs and squeezes Raphael's shoulder. "Or business." He ruffles Raphael's hair, then stretches his hands over his head, popping his knuckles and yawning.

"I have to be in California in three days," Raphael says. "I'm meeting my girlfriend in San Francisco on Thursday. I'm not stopping except to sleep." He takes a deep breath, then delivers the punch. "Maybe I should take you to some likely-looking place and let you out. You could get a ride with some-body who's taking his time to see the country."

Willy cocks his head. "Your car is not healthy?"

"My car is just fine."

"You are in luck. I am a mechanic." Willy pulls a film can and a pipe from his shoulder bag. "You want to get high?"

Raphael hesitates. He has never smoked marijuana. To accept this hospitality is to choose to allow Willy to continue on. He thinks of the temperature gauge on the Rambler, which for most of the day hovered near boiling. He studies the pipe, which Willy has thrust into his hand.

The pipe is small, hand-molded from some jade-green clay. It fits comfortably in his palm, a compact, tangible correlation of the vast, extraordinary, unimagined experiences that await him, of the gap between the whitewashed world that has penetrated to the remote hills and hollows of his childhood, and the vast, astounding, seductive, inviting world as it really is. He takes the pipe to his lips. In this gesture, in this moment his world divides and complicates itself, a geometrically progressing mitosis whose end he cannot foresee or imagine.

"That woman, with the pink things in her hair," Willy says. "She insulted my accent. I have no accent."

Raphael demurs tactfully—he is a Southern boy, he knows his manners. "Just a *little* accent."

"A *bitch.*" Willy says, with feeling.

For the first time in his life Raphael finds himself siding with the curler-headed motel managers and greasy-spoon owners of the hinterlands. "A Kansan," he says. "An American. A *true* American. What do you expect?"

"Cowboys," Willy says. "At least, that is what I am looking for. But we are not yet far enough west."

Willy strips and climbs into bed. Watching from the corner of his eye, Raphael sees that he wears small, tight underwear, striped in some pattern of green and navy blue. Raphael's groin tightens. Resolutely he turns his eyes to the wall and steps out of his jeans, but his eyes have taken on a life of their own—they know what they want, and it is stronger than what his mind wants, and he cannot keep himself from turning and looking. He retreats to the bathroom, where he shuts and locks the door.

Lingering over his toothbrush, he considers those parts of his life that until a very few weeks before he assumed no one in the world shared. Then he went for his induction physical, to encounter its questionnaire's forthright acknowledgment *(homosexual tendencies?)* of the slow, swelling, subcutaneous movements that until then he had allowed himself to acknowledge only in secret, and then only long enough to deny that they exist.

Why has he encouraged Willy's talk of free morals, free love, free sex? Why did he pick up this strange red-haired man in the first place? Why has he allowed Willy to stay? Raphael leans his head against the mirror, staring down his reflection.

Leaving the bathroom, he crawls under the covers, still wearing his underwear, his T-shirt, his socks. He is settling himself when Willy flings an arm over his shoulder, carelessly, as if Raphael's back were the most convenient armrest.

The mattress sags, hopelessly. Raphael clings to its edge to keep from sliding downhill into the hollow created by Willy's weight. He lies on his stomach, crushing his arms to pins and needles, until long after Willy's feigned snores have given way to shallow breathing.

His nails dug into the mattress, Willy's hand dangling before his eyes, Raphael falls into a place between waking and sleep. Behind his eyelids the road unrolls endlessly. At his side sits a California woman, blonde and tanned—but Raphael turns, and it is red-headed Willy, in a Stetson hat and a pearl-buttoned shirt.

Raphael wakes. Overhead, nesting in the wigwam peak, sparrows chatter. The paper blinds blink: gray with dawn; lurid with neon light. In his half-sleep he has turned over, slid down into the bed's hollow. Willy's hand is working its way under the elastic of his underwear, his fingers lingering in the curl of Raphael's pubic hair.

Raphael lies stiff, frozen, clammy with sweat. He tells himself that this is not happening, that he is not here, that he wants only to be in California, where he will find what he is looking for. He wants only this: to get where he is going. At almost nineteen years old, is this so much to ask?

At the thought he rises abruptly. Willy's hand flops against the bedclothes. Raphael heads for the shower, where he stays until he is certain the hot water has run out, and that Willy's shower will be cold.

Desire, the parish priest told the boys in Raphael's eighth-grade class, is a many-pointed star, turning and pricking in the heart. Their consolation was to know that with age its points would be worn smooth, even if the turnings never ceased. Tailgating farmers across the flattening plains, Willy at his side, Raphael remembers this wisdom, and wonders how long he will need to wear down his points.

Kansas drowns in rain. Raphael considers putting Willy out but argues himself into letting him stay. The Rambler's temperature gauge continues to rise, and Willy is a mechanic. Raphael points out to himself that in the crunch, he did not give in to the prickings of desire. He is still in control. Over the cheerful slap of the windshield wipers, he makes small talk.

They approach Dodge City. There is a bypass. Willy, who is driving, ignores the sign. "We'll take the bypass," Raphael says.

"You will pass by Dodge City?" Willy is incredulous.

"Dodge City will be just another tourist trap."

"There will be cowboys in Dodge City."

"Willy, there are no cowboys." The bypass signs loom, green and white. "We're taking the bypass. I'm on my way to school. I *have* to be in California in two days."

"Just for lunch." Willy digs a finger into Raphael's side. "Maybe you will find your*self* a cowboy."

The bypass is upon them. "Willy, it's my car and my trip and my gas. If you want to walk, get out and walk. Otherwise, take the goddamn bypass."

Willy wrenches the car into the right lane. Oblivious of oncoming traffic, he cranes his neck to cast a straining, wistful glance south, over the soggy brown plains. Raphael folds his arms and stares out the window.

They are in Colorado before he unclenches his jaw. Near sunset they approach the mountains, to stop outside Las Animas. Willy is in the motel before Raphael can step from the car.

Again Willy rents a room with one double bed. His back aching from the day's strain, Raphael flops down. Willy sits on the foot of the bed. Raphael hears one shoe drop. When the second drops, he promises himself, he will sit up and insist that they switch to a room with two beds.

The bed lurches, Willy's elbow brushes Raphael's foot. "You touch me and I'll break your neck," Raphael says, shocking himself.

Willy scoots over, reties his shoes. "I am going. I will walk." He picks up his shoulder bag and his suitcase.

"Get some cowboy to give you a ride," Raphael says, turning his back. He hears Willy open the door, and the thrumming of the rain on the pavement. Willy's footsteps splash away, crossing the asphalt.

Raphael lunges across the bed to peer through the curtains. Willy stands in the rain, staring up at the sky. He turns and retraces his steps.

His heart pounding, Raphael dives under the covers, feigning sleep. Willy tiptoes in, undresses, and climbs into bed, his underwear ghostly white in the room's dim light.

Lying awake into the night, this is what Raphael thinks: *I have been seized by something larger than myself. No one has prepared me for this, its size and power.*

The notion that he might be whatever he had the talent, gumption, perseverance, sweat to accomplish—this has formed the kernel of all his acts and thoughts; it was the kernel of all he has been told, by his parents, his teachers, his nation, his television set. And then an aging man with an accent and close-fitting underwear removes the bottom card from the castle, the keystone from the arch, and all Raphael has ever been, all his dreams and aspirations are falling to the rock-hard pavement and there is nothing, nothing between himself and his self.

The next day Raphael and Willy climb the high passes of the Sangre de Cristo. They drive fifty miles, stop to let the car cool, drive another fifty miles. At each stop Willy listens to the engine. Once he opens the hood. "A-OK," he says, making a circle with his thumb and forefinger.

It is dark when they descend from the mountains above Salt Lake. The city is awash with orange sodium-vapor light, extending exactly as far as its waterlines. Beyond the sharp line defined by that limit there is no light, no scattered farms or small towns, only darkness, reaching to the massive black shapes of the mountains to the west.

Raphael stops for gas. Willy heads for the bathroom.

Raphael fills the tank and moves the car forward from the pump. He sits for a single moment, his forefinger tracing the Flash-o-matic's luminescent dial; then he leaps from the car. He pulls Willy's suitcase and shoulder bag from the trunk and sets them by the pumps. As he drives off, he avoids looking in the rearview mirror.

He barrels out of the city, ignoring the speed limit, driving into the blackness of the mountains and the lake. He tries to conjure his vision of the woman who waits for him in California, tall and blonde. Instead he thinks only of Willy in his ass-hugging jeans, abandoned on the neon-washed apron of some Union 76. He rubs each eye with the heel of his palm. Is he so transparent, is his desire written across his forehead, that Willy so quickly sought it out? The thought brings sweat to his palms. He turns on the radio, sings along.

He exits and turns back.

Willy is at the gas station, sitting on his suitcase. Raphael stops and rests his forehead on the steering wheel. The roar of the trailer trucks along I-80 mixes in his ears with the car's lingering whine. Amid this din, Willy gently deposits his bags in the backseat and climbs in. "You have come back."

"Shut up," Raphael says, with his head still resting on the wheel. "Shut up, shut up, shut up."

They stay that night in Salt Lake. While Willy rents their room Raphael paws through his shoulder bag until he finds Willy's marijuana. With deep-sucking breaths he pulls at the pipe, then knocks the ashes from the pipe into the gutter. He returns the pipe to Willy's bag, then combs his hair in the car mirror while he tries to still his racing heart against what he is about to do.

Inside there are two single beds. Raphael sits on the nearest, high beyond words, hiding his humiliation.

Willy pulls on a fresh shirt. "I know this town," he says. "Near here they drove the Golden Spike—I saw it in a movie, with Barbara Stanwyck and Joel McCrea." He peers into the mirror, humming snatches of some familiar tune, combing his red hair. "I am going out now. I will be back late."

"Looking for a cowboy?" Raphael's voice is heavy with sarcasm.

"Perhaps I will get lucky. Should I return with one, or two?"

"You don't understand," Raphael says, but Willy is gone.

Raphael wakes the next morning to Willy bustling about the room, peering in drawers, opening cabinets. He turns up a Gideon Bible. "What are you looking for?" Raphael asks.

"Oh, nothing." Willy turns. Above his left eye a black-and-purple cauliflower blooms, flecked with dried blood. Raphael props himself on his elbows. "My God, Willy, what did you do to your head?"

Willy shrugs. "I went to a bar. I was watching. I asked for a cigarette. Then they turned on me, a foreigner, they said. A fag. I knew this anger and I left." He touches his bruise. "I did not leave fast enough."

Raphael turns to the wall. "You should put some ice on it. There's a machine in the hall. It's free—you don't need any money to operate it."

"It is nothing. You will see as much in your time. Maybe worse." Willy roots through scattered clothes. "I am not complaining. My cowboy followed me out. He took me to his place, to feed me drinks and nurse my wounds."

"So where is this cowboy," Raphael says to the wall. He hears the door open. "Taking your time in here," a voice says in a flat western twang. Raphael flips over. A tall, thin blond in glove-tight jeans and a pearl-buttoned shirt lounges in the doorway, smoking a cigarette. He wears boots studded with turquoise and tipped at their toes with silver. With the cigarette between his thumb and forefinger he inhales a last drag, then flicks the butt into a puddle outside the door. On its quick hiss Raphael's heart sinks.

"I beg your pardon," the blond says. He winks at Raphael. "I had no idea." He turns his back.

"Wait," Raphael says. "You don't understand."

Willy bends to the foot of the bed. "Good. It is found." He stands, clutching his shoulder bag to his chest. From the bag he pulls a patterned, lidded tin. He opens it and removes several bills. The blond takes the money, then shies from Willy's hug. Raphael watches him climb into a late-model Corvette. He guns the engine and rumbles from the parking lot.

Raphael leaps from the bed and slams the door shut. "Asshole. You told me you were broke."

"So I keep a little reserve for emergencies. Is this so terrible for a stranger in a foreign country?"

"That was no cowboy," Raphael says. "That was a goddamned whore. And you let yourself be hustled."

"Call him what you like. He helped me when I needed help."

"Much like myself," Raphael says. "Only *he* had the sense to get paid." He throws himself around the room, tossing aside Willy's clothes, pulling on his own jeans. "Well, I'm happy you found your cowboy. Or maybe I should say he found you. The guy who knocked you upside the head. *He* was the real cowboy."

"The man who hit me was *not* a cowboy. He wore a white shirt and brown pants."

"The only kind left," Raphael says. He strikes his knee

against the half-open drawer and kicks it shut, savagely. "Welcome to America."

In Nevada, fences drop away and signs crop up along the interstate: OPEN RANGE, CATTLE CROSSING. Every mile or so fake cattle guards are painted across the pavement to fool the cows from wandering. Yet they see no cows, no water, little wildlife, only endless sagebrush, with an occasional raven circling overhead or a black-and-white chukar winging up from the shoulder.

Traffic is light; Willy drives. Raphael has nothing to do but nurse his anger. "You will see as much in your time," Willy said to him only that morning. "Maybe worse." Raphael leans back, closing his eyes to imagine what might possibly be worse, to be confronted with a picture of himself, an aging man standing on street corners, provoking brawls in redneck bars, hiding wounds from a suspicious wife.

Climbing Battle Mountain the Rambler boils over. They stop, let the engine cool, start again, but the grade is steep and the car rebels after a few miles. Raphael cannot remember the last service station. He has no credit cards, little money. A few cars and trucks speed by, their drivers' eyes fixed on the road, avoiding Raphael's hopeful looks.

He turns to Willy. "OK, so earn your keep."

Willy smiles, rolls his eyes. "My keep? I do not understand."

"You're the mechanic. What do we do now? Let it cool? Push it over the mountain?"

Unbelievably, Willy's eyes fill with tears. In the roadside's parched glare, his fingers resting on the lump above his eye, he looks older, *old*. "I am no mechanic," he says. "I bought a used car in Canada, I was to drive it to California. I was to stop in Dodge City, in the Monument Valley where the movies are made, in the Death Valley with its twenty mules. Then I broke down in St. Louis. I had been standing by the road for hours. I looked at you. I liked you. I wanted to give you a good reason to keep me along. Everything else I have said is true. Only there did I not speak the truth."

Furious, Raphael climbs from the car. He raises the hood, to be confronted with a hot maze of wires and plugs and blades, all mysterious and to his eyes potentially lethal.

Willy stands beside him. "Perhaps if we let it cool—"

"You lied!" Raphael, who has never raised his voice to an older man, is yelling. "I could have left you sitting in Salt Lake. But *no-o,* I go back, looking for a mechanic. And what do I get. A liar. A fag."

Willy sets his chin, plants his feet. "That is enough. You turned back for me. You are old enough to face this."

"I turned back for a mechanic."

"You turned back for love."

"*Love,*" Raphael says. His voice trembles with contempt. "What can you know about love?"

Willy sits on the fender, crosses his knees, rests his chin on his fist. "Please," he says.

"Please what."

Willy waves his hand, an angry flick. "Please continue. I am waiting to have it explained."

Raphael crouches by the open hood, numbed from himself. He rests his chin on his hands, watching the radiator cap bubble and seep.

Willy touches his shoulder, and Raphael is so tired and angry that he does not shy away. Willy points to the north. The sky is searingly blue, but nearby a mustard-colored cloud boils upward. As they watch, it grows closer, until its mass separates into tens, hundreds of cows. Within minutes they take refuge in the car from a slow-moving river of bellowing, stinking, long-horned cattle.

Raphael looks back. Down the road men have blocked traffic. They must be yelling to drivers, but Raphael can hear nothing over the noise of the herd. To the front his view is blocked by the raised hood. He does not see the horse or its rider until he is looking at spurs, glinting at eye level from a battered, square-toed boot.

"What the hell are you doing here?" The voice comes from above. Willy is out of the car before Raphael can answer. "Stuck!" Willy cries. "Overheated!" Raphael pokes his head from the window.

The cowboy rides a gray-flecked quarter horse. Erect in his saddle, he wears faded jeans, a ten-gallon hat, a bandanna around his sunburned neck. He swings a tight-muscled leg over the saddle horn, tosses the reins to Willy, pokes around in the engine. "Fan belt," he announces. "Loose."

"You will be able to help us?" Willy asks shamelessly.

"Maybe. With the right tools."

"There's a toolbox in the trunk," Raphael says. "There's a couple of wrenches." He climbs from the car and retrieves the tools.

Standing in the spring sun, watching this stranger tinker with the engine, Raphael finds himself acutely aware of his world in a way he has never before allowed himself to feel. The warm tan of this man's boots against the asphalt; the leathery copper of his skin against the mud-spattered blue of his jeans; the heat of Raphael's own palms, burning to touch this handsome, hardened man.

Raphael forces himself to look away. He closes his eyes, trying for the last time to conjure a vision of the woman, any woman, who must be waiting in California . . . no luck. He has lost the art of outwitting himself, to the cowboy on the roan horse; to Willy, standing at his side.

The cowboy returns the tools to Raphael. "That should get you up and over the pass. But you need a new fan belt. Stop in Winnemucca at the Texaco, on the east side of town? Ask for Sonny Devine. I expect he won't charge you more than twenty bucks."

"Thanks for stopping," Raphael says. He would like to say more, but he has lost his voice to the heady smell of saddle soap and horsehair.

"A cowboy," Willy says. "An *American* cowboy." His hand slips from the bridle to the horse's neck. He fingers the saddle's worn leather. "A picture," he says. "Please wait, only a moment. I must have a photograph." He dives into the Rambler and retrieves his Instamatic. He hands it to Raphael. The cattle press too close to the car to allow Raphael to step back, so he climbs to the car's hood. He snaps Willy and the cowboy, standing beside the horse.

"You'll want one with the cows in it," the cowboy says. "For the folks at home. They don't make cows like this much anymore. A dying breed." He scrambles atop the Rambler before Raphael can object.

Raphael stands next to Willy, while the cowboy fits his eye to the viewfinder. "Closer," he says, waving them together. "I want to get them cows." Willy does not budge. Raphael hesitates, then steps to Willy's side to droop his arm around Willy's shoulder, casually, as if it might have dropped from the cloudless Nevada sky. "Say horseshit," the cowboy says, and snaps the picture: Willy and Raphael, grinning, Raphael's arm around Willy's shoulder, while behind them the long-horned cattle moil and balk under the glistening, snowcapped peak of Battle Mountain.

The cowboy returns the camera to Willy, mounts his horse and wheels around. *"Hasta luego,"* he says, and clops through the herd and across the highway, toward the rolling plain to the south.

Willy crows with laughter, clapping his hands and dancing around the car in little skips. "For this only, I would have come across the world!" he cries. He dances up to Raphael, takes his shoulders in his hands. "My thanks to you and your wonderful car!"

Raphael jerks back from Willy's hug. "We'd have been in California by now if it had been left up to me."

"But you see it is not left up to you." Willy executes a small bow. "These are the workings of love."

Raphael slams the hood and climbs into the car.

The herd clears the highway. In minutes Raphael and Willy are over the pass. Raphael puts the Flash-o-matic in neutral for the long downgrade. The pavement clicks by. The sun sinks. He lowers the visor against its brightness. Willy tilts back the passenger seat, closing his eyes.

Raphael steals a sideways glance. Above Willy's eye the lump swells, but a smile wrinkles the corners of his lips. The sun glints from his red hair as he hums a little song. Raphael fights the tune (where has he heard it before?) but it sticks in his head, leading him on to the place where he is going.

Guilt

[1981]

This was how Joe Ray Hardin came to sell clothes:

Woolett & Parks was the only clothing store in Jessup County. Spring and fall, April and October, Leo Parks made trips to Chicago (and later, with the rise of the New South, Atlanta), where he bought suits, dresses, slacks, and shoes to match the budget and measurements of everyone in Jessup County who wore more than bib overalls (those he ordered in bulk).

Taste was not a problem. Leo Parks determined taste, and he took care to ostracize the newfangled, the outré, the fashion statement ("as if anybody in Jessup County had anything to say," he told Joe Ray once, in a rare moment of self-revelation). Leo would study any Louisville-bought dress that showed up at midnight mass, or at a wedding, or at a funeral. "Poor box," he'd say, right out loud on the church steps, where the wives that bought and the husbands that paid would be certain to hear. And sure enough next season you'd spot that dress in the back left pews on a black girl whose mother had added a strip of red sateen to hide the tucks at the waist.

Men were not a problem. Know their family, know their genealogy, know their income and social standing (Leo knew all these), and you could look at a sixth-grader and tell what clothes he'd be wearing in thirty years.

Women were the problem. Women's sizes were *the* problem; women's sizes were the challenge of the trade. Women's sizes often changed between order and purchase. Leo would see Frampton Hughes driving out of town alone at a time of day when civilized people were sitting down to supper. Then he'd have to guess how much weight Millie Hughes would gain across the duration of Framp's latest affair. He'd have to anticipate whether to add a half or a whole size to accommodate the extra pounds. Then he'd have to present the new purchases to Millie as if they were the latest thing, taking care not to draw attention to the added sizes. And there was always the chance that Framp would tire of his latest fling before Millie bought the next season's dresses. She would be back to dieting, and nothing to do but put that dress on the sale rack.

Because Leo Parks had been a longtime acquaintance of Tom Hardin's, Joe Ray spent his high school summers working at Woolett & Parks. A few days to recover from his high school graduation party hangover and Joe Ray was headed for the military, headed for Indochina, until the Army got wind of his haberdashery skills. He spent two years measuring men for uniforms, then went to the state university on the GI bill, where he met Catherine. They had almost graduated, they were hopelessly "in heat," as Catherine came later to call it. Then Catherine discovered she was pregnant.

Wide through the hips, large-boned but small featured, Catherine was not that beautiful; but she was born to money. No great fortune; "middle-class," she called herself, like everyone Joe Ray knew, though her lawyer father earned enough that a maid came twice a week to their suburban home to pick up the clothes Catherine left strewn about. Joe Ray called himself "middle-class," too—he who'd gone into the Army because he couldn't afford tuition at the public university, and who'd never have gone to college at all but for the GI bill.

She had money; they had options. Her father was eager

to pay, no questions asked and hopeful that this experience might break his daughter of this relationship. Catherine promised she'd think over carefully what her parents said. They sent her to French Lick for a long weekend to be alone with her thoughts and the enormity of the idea that at twenty years old she would have a child. And she went to French Lick, and thought it over carefully, and believed she was choosing her fate and that of her unborn child; but there was no decision to be made. The tyranny of desire is absolute. Within a month they were married, and Joe Ray was back at Woolett & Parks.

Across his years in the store Joe Ray came to know (as Leo Parks had come to know before him) the breadth, height, inseam, and shoe size of every person in the county. The job required a diplomat's discretion, a banker's financial acumen, a writer's perceptive eye, a politician's dissembling, a gigolo's charm, a suitor's manners. From Leo Parks, Joe Ray learned these talents and more.

He was heir apparent to the store—Leo had two daughters, both married to prosperous suburbanites, neither interested in selling clothes in a small town buried in the hills, and anyway, as Leo pointed out on the first of the times when he took Joe Ray with him to Chicago, wearing was for women; buying was for men.

In Chicago they stayed at the Drake—Leo's room had a lakefront view. When Joe Ray met him there for late afternoon drinks, Leo had dressed for dinner in a tailored, three-piece silk suit. As Leo was knotting his tie Joe Ray stole a glance inside Leo's suitcoat: Carson, Pirie, Scott. It was a revelation to Joe Ray that Leo was capable of such extravagance. His own suit (polyester blend, bought, of course, through Woolett & Parks) smelled faintly of mothballs, which Leo kept in open boxes scattered around the store.

111

Looking over the lakefront view Leo mentioned that he was getting old, time perhaps to think of handing on management of the business. Before Joe Ray could muster a response Leo was ushering them down to supper. That night as Joe Ray lay listening to the muffled sounds of Michigan Avenue he calculated how many years it would take to buy out Leo's daughters, what it would be like to own a set of tailored dress clothes that didn't smell of napthalene. He fell asleep thinking of the store foyer, with its floor mosaic in hexagonal blue and white tiles:

Woolett

&

Parks

How much would it cost to have it retiled? Would *Hardin's* fill the wide entryway?

Then they built the bypass and it was over. Now it took only an hour to drive to Louisville. The women flocked to the malls, to be caught in traffic jams on the interstate or on Shelbyville Road, to park and walk a half mile across baking or freezing asphalt, to enter a vast warehouse where the help (just try to find them) was ignorant, aloof at best, abusive at worst; to choose from racks of poorly designed, ill-fitting, cheaply made—

Leo sold the Woolett & Parks building, with its high pressed-tin ceilings and hand-turned poplar banisters, to the highest bidder—a chain of hardware stores who had plans to use it to store paint. Joe Ray was too proud to beg and not sure what he would beg for. He worked wordlessly through the Christmas sale, the going-out-of-business sale, the final FINAL sale.

When looking for someone or something on which to fix blame for the course of his life, Joe Ray thought of those few trips to Chicago. Had he never been to the Drake, had he never seen Leo Parks in a tailored suit, he would never have imagined such possibilities. But once experienced they became not only possible but necessary, and falling shy of them was failure. This was America, after all, where (as Tom Hardin had often seen fit to remind his sons) the only obstacles to a man's career were his own faults and laziness. Joe Ray was not lazy, and he was by any standard smarter than Leo Parks, and with an education. That left only the intangibles of character. And so, in the months following the closing of Woolett & Parks, when Joe Ray cast about for someone to blame, he saw no one to turn on but himself.

The accident happened a few months after he'd moved his family to Louisville. The bypass siphoned away the few jobs left in Jessup County and anyway, who could work among these people who suspected his ambition, who'd seen him fail? Six months after the move and he had yet to find a job. The economy in Louisville was in terrible shape but in any case Joe Ray refused to work in retail, where he would encounter wholesale buyers, all of whom he knew, and maybe even a familiar customer the other side of the tape measure. To keep a roof over their heads Catherine went to work as a legal secretary at a firm owned by a friend of her father. Within two months she received a promotion.

Each day Joe Ray drove her to work, dropped the kids at school or day care, sat at home and had—yes, he acknowledged it (though not to Catherine)—a few carefully paced drinks. Then he picked everyone up at the end of the day.

Why did he drink? He asked himself this question with

the first drink of each day, and each time he gave himself this answer: Because he was weak.

But everybody was weak—he'd learned this from the Baltimore Catechism and had since seen plenty of evidence to support it. After all, not everybody drank. There must be more to his drinking than just weakness.

Was it possible, ever, to bridge the chasm between himself and the women of his life—Rose Ella, Catherine, his sisters, between himself and any woman, every woman whom he liked and wanted desperately to like him in return? *That* was why he drank. Drinking was the only time when he felt close to women, in touch, let in on their big secret that during his sober hours he felt only as a hopeless mystery. Looking up at Rose Ella's face the time she pulled him off the barbecue coals—the pain of the burn he'd felt not at all, he was too drunk. What he felt, what he remembered was the clarity of things. His man's layers of self-deception and vanity were dispensed with, at least until he sobered up the next day to find his neck swathed in bandages. The world expressed itself in frank and declarative sentences: Are you all right. Does it hurt. I love you.

That last he was almost certain Rose Ella had said to him, as they hustled him into a car to go to the hospital. This he saw as a tragedy: It was one of the few encounters of his life he would like to have remembered precisely, but he knew booze too well to trust his memory of specific facts or words or gestures. As for asking Rose Ella if she'd said what he remembered her saying—that was as impossible as the thought of quitting drinking.

Assuming she said it—Joe Ray assumed that she'd said it—it carried a load of irony. He knew perfectly well how women felt about him when he was drunk—you didn't have to be Dr. Freud to read it in their faces. But still he drank—it was worth it to have those edges buffed and softened, to get that mystery monkey off his back.

The day of the accident he'd spent working the crossword puzzle, watching the news, reading the paper, drinking three whiskies before he went as usual to pick up the boys. He was on his way to pick up Catherine, he was thinking about where on earth he would find a job, he was thinking about providing for his children when he ran the red light. His lightweight sedan was no match for the hulk of a station wagon (Country Squire, early '70s) that struck them. Even so his car demonstrated the triumph of foreign engineering—Joe Ray, who had his seat belt fastened (more evidence that he was sober) was not so much as bruised or sore the next day from an adrenaline rush.

Which was why, when he thought about it later, he hadn't immediately checked on the boys. If he himself was un-scratched, how could they have been hurt? Instead he'd leapt from the car. "I'm sorry, sorry, my fault, I didn't see it, didn't see the light," he cried to the other driver, a frowzy woman in faded, too-tight jeans, a loud print blouse, and a close-fitting hat. Who wore a hat, in 1981? He couldn't help but notice clothes even now, even as she was saying, "Don't call the police for God's sake, no police, this rattletrap isn't worth what it costs to insure," and he was still stunned by his luck in get-ting off so easy when he realized that the boys, contrary to his explicit command and their longtime training, had unfastened their seat belts (maybe they'd never fastened them? Had he remembered to check?), that a rear door had popped open, that Sean was silent while Michael was just plain not there, his absence an immediate and accusing presence.

Sean, the younger, would be all right, after a few days of hospital supervision and some nightmares. Michael, the eleven-year-old, no. He had been thrown from the car, struck his head, unconscious, blood, bleeding, ambulance, hospital, emergency room, no visitors, waiting.

Waiting, this is what Joe Ray thought.

It might have happened to anyone. And this was true—the route was still new to him, another few months and driving it would have been intuitive, this would never have happened at all. There had been many accidents at that same corner—a small rise concealed oncoming cars, neighborhood growth had outpaced the intersection's ability to handle the late-afternoon traffic. He'd had only three drinks all afternoon, one as part of a large lunch; he was sober, so obviously sober that the police (who did come) never suggested a sobriety test. It wasn't *his* problem that the other driver was too poor to insure her car. Someone who would drive a car without insurance was likely to drive irresponsibly. Maybe he hadn't run the light at all.

Waiting that first afternoon for Catherine to arrive at the hospital, he thought these things, cursed himself for thinking them, dwelt on them all the more. To think about anything else was to think about the unthinkable—what was happening, what was going to happen to Michael? To his horror he found himself wanting a drink—he looked down to see his fingers curling as if forming themselves around a glass. If he'd had a knife he would have cut them off. He transformed their curling into a circle made of thumbs and forefingers, a dial at which he stared, a clock with hands that he could turn back to a time when this hadn't happened and he might have stayed home, he might have drunk himself so far under the table that driving wouldn't have been an option. Or maybe he could have confessed that morning to Catherine and gone to an AA meeting and he would have been there instead of on the road.

When Catherine arrived in the waiting room, this is what he told her:

The frowzy woman had been driving without insurance. The last time he'd *seen* the light it was green, though it had all happened so fast he couldn't of course be absolutely certain of all the details. By hedging this point he hoped to lend verisimilitude to his story—the judicious heart, making allowance for its own fallibility.

"It could have happened to anyone," Catherine said. "Don't think about it anymore. Think about the future. Think about Michael's getting well."

Rose Ella, who drove straight to the hospital from Jessup County, was not so generous. Once alone with her son she came straight to the point. "You'll forgive my asking, Joe Ray."

"Mother, I wasn't drinking." He thought of what this small lie entailed. The universe was filled with mysteries—the greatest scientists admitted it. Who was to say that there was no celestial scale balancing the son's life against the father's virtue? Joe Ray turned from his mother to face the wall—a cheerful floral pattern; he'd have preferred the nubbled vomit brown of the hospital where Sean and Michael had been born. "I had a highball at noon," he said. "That's all, Mother, I swear to God that's all."

"Merciful Jesus in heaven," Rose Ella said, and fell silent. Then she stood. "Your son did nothing to deserve this, and you never did anything to deserve it either, except this tiny little thing, and that was to have those drinks and then go out and drive your sons on the open road. But you're old enough to know that this is not a forgiving world. I won't say anything else. I won't ask anything else. What you tell Catherine is your business and you know I mean what I say. But you had better think about talking to the Lord, because there's not much anybody else who's going to listen."

Tom Hardin stayed away. Once or twice Rose Ella apologized for him—Tom Hardin was getting close to retirement and working hard, wanting to leave his job with everything set and ready to go for whoever took his place. Joe Ray waved off these excuses. He was his father's son—he knew why Tom Hardin stayed away. In the face of matters of such enormity Tom Hardin would be wordless, frozen into silence, his only course of action either tears (out of the question) or a violent outburst.

Michael did not improve. Waiting alone while Catherine sneaked cigarettes in the parking lot (a disgusting habit—Joe Ray himself wouldn't be caught dead smoking, but for the sake of domestic tranquility he went along with the fiction that Catherine had quit), Joe Ray stared at the floor and made promises. If Michael survived he would never touch another drink. If Michael survived healthy he would contribute time, money, to—someone, somewhere. Across their marriage and at Catherine's insistence, for the benefit of giving an example to the boys Joe Ray had attended mass, but he had never prayed even when early in their marriage they'd gotten on their knees as a family with rosaries in hand. Often as not he rested his forehead in his hands and fell asleep. He felt stupid praying now—as if he'd ignored a casual acquaintance for years only to call him up and ask a favor. A big favor. But he did it, he got on his knees right there in the waiting room, all that fifties stuff. Under such circumstances, what resort was there but superstition?

A few days after the accident he woke to find Catherine gone. Her clothes, which usually she left scattered about for him to clean up, were hung neatly in the closet. But her black pumps were gone, and her dark skirt. When he called the office she said, "Well, at a time like this we can't risk losing our health insurance," and of course she was right.

That was the first day he pulled out the bottles. Anything that contained alcohol he placed around the house so that all day he was never out of sight of liquor, until just before Catherine came home. Then he replaced the bottles in the liquor cabinet, but any old way—in case Catherine checked, he wanted her to think he was still drinking. If she discovered he'd given it up, she'd have one more bit of evidence that he was guilty.

On the bathroom vanity he set a bottle of Irish whiskey— his favorite—then arranged the mirrors so that they reflected it again and again. Each time he went to the bathroom (he went often; he was drinking too much coffee now that he wouldn't allow himself alcohol) he contemplated this diminishing infinitude of temptation. And still his struggle was not great enough. The penance did not begin to fit the crime.

And so he called the frowzy, hatted woman, whose number he still had on the scrap of envelope where she'd scribbled it after the accident. He called her up, not at all sure why except that—well, maybe she would admit something. He would buy her a drink, then another. She would be flattered at his attentions. "It was as much my fault as yours," he imagined her saying after a couple of martinis. "My mechanic told me ages ago to fix my brakes and I just haven't found the money to get it done."

That afternoon at the hospital, Michael spoke for the first time since the accident. His eyes opened, he looked straight at Joe Ray and said, "Mother." Then his eyes closed.

"Michael," Joe Ray said. "This is your dad." But his son's eyes stayed shut—those eyes that were inherited—Joe Ray's eyes, impossibly wide-set (like Joe Ray, he would always have trouble using binoculars) and blue. Put a hand over Michael's eyes—Joe Ray did it now—and he was Catherine's son. But take the hand away, and there was no mistaking those eyes.

Joe Ray left his hand in place until Catherine arrived from work.

"A little bit of good news," she said as she entered. "They've given me a raise."

"Michael spoke today," Joe Ray said. "The doctor thinks that's a good sign. Evidence there's no brain damage."

"What did he say?"

"He asked for you," Joe Ray said. "I told him you were off at the office."

Sitting at a local bar, waiting for the driver of the other car, Joe Ray looked at his watch. Why not stand her up? Because he'd made an appointment—he had a duty to honor that, and he believed in duty. Besides, he'd been responsible. It had been his fault.

Except that he hadn't been responsible—at least, not entirely so. He checked his watch again. If she was so much as a minute late, he was out of there—but then she arrived.

Her name was Flora MacKenzie. She was unemployed, she too had two boys, about the same age as Joe Ray's. "I'll never forget walking around the car and seeing your son—" She shivered.

Why was he listening to this? "Nice hat," he said, and it *was* a nice hat, a tight-fitting cloche of real felt, though he would never have matched it with that loud blouse. If he'd have advised such a hat at all.

"Thanks. Four bucks on Canal Street."

"Oh, yeah? Is that a boutique?"

And so it went from there. They talked about New York, where she'd been a model. "Oh, I know it's hard to imagine now," she said. "It might have been hard to imagine then. But since when have talent and ambition gone hand in hand?" She talked about her career (ads in *Redbook*, *McCall's*), the expense of living in New York with two children, her move back to Louisville, where she'd been raised as the oldest daughter of an autoworker's ten kids; her divorce. Talking about this and that, and they weren't talking about the accident. And then as Joe Ray was paying for their drinks (her martinis, his soda water), thinking he might yet make it out the door, she laid a hand on his arm. "Look, I just want you to know I'm sorry. Two kids and a totaled car—your rates will go through the roof. And your son—that's too big to talk about. You just hold it in your heart and hope."

"Well, my rates might not go through the roof, if it comes to that."

"Then your insurance company is nicer than mine is. Or was, back when I had insurance."

"It depends," Joe Ray said carefully. "If I tell my insurance company I wasn't at fault then everything gets a lot more complicated."

"Well. Whatever it takes to make you feel good," she said coldly, and stood to go.

Joe Ray took her hand in his. "It made me feel good to have somebody to talk to about it," he said, and like Catherine, like all the women he knew, she couldn't reject an appeal so direct.

"You buy the drinks," she said. "I'll provide an open ear. It's not like we've got somewhere to be from nine to five."

"Oh, I'm just between jobs," Joe Ray said, and then saw her to her car, the same old blocky station wagon with flecks of paint from his car on its dented bumper.

That night he dreamt:

He is talking with a woman who has no features that he recognizes but who is from and of the city—he hears this in her uninflected voice, he sees it in her smart, dressed-for-success clothes. She is a vegetarian—a new concept to Joe Ray—and she has just denigrated suburban men, husbands and sons, who pick up their hunting guns each November to go play at what she calls Caveman in the Hills.

Suddenly Joe Ray is trembling with rage. He seizes her shoulders. "My family survived on the meat we shot each fall," he says. His voice shakes—tears of outrage and self-pity course down his cheeks. He is ashamed of this maudlin performance but he has one thought only—to make this woman feel bad about her silly generalizations. "Don't talk to me about living off vegetables," he says. "We had a two-acre garden and if it failed, if there was too much or too little rain or sun or whatever, then we went hungry for a year. Now you city folks eat broccoli flown in from California on a gas-guzzling jet and then lecture me about killing deer." He chokes on his words— he is unable to continue, and in his fury at his inarticulateness he slams the woman against the wall with such force that he jolts himself awake.

Joe Ray looked at his hands—they trembled still. Craziness—maybe from cutting off the booze? He didn't even care much for hunting; he went mostly because he saw it as a family obligation to Tom Hardin. Yet the anger, the violence in his hands had been absolutely real, against a woman whose face he couldn't even recall.

Over the next few days Michael improved a little. He opened his eyes, he looked around the room, he seemed to understand where he was and what had happened. The first time this happened Joe Ray relayed the news to Catherine; then he called Flora MacKenzie.

They met that afternoon and every weekday following,

between afternoon and evening intensive-care visiting hours. By spoken agreement they talked about anything but the accident. Each meeting began with Flora asking, "How's your son?" to which Joe Ray gave a noncommital reply. Then it was on to some other, brighter subject.

She had a model's wardrobe, an endless array of materials in colors and styles that she put together in some implausible way that somehow worked. Most of them she'd bought from the poor box—no one in the clothes biz was about to get rich from her.

He felt guilty at enjoying these afternoon meetings with Flora but he did enjoy them; he told her as much the fourth or fifth time they got together. She took his hand. "Look. Torturing yourself is not going to help your son get better. You're doing what you can. Your wife is doing what she can." After this he placed his hand where it invited being taken, though some not-so-secret voice still spoke of a connection between this unseemly frivolity and his son's fate.

They talked about clothes. "You are what you wear," Joe Ray said. "Clothes make the woman as much as the man."

"In Louisville that doesn't give you room to make much," she said. "I have the greatest double-breasted white suit that I picked up for ten bucks in some secondhand store down by the river. Ivory buttons—must have been made in the thirties."

"Double-breasted suits are coming right back," Joe Ray said generously. "But white is a problem for—full-figured women."

"I wore it one time, long enough for some guy stopped at a traffic light to douse me with a cup of beer and call me a dyke."

"Let me get this straight. This is a *man's* suit you're talking about?"

"Well, sure. You don't think I'd wear one of those boxy

skirted things they make for women. I'd look like a gabardine tank."

Her frankness was disarming—he had made pretty much the same observation to himself, after all. But there were larger considerations. "Men's clothes are cut for men, women's clothes for women."

"Myth," she said. "I'm as broad in the shoulders as you, and if it comes to that, not much wider in the hips. Anyway, every man should be required to go out in serious drag at least once in his life. Society would transform itself overnight."

The notion scandalized Joe Ray into silence.

They might have ended up in bed—the thought crept up on Joe Ray in the mornings after Catherine had left for work and he was horny (weeks, now, since they'd so much as touched) and Catherine had left him not so much as a blouse to hang up or a cereal bowl to wash.

While they were still in college Catherine thrust money in his hand and asked him to do her shopping. Even now, after years of living with him, she'd pull on a plaid blouse with a flowered skirt, then drop them both in a clashing heap on the floor at the end of the day. But since the accident she hung her blouses on hooks, clipped her skirts to hangers, matched her dark skirt with black pumps. The toothbrushes were in their holders. The floors were swept and mopped. When was she doing this? Joe Ray wondered. The why he could not bring himself to question.

An afternoon came when Flora talked about her own nightmares. "I dreamed last night of the three agonies," she said.

"What's that?"

"I don't know. All I remember is that phrase. I thought you might know—it sounds so Catholic." Flora had been raised in one of those social circle Protestant churches and now was an atheist—something else she'd picked up in New York.

"There are the Seven Sorrows of Mary, and the Sorrowful Mysteries of the rosary," Joe Ray said. "But three agonies—nothing I can remember."

They set about figuring what these might be. Flora decided they'd each choose one agony and then agree on the third. "Like ordering in a Chinese restaurant. Except no death—it can't include death. For all the grief at least death is final. Agony implies something ongoing, a situation you can't do anything about but just have to endure."

"Like unhappy marriage."

"I'll buy that," Flora said. "See? We've already found the one we agree on. Two more to go."

"You name yours first."

"Failure," she said promptly.

He wasn't so certain about that. "We learn from our mistakes. You can always find a second chance. Or if you don't get one, you can make one."

"That might be true for men. Not for women."

"Well, it's your choice. Why should you care what I think?"

"Sure I care. Anyway, it's your turn."

"I can't think of anything," Joe Ray said, though what that meant was that he couldn't think of anything that didn't involve Michael dead or disabled. Which of those would be worse? He gave his head a sharp shake to dislodge that fear. "Time to go," he said, and pulled his wallet out to pay their bill.

"Money," she said. "Or lack of it."

"Pretty hard to bear," he said. "Though you can always get out of that one."

"Men," she said, and there was that helpless tone in her

voice that appealed to him. He pulled a couple of twenties from his wallet and pressed them on her. "I won't refuse," she said, tucking them in her purse. "I saw through that one long ago."

At home or at the hospital, Catherine spoke only of her hopes for Michael's improvement, never of the accident. Joe Ray had handed her the weapon to destroy their marriage, maybe to destroy him, and she was being civilized, she was choosing not to use it, but it rested in her hands all the same, real as a dagger. A part of him wanted her to go ahead and use it, get it over with; because even if Michael lived, even if everything turned out fine it would still sit in her hands, the ultimate weapon, there for use at the time of her choosing. And if that time came, *when* it came, he had only one defense: She did not know, she had no *proof* that he'd been drinking.

Michael stabilized but wasn't much improving. "He's holding," was how the doctor put it. "This happens a lot. The body cures itself a little, then takes a breather."

"What happens after the breather?" Joe Ray asked.

"You've asked a very important question," the doctor said.

That afternoon, sitting at the side of his sleeping son. Except comatose, not sleeping, but he looked as if he were sleeping, excepting the wide shaved patch on the left side of his head. Joe Ray chose to sit on the right, as did everyone who came in except Rose Ella.

How long had it been, a few weeks only, since his son had seemed as indestructible as any eleven-year-old? Now everything about him seemed fragile, his flesh thin as voile, his eyelids all but transparent and behind them his father's eyes, Joe Ray's own eyes. Joe Ray reached to touch his son's right hand, flung outward and open like a baby's, as if waiting for a finger around which to curl.

At that moment Michael began to hum, a clear tuneless

hum that rose and fell without form or direction. The song of delirium, and as it babbled on, Joe Ray's hand trembled above his son's, big over small, and his heart was breaking, breaking and there was nothing he might do, no atonement under the sky, no possible absolution for a sin so great, nothing to do but sit, weep, endure.

The next day he called Flora MacKenzie and asked her to meet him for a walk—the first time they'd met outside a bar. She proposed the riverfront but he was afraid Catherine might wander from her law office job to lunch on the Belvedere. They met instead in Cherokee Park.

He waited for her at the main entrance, below the statue of Daniel Boone, sculpted here as an adventurer, conqueror in full bold stride of certain purpose. The statue offered no hint of Boone's later fate—bankruptcy, exile from the lands he'd opened up for others to make their fortunes, and then after death the final indignity of being dug up (assuming they got the right corpse) and transported to a hero's burial in a fancy mausoleum overlooking the land they'd taken from him when he was alive. Joe Ray knew this story—had committed it to heart—the story of a brave man, a man among men unable to find words to claim and defend what was rightfully his; a man of action, out of place in what had become a world where a man needed to know not how to act but how to obfuscate, postpone, equivocate, lie.

For a week it had been cloudy, until the night before when a storm had rumbled through, one of those late, late summer storms mostly flash and dazzle and not much rain, but the air today was crystalline and with an edge. How could autumn have crept up without his realizing it? Joe Ray wondered, and then realized that during these weeks of clouds and hospital rooms the sun had dropped lower in the sky, the light had taken on a sharper slant.

When Flora arrived they walked down paths, past a playground where razor-sharp children's screams rent the still fall air. Flurries of leaves whirled around them. "Remembering," he said.

"What's that?"

"The third agony, that you can't do anything about but just have to endure. You can't make yourself forget things. That just has to come on its own time. If it comes at all."

"But there are good memories."

"Even with those it hurts to know they're gone, they're in the past. Name me a memory that doesn't hurt. It doesn't exist."

"You're just torn up about your son," she said. "He'll be OK, and then you'll get over it."

"That's what I'm afraid of." He took her arm. "You're really sweet to see me through all this. My wife—" he stopped for a second. "It's not her fault. I'd be the same way to her if she'd been driving. No, worse. But she can't forgive me, and it's hanging there all the time, like she's accusing me."

"It could have happened to anyone," Flora said.

A cloud moved over the sun—a single dark cloud filled with rain, a stray from the storms of the night before, that came along with the express purpose of driving them back to the shelter of the car, where she removed her hat to blot at the raindrops with a tissue and Joe Ray put his arm around her shoulder and kissed her, a brief kiss with more intent than passion.

She broke away, but left her hand in his. "I'm sorry. Maybe I've given you the wrong impression."

"Oh, no," Joe Ray said, and he was certain that he had her, she was his to do with as he wished, as surely as if they were lying in her bed at her apartment. From there it would be a short step to asking after the details of her clunker car; to a concession that, yes, perhaps she shared some responsibility for Michael's fate. She would do this for him.

He searched his heart for triumph, security, peace. He felt only a rage not much shy of murderous, that once again he, a man with reasonable expectations, had been reduced to some kind of emotional dependency on a woman—this woman, who in this slanting, aging, autumnal light seemed less attractive than ever.

He started the car and drove aimlessly through the park. As yellow leaves from the shedding gingkos fluttered across the windshield he thought this: *Women.* He was surrounded these days by women, except for his sons, and one of those he'd come close to killing. Women, with whom everything boiled down to emotion, whose love and forgiveness and vengeance operated on terms too simple to accommodate the duck-and-cover, sleight of hand of men's logic.

He drove them back to her car, parked below Daniel Boone. "Even his damn doctor is a woman," he said.

"You're a good, kind man," she said. "Go easy on yourself. Forgive yourself."

"No." He gave a bitter little laugh. "I'm not a good man. Anyway, how can anybody forgive himself? What difference would it make? Forgiveness has to come from outside. Otherwise we'd forgive ourselves for anything and everything we did, no matter how terrible."

"Well, then, I forgive you. Does that make things any better?"

"You sound like you think I did something that needs forgiving."

She held her tongue until he turned to look at her. "Has

it ever occurred to you that someone might love you without conditions—for no reason other than who you are?"

He pulled out his wallet then, and held out a hundred-dollar bill that he'd brought along in case things got to this point. "We have to go awhile without seeing each other," he said.

"Ah," she said. "I see."

"We can stay friends," he said. "I'd like that. I like your company. But you have to understand. I'm married."

The bill stayed poised in the air, a small but adequate barrier. "To a wife who loves you."

"How do you know she loves me?"

"Well, she's stuck with you through this."

"She's only waiting to lower the boom."

"How do you know? Maybe *she* loves you for who you are. That's what's so mysterious about love. The way it brings you to embrace even the weaknesses of the other person. Like your drinking."

"Who said anything about drinking," Joe Ray said, but the color rose to his face and he turned away.

She lifted the bill from his fingers. "Who needed to say anything? It takes one to know one."

At that moment he felt gathered in the delicate bones and blood of his right hand all his fear and rage and resentment of the past days, months, years. His hand knew the answer for this, an answer beyond his heart and head, and it gathered itself into a fist and flew of its own accord into her face. Then he found himself staring at it, wondering at first what it was that caused this woman to clutch at her head (now bare—he'd knocked her hat into the backseat) and moan with such sharp cries. "Are you all right," he said, though at bottom he dwelt still in the hot glow of triumph at this indisputable victory.

And then the wave of remorse, as the facts of what he had done penetrated. He turned then to apologize, to comfort her in earnest—my God, what had he sunk to? But she was gone, she had opened the door and was running to her car and then she was in her car and gone, and he sat frozen, afraid to comprehend what he had done.

He reached over, closed her door, started the car. He took comfort in its mechanical precision. Men had conceived, designed, engineered, and produced this vehicle—trace its history from where he sat driving it now back to its inception and Joe Ray would bet on this, there'd been hardly a woman at any stage of the process. Either it worked or it didn't, and if it didn't work there was an answer to its problem that a man could identify, puzzle through, and solve. He could drive—he could keep driving until he wore this car out. And then he would get another, and another after that. Computers, he thought. A man could make a living in computers.

In front of her office he picked up Catherine, then slid across the seat to let her drive to the hospital (since the accident she insisted on driving when they were together). They were on the road and stopped at a traffic light before she glanced back. He saw her head turn, then turn back, then glance back one more time. The light changed. She accelerated. "Who does that belong to?"

"What?"

"The hat."

He'd forgotten it was there—if such a thing could be *forgotten*. "Oh, that woman. The woman who hit me in her car."

A long silence. "And I suppose her hat flew into your hands that day and you've kept it lying around until you can return it to her."

"She left it in the car by accident." A silent moment, then

the plunge. "We've been getting together every once in a while, just to talk."

"How wonderful that you've found a friend. And does she have a regular job? No? That's great. I've been so concerned at the thought of you sitting at home alone all day and nothing to do but brood about all this until it's time to go to the hospital. We should have her over for dinner. After Michael is out of the hospital, of course. The thought of having some kind of real life outside that place—hard to imagine, isn't it."

They were approaching a traffic light. Catherine braked with a great show of care, then let the car edge forward a few inches at a time until they sat almost in the intersection. An approaching car blared its horn. "Catherine, for God's sake," Joe Ray said.

She threw the car in reverse and backed up. "I asked for it, marrying a redneck for whom booze is more important than love."

They arrived at the intensive care unit to find Michael's bed empty. For a moment Joe Ray felt the world drop away— Catherine, the hospital walls, the floor itself fell away and he was drowning in an infinite ocean of fear, grief, despair—the fate he deserved except too kind. Then a doctor rounded a curtain. "Oh, no one told you?" he said nonchalantly. "Your son's out of ICU."

In that moment he understood this, that he had appeased his fate, that he had brought down on himself enough pain and suffering; that he had begun, perhaps, to approach the possibility of atonement. On the walk to the new ward, up two flights of stairs and to a room in a different wing, he took Catherine's hand. She did not pull away.

Back at home: he climbed the stairs to the bedroom on some trivial errand. When he came down Catherine was sitting at the kitchen counter, where she'd poured an inch of Bushmills in each of two glasses. "We might as well celebrate," she said. She raised her glass. "To Michael's health."

"Thanks, but I'm not up to drinking. Not right now."

This, he thought as he watched her sip, was love's place: to seduce the lover into supporting the beloved's obsessions. And all the women who loved him allowed themselves to be drawn in, in the hope (he supposed) that by participating they might earn his love in return. And this much was true: In Catherine's hopeful, hungry eyes he felt, for the moment anyway, overwhelmed with love, or something like it: because he had brought her to this sacrifice; because she was willing to make it.

That night, lying next to Catherine—for the first time since the accident she slept soundly—Joe Ray spoke aloud in a thick voice not at all his own, that might have belonged to some inhabiting spirit. "What terrifies me," he said, "is the way love works at cross purposes with itself." This was not the language he normally spoke. "Good intentions are not enough," he said.

He glanced at Catherine—she slept on. In sleep, her face relaxed, she shed years. Except for some puffiness around her chin she might be the woman he'd lusted after in college: a well-to-do, white-collar pedigree; thick, waving black hair (cut short now—a married woman's prerogative); full lips that dimpled in the middle. Michael's hair; Michael's full, sensuous lips—"girlie lips," the other boys called them. "It's OK," Joe Ray remembered telling Michael two or three years before. It had been early summer, he saw as if he stood there now the green brilliance of the tree under which they'd been talking. "You'll be a great kisser, when that time comes."

Their marriage was woven not from respect but from

blind need: She cared for him; he gave her something to care for. Sleeping and waking and going or not going to work, drinking or not drinking—it was all one smooth, boundless, neutral, tightly woven bolt of some functional material suitable for tablecloths or dish towels or aprons or traveling clothes, until this accident (if it could be called that) came along and the tangled threads of their lives were revealed to them. "Oh, what a tangled web we weave / When first we practice to deceive," the voice of some nun with a downy lip and white tennis shoes came to him across time. Was it possible to negotiate one's way, backward or forward, through this tangle of memories and desires, lies and consequences?

How big love is, how immense and powerful its weapons! That love might exist without conditions—that Catherine might love him for who he was, rather than who he might become—before the accident he could never have accepted this; he had too many layers of pride between himself and such love. Now he had the strongest evidence of its existence in hand, and the immensity of its challenge daunted him. Being worthy of her love required nothing less than acceptance of his complicity in his fate, of the way things really had been: Michael lying on the pavement; his fist striking Flora MacKenzie; Catherine with her glass raised in a toast.

But that was the way of memory: the third agony. Well, he knew how to take care of that.

He rose and dropped his underwear to the floor, pulled off his undershirt. He strode naked to the closet, where from behind a pile of shoes and dirty underwear (his underwear—since the accident Catherine had been washing hers) he retrieved the hat. He tried it on—it was, of course, too small. He jammed it into place—that would ruin its form for good, tight little well-made cloche that it was, but he had no intention of returning it. He'd have it buried in the garbage before dawn.

He poured himself a stiff shot, the solitary drink that he'd known he would have from the moment of his first promise not to have it, when Michael lay in a coma in the hospital and no one had known how this would turn out.

Except that he'd always known how it would turn out. Michael dead, Michael crippled for life: God, the gods, fate could never have been so cruel to someone—himself—who meant so well, whose intentions had always been of the best. Leaning against the sink, the stainless steel cold against his buttocks, the tight-fitting cloche crowding his thoughts, Joe Ray wanted to be sure of this; though he knew only one way to achieve certain sureness. He raised the glass to his lips and drank.

Scissors, Paper, Rock

[1988]

For the first time in Rose Ella's memory, Raphael came home from San Francisco without a friend. Surely that should have told her something, but over the years she'd been careful not to ask questions of Raphael or his California friends and everyone, including Raphael, seemed to like it that way.

And on top of this there'd been the party. Since the time of Tom Hardin's great-grandfather, people had come from all over the south end of Jessup County for the Hardin parties. They brought themselves, and their families, and a bottle, and instruments—banjos, fiddles, guitars—that hadn't seen paying work since the ragtag bands that in the 1920s played the Kentucky dance hall circuit. Rose Ella and Tom Hardin had quarreled more than once over the expense of these parties, Rose Ella pointing out that it was *she*, after all, who would be left with seven children and a rented house, if an accident at the distillery should lay Tom Hardin up, or out.

Party, party. Tom Hardin spent their money anyway, and no accident ever happened. Instead he lived to suffer the indignity of layoff—first the country stopped drinking whiskey, then the company shut down the distillery no more than a few months before he was to retire. Then to add injury to insult the diseases of old age—cancer in the gut, from which he'd recently been salvaged by the surgeon's knife.

But no sooner was he home from the hospital than he sent out the word—party, party; if people were to stop drinking whiskey it wouldn't be on his account. Of course it was left to Rose Ella to pull it off. And so even with Raphael back from San Francisco alone, even with that blackness hovering over his head, she asked no questions, she just kept putting the party together, making it happen, talking talk.

"You start with all the sons and daughters, and their wives and husbands and children and Andrew, can't forget Bette C.'s Andrew." Rose Ella licked her finger and numbered guests in the air. "Then there's old Tice Flaherty, his great-nephew Dwight's driving him over, hard to say whether Tice is more interested in playing his banjo or flirting with Miss Camilla but he has arthritis so bad I'll be surprised to see him play a note, old Mr. Flaherty, that is, not Dwight. Dwight got arrested for growing pot last summer, the government looked at every electric bill in the county and that's how they caught him, can you imagine, he had a whole basement full and the lights running twenty-four hours a day and his father head of the Knights of Columbus. They said it was practically a jungle, except for one tiny corner he kept clear for his mother's ironing board. She told the bridge club she thought they were toma-toes. Tomatoes! And there's the Handleys, I never thought I'd see the day when Tom Hardin would eat at the same table as a Handley but I feel sorry for them out there on that poor little farm and Frances just drying up like a leaf, and her just as cute as she can be and with a darling personality. And Nick in practically the same boat, you'd think it runs in the family except that their mother was such a popular girl, and artistic, too, Nick, that is, not Frances. And of course you've got to count your monks twice over, each of 'em eating twice as much as a normal human, not to mention the drinks. And then Miss Camilla will wander over from next door, if only to criticize our grammar—it's a good thing we all don't talk like she does, else she'd have to stay home. I'll set a table for the hospital staff—Tom Hardin had to invite all the doctors, and he's got to pinch the nurses' behinds once more for luck. The Ellises have all moved to Florida, she had a sister down there, you remember her, long-necked girl with the teeth that stuck out, she was in your class. Or was that Bette C.'s? The Pattersons are off in their RV to Michigan—heat, they say, drove 'em north, like they'd never lived every summer of their lives watching it get hot around here. I say they spent so much money on the damned thing they got to get on the road to show it off. And how did they come across twenty-five thousand in cash? It don't pay to ask questions, is what I say, but what do you talk about when the answers are growing in the creekbed you've set traps in for forty years? The weather I guess. The McCrearys are all in the graveyard, and the Muhlenbergs, you remember Ittybit Muhlenberg, she was the Altar Society treasurer that year you broke the stained glass? They've all moved to Louisville except for the ones that are down there keeping company with the Mc-Crearys. That leaves Tom Hardin and me, but somebody's got to sing the funerals. Su'vivors," she said gaily, "we're just su'vivors."

"You could say that about us all," Raphael said.

The silence that followed grew into something she could touch, the size and shape of themselves. Raphael said nothing more, and as for the questions that crowded Rose Ella's tongue, each looked like a door closed on things she knew but didn't want to know and in any case couldn't bring herself to speak the words she'd have to say to learn more. All this with Tom Hardin not long back from the hospital and none too well himself, and a mob of people about to show up on her doorstep hungry and thirsty and expecting a good time. In the end Rose Ella said nothing but took up her kitchen hatchet and led Raphael outside to the carriage rock.

Already the Hardins were scattered about the yard, clustered under the trees like barnyard animals in a heat wave. For the first time in years Rose Ella had strong-armed all of her surviving children into the same place at the same time, along with in-laws, out-laws, grandchildren. The younger men were inside watching baseball; the older men were gathered at the bar set up under the old dogwood, from whose outstretched limb hung the flag from Clark's coffin—Rose Ella brought it out on special occasions. The younger women watched the next generation and compared brood notes on the patio; the older women were inside fixing supper. Old Tice Flaherty was climbing from Dwight's van, customized metallic blue with golden flames roaring down the sides—Dwight had pulled right onto the grass, so as to unload his stereo. At the last minute Dennis appeared—Elizabeth's high school boyfriend. He'd been down from Louisville, he explained, visiting family, had seen the cars in the Hardin driveway, and thought he'd stop in. Rose Ella had her doubts, but sacred manners won out—she had Joe Ray fix him a drink. In the outer reaches of the long, sloping yard the older grandchildren flew about like chickadees, alighting first on the horseshoe pit, then fluttering to the swing set; flying over the grass, so dry it crackled underfoot; in and out of the apple orchard, until settling finally to red rover, where for referee they installed Michael, Joe Ray's eighteen-year-old, in an Adirondack chair on the sidelines.

While his great-aunt Galina was still alive and holding forth in this very house, Tom Hardin had hauled and cursed the old carriage rock to the edge of the barbecue pit. Rose Ella slapped the fish down on it now: a fifteen-pound, steel-blue channel cat, iridescent against the bone-white limestone. "Global warming," she muttered. She turned to Raphael. "Was a time when your father and me'd set a dozen trot lines, we'd catch two dozen fish. Yesterday I caught exactly one, but at least he's a prize. Speaking of su'vivors. Look at the meanness in him." The fish glared up at her. There was a resemblance, though Rose Ella would never have admitted it; the same broad chinless grin, the same boxy figure tapering to next to nothing—ankles, in her case, which she took care to show off; she always bought her slacks a little short. Since the change of life she could even sport whiskers, but fortunately for her there was Nair.

She stood aside and waited for Raphael to do what men do—take this hunk of fishy meat by its tail and slam its life against the rock. Raphael studied the hot blue sky. "Doesn't look like much chance for rain today, either."

The fish lay quiet, gills gasping. "City boy," Rose Ella said. She whetted the hatchet against the rock's edge, clutched it in clenched fists, raised it above her head, plunged it into the fish's flat skull. Then she handed the hatchet, the fish flopping and twisting on its blade, to her son, along with an apron. "Better for the fish to slam it against the rock—at least that's what your father says. But I could just never bring myself to do that." She went inside to fetch a bucket of brine, leaving Raphael holding the hatchet.

Raphael spread some newspapers, laid the catfish across the headlines. He'd hesitated not from squeamishness. As a child he'd killed his share of animals, hunting and fishing with Tom Hardin—those days when his father taught him to wield a weapon or gut a deer were among the few times they'd spoken without anger.

Now Raphael was in a place where life and death seemed more fragile. Had the living fish been left to him, he would have flung it back into the shrunken river, a demonstration that it was humanly possible to thwart fate. But he was here,

and the run-through fish was here, and there was only one possible end to this particular chain of events. Raphael worked
the blade free from the fish's skull, then took up a knife and
slit its gut.

From Tom Hardin he'd learned to kill and gut fish and
deer; from Rose Ella he'd learned to clean and cook them. She
taught him that, then she got him off to California. "You take
that money and vamoose," she'd said to Raphael when he won
a scholarship to college, and when he announced he was going
to California she raised ringed fingers and danced a little jig.
"On the condition I get to come to visit," she'd said. "He'll come
back a damned hippie," was what Tom Hardin had said, but
Rose Ella silenced him with a look. "It's no place for this one
around here," she'd said, and even Tom Hardin gave ground
before her determination.

Each passing year Raphael grew more distant from these
parties, as he grew away from this place. He wore his pants
pleated and pegged now, he had his hair styled, flat up the sides
and long on top, except where it was thinning at the crown;
he wore spectacles (when he wasn't wearing contacts) with
round, imitation tortoise shell frames with high-tech lenses. In
this vanity he was closer to his nephews, with their perms and
gold chains, than to his older brothers. "City boy," Rose Ella
had called him. Among these country men he *was* the city boy,
in city clothes and city ways, as out of place as the catfish on
the carriage rock; as out of place as he himself had once been
on city streets.

But if not this place then what place? Here in the South
places laid claim to people, not the other way around, but
California laid claim to no one—it was too vast and grand,
too young and full of itself for that. People came and squatted
on its living, trembling earth, which in a given year might or

might not tolerate their presence. How did a man go about establishing himself in the heart of a place? Raphael wondered. By loving it over a long time, he guessed. And how much time, how many generations would that take, in that cheerfully rootless place? More time than was likely to be left to an HIV-positive man, of that much he could be sure.

This was his place in the world: a shell of thought and emotion wrapped around a core of anger and grief so bitter that he saw these as his choices: Dwell in anger, or forgive and forget.

He admired those men and women who, driven by righteous anger, shouted accusations from balconies, chained themselves to bureaucrats' doors, seized the Golden Gate Bridge and transformed it into a media event. Insofar as things were better for him than for his friends who had gone before, it was due to these people's courage and boldness, their love for each other and for him, a man whom they'd never met. He understood all this but he remained on the sidelines. He gave money, volunteered, marched—he was always marching; but when the bullhorns and handcuffs came out he was always to be found safe on the margins. The deaths he'd witnessed drove him less to action than to inaction—a resignation just shy of despair.

Accept. Only accept. Raphael found himself ambushed by this mantra as he stood on busy street corners, or in the middle of crowded parties, or (worst of all) alone in his bed, awakened by its insistence at some odd hour in the middle of the night. It welled up from some place deep within: Only accept this fate, but he could not accept, and with each refusal to accept he grew more bitter, his heart hardened to a callus.

He was washing blood from chunks of catfish meat when the monks pulled up in the monastery truck, whooping and chattering like schoolboys set free. Years before, hunting on monastery land, Tom Hardin struck up friendships with the brothers he found laboring or praying in the fields. Tom Hardin preferred the company of men; he'd have been a monk himself, he said this often, except that he was allergic to religion.

In the years since, the Hardins had seen abbots lax and strict come and go, but always some of the monks managed to slip out of the enclosure for an occasional evening with the Hardins. Eusebius, Hippolytus, Anselm, Cyril, Samuel—for Raphael their names opened back into time, bringing to life here in K mart Kentucky the memory of medieval scholars and martyrs, the continuity of all that, how very close it was in the scope of things to their own time: twelve aged men and women, linking hands, might join his own hand to that of Saint Anselm; twelve more pairs of hands would join him to Jesus.

They were Yankees, these monks, veterans of one or another war or children given gratefully to the Church by families from the Catholic immigrant ghettos of big Northern cities (one less mouth to feed; spiritual collateral in the event of a God). As a child Raphael had heard a foreign country in their flat nasal vowels—a place with elevators, baseball, blizzards. They'd brought a glimpse of a world almost as fantastic as California, with Samuel, born and raised in the heart of Harlem, the most exotic of them all.

On this hottest of summer evenings they wore their formal dress—"party clothes," Samuel called them; white woolen albs over brown woolen surplices, belted at the waist with plain leather bands. They gathered around Tom Hardin, standing at the bar.

Eusebius clapped Tom Hardin's shoulder, then drew his hand back. "Maybe I shouldn't be so rough. How's it going? How are you doing?"

"Just fine," Rose Ella said. "The doctor is almost certain he cleared out every bit of trouble, and what's left he'll catch with chemo."

"I'm not going to let him do chemo," Tom Hardin growled.

"Now isn't he just a pill?" Rose Ella took Eusebius by the elbow. "Go on, you have Tom Hardin fix you all a drink while I get some lard for the skillet." At her cue the monks lined up. Tom Hardin poured stiff whiskeys, then excused himself to the kitchen. A few minutes later he emerged with a glass of water, and Raphael understood that there would be no more drinking for Tom Hardin, not in this life.

Rose Ella returned with a tub of lard. She greased the skillet, then called Raphael to the grill. She lowered her voice conspiratorially. "Rafe, you keep a eye on Joe Ray. You don't need to tell him I said so but you know how he gets after a few highballs. I don't want you pulling him out of the fire again."

In his younger days Raphael would have insisted on facts—how could he have pulled Joe Ray out of the fire? He was living in San Francisco by then. But Rose Ella lost no sleep over facts. "If you weren't there you ought to have been," was what she'd say. As for Joe Ray, he still carried scars scattered like coals up his neck.

Brother Eusebius: tall, thin, serious; he had been an orphan. He retrieved his drink from the bar and stood at Raphael's side, watching as he dredged the fish in flour, then gently lowered each slab into hot lard. "And which is this? And which is that? And how do you know?" he asked.

Raphael pointed with a fork. "Crappie. Bluegill, from the freezer, with the little spots on their gills. Catfish. Fresh from the river."

There was a screech, then a deafening howl, then a guitar riff echoed through the yard—Dwight Flaherty had the stereo up and running. "Turn that thing down!" Elizabeth called. She was their other Californian—she and Andrew, her boyfriend, had flown in from Los Angeles the day before. She wore a bright flowered blouse that Rose Ella would have called tacky on anybody else's child.

"I thought you Californians would be used to that kind of noise," Joe Ray said. "They have to play it loud, you know that. What they lose in quality, they make up for in volume."

One of the grandsons groaned. "Another lecture from the middle-aged set." He made quavery, trembling motions with his hands. "You stick with selling computers, Uncle Joe. Let the musicians handle the music."

"There's not one of 'em could play next to the greats," Joe Ray said. "Buddy Holly, Little Richard, Roy Orbison. Even Elvis, for God's sake. These guys you listen to now—they're three generations removed from the real thing. It's nothing they can help, but there it is."

"When's the last time you listened to a live body play a guitar?" Andrew asked.

"They're not playing guitars anymore, they're playing computers," Joe Ray said.

"Well, thank the Lord they're buying computers," Rose Ella said. "It's good for your business."

A battered farm truck pulled up—Nick Handley, with his sister Frances. Tom Hardin pointed with his cane. "Are we scraping the barrel for guests or are they just showing up because there's a free meal to be had?"

"Oh, hush," Rose Ella said. "I just thought it'd be nice to have somebody Rafe's age among the Geritol set."

"Bottom of the barrel," Tom Hardin said.

Rose Ella made an extravagant show of greeting the new guests. She threw her hands about in wide gestures that took in the family, the guests, the monks—the whole heat-seared yard.

Nick Handley was in his thirties, with a farmer's wiry muscles and red raw skin, his brown hair shot through with sun-streaks. He and Raphael had graduated together, then had hardly seen each other since Raphael went away to California. Now, watching Nick cross the yard, Raphael was struck by a newer, deeper sense of recognition. Nick carried himself with the distance and gracelessness of a man who could not allow himself to be touched, who from his earliest self-knowledge had placed himself beyond touching. He had been hardened by sun and dirt and work, yes, but more than that by years of turning in on himself. He was high-strung like a banjo drone, taut and fine-tuned to the point of breaking, and singing with desire so urgent it announced itself, singing out of its own accord in his awkward handshake, in the trembling of his fingers as he lit a cigarette, in the nervous flexing of his shoulders as he stood at Raphael's side, and all the while Nick himself clearly so certain of what he needed to believe: that nobody saw his wanting, not his sister, not his neighbors, not the townspeople whose eyes he avoided on the street. As for them, they were relieved to aid and abet.

Raphael knew this apartness. He tucked in his shirt, straightened his bloodstained pants, passed a hand over his thinning hair, raised his hand to touch Nick's shoulder. "You're looking sleek. Working the farm must do you good."

"Frances told me you were in town. Welcome home," Nick said, but he drew back from Raphael's touch. His hands roamed like a raccoon's—searching out small objects, picking them up, turning them over, testing their edges. He seized a platter from the carriage rock. As Raphael lifted chunks of fish from the sputtering lard, Nick arranged them on serving dishes.

Now they were ten around the fire: Raphael and Nick, Joe Ray and his wife Catherine, Eusebius and Nick's sister Frances, Elizabeth and her boyfriends past and present—Dennis and Andrew; and nearby Rose Ella, keeping peace among the younger children.

Raphael speared some frying bluegills and handed them to Nick. "So how are things on the farm?"

"Could be worse, but I'd need a lawyer to tell me how."

"Mother tells me you're about the only one around here who hasn't gone into pot."

"We wouldn't touch the stuff," Frances said.

"We find it all the time," Eusebius said. "Practically inside the enclosure. They figure the police won't come onto monastery land."

"They'll quit growing it when the government builds that dam," Joe Ray said. "That's half the reason they're putting it in—flood out the pot growers."

"We'll have lakefront property," Nick said. "I'll tear down the tobacco barn and build a marina."

"You and what bank." Frances pulled a cigarette from a pack and took a lighter from her purse, but Eusebius had a match already struck. Frances pulled back her hair and bent to the flame. "You see that, Nick? Gentlemen live!"

"You don't want a lake," Elizabeth said. "People from Louisville out every weekend. Breaking into your houses, leaving their trash. Paying cash three times what you'd think of borrowing, to buy an overgrown piece of knobs. You won't be able to afford your own land."

"I live in Louisville and you can put me down for a lot at whatever price you name," Joe Ray said. "I'd quit computers in a heartbeat. I'd have a little air-conditioned store to keep open on the weekends and fish in between."

"No fish in a Corps of Engineers reservoir," Raphael said.

"You think we can't stock 'em?" Joe Ray asked. "You *have* been in California too long."

"Damn right," Elizabeth snapped. "We've seen the future and it's Los Angeles."

"I liked Los Angeles," Rose Ella said, looking up from the children. "So much to do. I'd love to go back. That's a hint."

Catherine took Joe Ray's hand. "We need a man in the kitchen, to get the heavy dishes down."

"Here's Miss Camilla, just in time for her spot of whiskey," Joe Ray cried, pulling his hand free. He seated her in the folding chair that Tice Elaherty had pulled out. Tice parked himself in a neighboring chair. He threw his hands in the air and slapped her knee. Finally his hand rested itself on her thigh, where it sat like some forlorn object, neither refused nor welcomed.

Next the hospital staff arrived, dressed at Tom Hardin's request in their hospital whites—Tom Hardin thought the nurses were sexy in their uniforms. They flocked around the bar. One of the nurses struck up a conversation with Dennis, who spent most of his day on his feet selling cars and who had problems with his back. He was swearing by a treatment he'd first seen described in a holistic newsletter—each day he hung upside down, his feet clamped in antigravity boots, while he listened to alpha (or was it beta?) waves broadcast through a Walkman attached to his belt.

Catherine circled the yard calling in the grandchildren. It was time to eat.

The children roared across the patio, lining up to wash their hands at the hose. Catherine was all over the yard and the house, bringing out plates, tearing off paper towels for extra napkins, picking up glasses before they might leave rings on the big Adirondack chairs that Samuel and Tom Hardin had turned out from Tom Hardin's woodshop. Catherine ushered Raphael into the kitchen, where she put him to work rooting condiments from the refrigerator.

Joe Ray sailed in, to throw his arm around his wife. "My Queen of Clean," he crooned. Pulling plastic forks and knives from the cupboard, Catherine eyed him coldly. "Just warming up to sing," he said.

"Try not to get too warm. Just this once." She lifted the drink from his hand and replaced it with a tray of banana croquettes. "Take those to the outside table. See if you can make it without tripping over the steps."

He balanced the tray on one hand, snapped the other hand to his forehead. "Yes, *sir*."

Raphael watched his brother negotiate the back stoop, past kids reaching after croquettes, over pets and toys. He didn't spill a thing—he wasn't *that* drunk, not yet. With the high-leaping steps of a racking horse he deftly avoided all obstacles and set the tray atop its three-legged stand. He turned and bowed in their direction.

The commotion shifted from the patio to the front door. The grandchildren were fighting over who would ring the dinner bell, a great iron thing that could be heard in the farthest reaches of the fields. Rose Ella struck a compromise. The bell rang out. Family and hospital staff crowded around the patio.

Rose Ella took two of her grandchildren's hands in her own. "Give us some of that Yankee grace, Samuel."

Samuel stood and bowed his head. The family joined hands to form a circle for his grace, then Rose Ella raised the clasped hands of Tee Junior and Michael, the youngest and oldest of Joe Ray's three sons. She nodded at the flag hung from the dogwood limbs, unmoving in the still, late afternoon heat. "And don't forget Clark, who lives still in our hearts."

"And Leola Ferber." This from Brother Samuel.

"And Gaspard," Rose Ella said. "Though I don't know that Gaspard died—he just disappeared, about the time they took Leola off to the Little Sisters."

"Speech, speech!" Joe Ray called—he had hooked up his video camera.

"Food first," Rose Ella said. This brought a cheer from the grandchildren.

"What about Frances and Eusebius?" Andrew asked.

"They've gone for a walk," Rose Ella said.

"To the cemetery bench," Joe Ray said with a broad wink.

"Eusebius can do better than that," Tom Hardin said.

"Just as cute as she can be and with a darling personality," Rose Ella said.

"Oh, Mother, please." Elizabeth paused in the middle of filling her plate. "We all know Frances is plain as a plank and tough as nails."

Joe Ray snapped off the camera. "Here we have an illustration of the subtlety of California conversational technique."

"That's not to say I don't like her," Elizabeth said. "It's just the truth, is all."

"I think the world could use a little less truth and a little more manners," Rose Ella said. "Bette C., do me a favor and go check on the cornbread."

At one end of the long table were platters of fish, huge blossoms of rich white flesh. Around the platters' edges small flat bluegill fanned out, petals around a corolla of catfish fillets encrusted with golden cornmeal. In the center were the delicate-meated fighters—large- and smallmouth bass, crappie. Stalks of leafy celery, feathered radishes, carrot sticks, and small round hush puppies ranged among the piles of fish—Nick had been at work here.

Next to the fish were bowls of dark green kale cooked since morning with a side of fatback, with cider vinegar at hand in Rose Ella's great-grandmother's silver-and-crystal cruets. A gilt-edged platter carried a small mountain of thin fried potatoes, encircled by a moat of Rose Ella's green tomato ketchup. Quartered watermelons showed speckled crescents next to pyramids of homegrown tomatoes, yellow and red. Deviled eggs peered up at the sky, their scrambled yolks bloodshot with paprika. A pile of corn on the cob filled a silver platter. At the center of the table three jam cakes iced with caramel ringed a cut-glass punch bowl filled with layers of fruit cocktail, cubes of electric-green Jell-O, Cool Whip, and miniature marshmallows, topped with a sprinkling of toasted coconut and luminescent maraschino cherries. "Heavenly hash," Rose Ella said proudly. "It's my own invention." She had changed into a fluorescent scarlet blouse. As she served potato salad Joe Ray shielded his eyes. "I'd better be careful around that— you'll blind the camera."

"Elizabeth brought it," Rose Ella said. "I don't ask questions, I just wear what she tells me. She says they're all the rage in California."

"Oh, well. *California*," Joe Ray said.

The line snaked along the table to bunch up at one end, where Joe Ray set up the camera to interview every hungry person down to Tee Junior himself.

The Hardin brothers and sisters, Rose Ella, and Tom Hardin sat at a single long table, covered with floral tablecloths and real glassware—Tom Hardin refused to eat from a bare table or a paper plate. Always Rose Ella kept a place set and empty for Clark—she'd remembered hearing somewhere that Jewish people do this, and she liked the thought that in some way he was sitting down with them for hush puppies (his favorite) and fish. In-laws and grandchildren and friends and the hospital staff sat at side tables, clustered in a circle around the family. Of the grandchildren only Michael, Joe Ray's oldest, sat with the older generation. Years after his accident and he still needed someone to help him with delicate movements—writing, or holding a fork.

Elizabeth waved at Dennis, who was wandering about alone, a loaded plate in his hand. "Take a seat," she said. "Ex-lovebirds are allowed."

"Not if I have any say in it," Andrew grumbled, but Elizabeth hushed him with a kiss.

A few minutes and the evening settled into a mealtime quiet. In the silence that followed loading the plates Joe Ray started a joke. His voice rose to the punchline. Michael laughed, too early and too hard.

Tee Junior carefully rested his plateful on the table next to Samuel. Standing on tiptoe, he reached toward the monk's head. The monk lifted the boy into his lap. "What you want, little boy?"

"To pat your head," the boy said. "Grandfather told me I get a wish every time I pat a nigger's head."

Silence.

Catherine stood and swooped up her child. "Your grandfather said no such thing."

"Let's every one of us here take a last look at that platter of fish," Rose Ella said. "A man can outcook a woman over an open fire—I don't deny it—but it takes a woman to make it look pretty."

"Nick arranged the fish," Raphael said.

A smaller silence.

"Well, I ought to have known," Rose Ella said. "You ought to see what he does for the Advent altars. Milkweed pods and devil's walking stick and crown of thorns, can you imagine, and he turns them into something positively *holy*. I don't know what the Altar Society'd do without him. He's so artistic."

Joe Ray gave Nick a sympathetic nod. "I have to admit I've wondered all these years, and I'm sorry to hear it now. But all of us have to work with what the Lord gives us. I've read where some kids can't even talk to their teachers, they're just in a world of their own. You don't look like you've got it that bad."

"*Art*istic," Catherine said. She lifted a drink from Joe Ray's hand. "An entirely different thing."

"You better believe it," Raphael said.

"He's not artistic," Tom Hardin said. "He's just a damned tobacco farmer."

"There's an art to farming tobacco," Nick said.

"Why don't we just skip supper?" Joe Ray said. "Catherine can put Tee Junior straight to bed and we can start singing." Tee Junior, searching one grownup's face after another for clues, let loose an anguished howl.

"Just leave the boy alone," Tom Hardin said. "Samuel don't mind. Do you, Samuel."

"Don't mind a bit," Samuel said cheerfully. "Tee Junior, you can pat my head anytime you want."

Behind Samuel's back, Rose Ella pointed at her open mouth with a wooden spoon. "Cornbread," Catherine said, "and high time. Samuel, you take your pick."

There were baskets of cornbread, hot from its cast-iron molds—heart-shaped muffins and the long pones. For years Rose Ella had kept track of the last cream-producing cow in the county and now she brought out a mound of butter criss-crossed with her trademark slashes.

Eusebius and Frances came trotting up then, a little breathless. "You all took so long loading your plates we decided we'd take a little walk," Frances said. "The black-eyed Susans are so pretty this time of year. Mind if I sit down?" She squeezed herself into the empty place at the foot of the table, between Rose Ella and Raphael, then scooted over to make room for Eusebius.

"That's Clark's place," Raphael said.

"Hmm?"

Tom Hardin stood and went to the bar, leaving his plate untouched. "Don't move on our account," Frances called after him. "Oh, don't pay attention to him," Rose Ella said. "Since the operation he just has a little trouble sitting for long spells. Isn't that right, Tom Hardin?" Standing at the bar, Tom Hardin turned his back.

Andrew turned to Dennis. "So where's Crystal?" he asked—Crystal was Dennis's wife.

Rose Ella lowered her voice. "They're working out their differences."

"They're considering a divorce," Elizabeth said in a loud, cheerful voice. "Which Andrew knows perfectly well, since I told him only yesterday. Well, there's no point dodging it. They haven't lived together for the last three months."

"Which is no reason for their situation to become supper table conversation," Rose Ella said.

"We're not considering a divorce. We're just—working out our differences," Dennis said. "Just because people in California live together for a lifetime without making some kind of commitment doesn't mean that's the way it's got to be every place else."

"Well, these things happen," Elizabeth said. "You can't expect people to live out their lives in a monastery, hmm, Eusebius?"

Tom Hardin spoke from the bar. "You can expect people to abide by their word. Once was a time you gave your word, you stuck by it. They got married, they gave their word. There's such a thing as being loyal, even when it don't suit your ends."

Dennis took on the stony face of a man forced to talk about things he'd prefer left unsaid. "I couldn't agree more, sir. This is temporary. It's just like Mrs. Hardin said. We have too much commitment to our family to consider anything else."

"Well, you don't have to be married to be part of a healthy family," Andrew said. "Elizabeth and I have a healthy family, if it comes to that."

"Not by my standards," Dennis said.

"And what might those standards be?" Andrew asked.

Dennis waved at the crowd of relatives. "People that you're tied to by blood. What's the point of a family if you can just up and leave it anytime things get rough?"

"What's the point of family if all it does is make you un-happy?" Andrew asked.

"Yes!" Dennis said. "I mean, no!"

Andrew smirked.

"We wouldn't even have a family if it weren't for Reach Out America and Supersaver fares," Elizabeth said.

"A telephone call is great but it's no substitute for Catherine's chicken soup," Joe Ray said.

Dennis tapped Andrew's chest with his forefinger. "It's a man's place to be responsible. You and Raphael—you might like your friends, but you don't have kids you're taking care of."

"Instead I'm taking care of friends who are dying," Raphael snapped. "A lot of them a thousand miles from parents or brothers or sisters who could care less."

Silence.

"There's a time and a place for this conversation and it's someplace else and later on," Rose Ella said. "Right now we're all in good health and happy to be here."

Dusk fell. Some of the hospital staffers left for late shifts, others joined the family on the patio. The children adjourned to the television room—Joe Ray had hooked his video camera into the television set and was showing the tapes he'd shot earlier that evening—"an interactive family video installation," Andrew called it. Tice Flaherty sent Dwight crawling into the van to dig out his ukulele. "I don't know why you asked me to set up the stereo, if you're not going to listen to it," Dwight said.

"I don't recall anybody asking in the first place," Joe Ray said.

Sitting on the patio glider, Tice Flaherty picked out a tune. On a visit to San Francisco, Rose Ella had bought a fake grass skirt on Fisherman's Wharf, which she pulled out now for Brother Hippolytus to wrap around his robe. He and Brother Cyril climbed atop the carriage rock and threw familiar arms around each other and sang Broadway musical hits in harmony, Cyril launching into a falsetto to counter Hippolytus's contrabass. With the first plink of the ukulele Joe Ray brought out spoons, which he banged while Tice Flaherty played. "Now it's Mother's turn!" Joe Ray cried, and though she argued and balked, in the end Rose Ella let herself be hoisted to the rock, where she sang while Cyril and Hippolytus improvised a little soft shoe. Tice Flaherty wound things up with a hot little ukulele lick. "The best in the county!" Joe Ray cried. "There was a time—I was there, Mr. Flaherty, don't you deny it—it was at the county fair, and Bill Monroe, and one of his boys got sick."

"Accident," Rose Ella said. "He'd had an accident."

"Whatever, it was last-minute and they got Mr. Flaherty

up there with his banjo—none of this ukulele business—and he played like the dickens. And at the end of the night Bill Monroe himself turned to him and said, 'Mr. Tice, you can play in my band anytime you want.' Isn't that true?"

"It's the ones that went before—you take Samantha Bumgardner," Tice Flaherty said. "She's lost even to the rememberers, her name don't mean nothing to nobody no more. But she was a real player, she and the ones like her. They played all the old songs and played 'em best, because they never had to learn 'em—they were born with 'em in the blood and grew up with 'em in the blood. My daddy he played good but not so good as them, and all I do is try to remember how he remembered how they played it, is all. The ones of us that remember best are the best ones left."

Joe Ray looked around mournfully. "It's not like it once was," he said. "Was a time when there'd be seventy or eighty of us, and four or five different circles all singing, and everybody with something to make music."

"There was a time when we had to walk a hundred yards in the snow to get to the outhouse," Elizabeth said.

"I don't see any frostbit toes, Miss California," Joe Ray said.

"Where are all those people now?" Cyril asked.

"Oh, here and there," Rose Ella said vaguely. "Those that are still alive, of course. I'd show you pictures—photographs— but you'd have to ask Miss Camilla's father for those." She told her story then, the old story whose many versions they all knew—how Miss Camilla's father had come through and taken Rose Ella's parents' wedding photograph, only to run off with Miss Camilla's mother, a local girl who was never seen again, any more than the photographs themselves.

"'Course, it wasn't Miss Camilla's fault," Tice Flaherty

added generously. "For all she knows those pictures never even turned out. Ain't that right, Camilla?"

"I expect my father had his mind on more important things," Miss Camilla said brightly. Rose Ella managed a polite laugh—it was as close to a joke as Miss Camilla came, at least on this subject.

Joe Ray was shooting again—he had attached a spotlight to his camera and was taping at the picnic tables, where Dwight and the Hardin grandsons were playing poker with a scrabbling of bills and change anted up. "In those days we'd take up a collection for Mr. Flaherty," Joe Ray said, "and feel honored to empty our pockets."

"Can't dance," Dwight said.

"Joe Ray, why don't you see if anybody needs a refill," Rose Ella said.

Catherine lifted the video camera from her husband's hand. "It's getting late. And when it gets late we get hard to deal with."

Joe Ray clapped Tice Flaherty's shoulder. "Mr. Flaherty's careful with his talent—that's because he's good. But stick around till midnight. We work on him long enough, he'll get that banjo out. That's when the party really takes off." But Mr. Flaherty tucked his ukulele back in its case. "Airish out here," he said. "Fingers are too stiff."

"What the hell is wrong with this family anyway," Joe Ray said, but already Dwight had the stereo cranked up—they weren't going to suffer silence on *his* account.

Nick pulled Raphael aside. "They're still growing great pot in Kentucky," he said. "In case you're interested."

They walked out behind the garden, where they were hidden from the party by the old, gnarled trees of the apple orchard.

That spring Tom Hardin had been too ill to prune the orchard or to plant a garden, and with a supermarket at hand Rose Ella didn't see the point in all that work. The garden had grown rank, a weedy jungle of volunteer tomatoes and potatoes overwhelmed by head-high lamb's quarter and amaranth and a few spikes of bright yellow mullein. The unpruned trees bore hard, wormy fruit, dark little globes against the darkening evening sky.

Nick tapped marijuana from a matchbox into a cigarette paper creased between his fingers. "You think I could make a living in California?"

"It's not as easy as people believe," Raphael said. "Picking up and moving twenty-five hundred miles."

Nick gave the joint a practiced lick. "I hear San Francisco is a crazy place."

"Don't believe what you see on television."

Nick handed the joint to Raphael, then struck a match on his jeans. His face loomed large in the flaring light. "I'll bet you seen it all."

"Not all," Raphael said, then, "a fair amount."

"Tell me some of the things you seen."

Raphael sucked on the joint, smoke leaking from his lips. "Nothing you don't see here in Jessup County. Just different, and more of it."

"You seen guys kiss other guys."

"I've seen that," Raphael said. He let the smoke ease out, a white cloud against the black branching apple trees. "Plenty of that. But don't you believe that doesn't happen right here in Jessup County."

"I know that. I know that myself."

Only the white limestone cliffs across the valley stood out now, and the fireflies, no more than a few in this dry summer, scattered across the fields that rolled to the dark fringe of

woods bordering the ravine. Music boomed from the yard—
rockabilly music now; Dwight's concession to the old order.

In this hot weather Nick wore only an old cotton work-
shirt, worn so thin that even in this dusky light his nipples
showed as two dark circles through the cloth. Half-moons of
sweat darkened his underarms, and on the still night air his
scent brought a surge of blood to Raphael's skin. Desire was
something he thought he'd left behind, that had been crowded
from a heart too full of fear and anger and grief.

Nick stepped to Raphael's side. "Stand here next to me.
No, closer. Open your mouth." Nick reversed the joint. "Shotgun," he said. He took its burning coal into the hollow of his
own mouth, holding the joint between puckered lips. He put
his mouth over Raphael's and exhaled, blowing a thick stream
of smoke from the tip of the joint into Raphael's parted lips.

Lust rose in Raphael's body, a shiver through his shoulders, a fist in his throat. How long had it been since he'd been
seized by desire so strong it created its own demands, outside
of time and place? Nick's long, narrow self under his own
body, hard as a plank and permeated with the musky, sour
taste of tobacco—this old, timeless, fooling, joyful thing, with
its own ways and means.

Above the music they heard Catherine's voice, sharp-
edged. "Right *now*, young man!"—then an explosion of laughter.

"You ever kissed a guy?" Nick asked.

"It's been known to happen."

"When you were a kid?"

"Well. A *kid*. The first time I was out of college already—
twenty-one, or twenty-two. Does that make me a kid?"

"No. Not a kid."

A firefly flashed nearby; Raphael snatched it in midflight.
Its golden glow filled the cup of his hand.

"Did you like the guy?"

Raphael told his story then. "I was right out of college—I was twenty-two—I'd just moved to San Francisco. I'd never lived in a city before, not a real city—you don't know what it's like to be alone until you're alone in a city. And I was alone, I hardly knew a soul, and then I met this guy at a party and we got to be good friends, for a year or so." The firefly reached the tips of Raphael's fingers. It spread its wings, but Raphael flipped his hand and the firefly began its climb again. "He lived in the suburbs and I got up every Saturday morning at six A.M. and biked fourteen miles to his house, and sometimes on Sundays, all the time thinking we're just friends, except that we were calling each other every day, sometimes twice a day, and we couldn't wait to get together every weekend and sometimes in between and hang out.

"One time before all this I'd picked up this hitchhiker—he tried to put the make on me but I held him off, I wouldn't let myself do it. And then once I got to California I held myself off, I just didn't allow myself to think about love, or even sex, I couldn't let myself believe they could happen, at the same time that they were the only things I thought about or believed in, you know what I mean?"

"I know what you mean."

"And then finally I invited my friend on a bike ride and sat him down in Golden Gate Park on the benches in the bandshell, and I was scared shitless but I couldn't stand it anymore and I said, 'There's something you ought to know,' or some such line. And it turned out he had wanted to say the same thing to me but I'd talked about a girlfriend in college or something like that and he thought—well, he *had* a girlfriend, right then, right when I knew him, for Christ's sake, how was I supposed to know he was interested in me? We used to sit around arguing who was straighter until—for a long time, anyway. Anyway, so we're sitting in the bandshell and jumping out of our skin to make love and nowhere to go, I wouldn't take him home in front of my roommates—"

"Why didn't you go to his place?"

"He was living with his mother. He was living with his mother and I was working in San Francisco. I was a workaholic until then, I was twenty-three—"

"Twenty-two."

"Twenty-two when we met, twenty-three by this time, and I was determined to prove to myself that I could make it in the city, and I was working till eight or nine at night and on weekends and then all of a sudden I started leaving the office every day at five-oh-three, because if I left the office at five-oh-three I could run like hell and make the five-twenty-one Southern Pacific—that's the commuter train. He drove this souped-up, scarlet GTO with a broken muffler and he would roar up to the Southern Pacific station and I'd hop in and we'd drive like bats out of hell to his mother's house—we'd get there about five after six and we'd have maybe twenty-five minutes before she got home from work. And we'd go in his room and make love." Raphael grinned. "I'd tear his clothes off. He wore singlets, you know, not T-shirts but the kind of undershirts with straps—"

"Like basketball players. Or track stars."

"Yeah. We'd be unbuttoning our shirts while we were roaring down El Camino and we'd be down to our undershirts by the time we got to his mother's place, but one time we were running a little late and we only had maybe fifteen minutes and as soon as we were in the door I grabbed his undershirt and just ripped it off him, tore it right down the middle. And after that it got to be kind of a ritual, he would always wear one of those sleeveless undershirts and I would rip it off him as soon as we got in the door."

"And his mother never caught you."

"Never. Well, she always made a lot of noise driving up. What does that mean?" The firefly reached the tips of Raphael's fingers, spread its wings, and flew into the dark. "We must have gone through a dozen and more packages of undershirts, three to a package, that summer. You go through a couple of packages a week, that underwear gets expensive." He turned to face the sky, studying the stars through the trees. "One day at the last minute my boss asked me to stay late and I turned him down, made some kind of lamebrain excuse and Sarah, the woman who sat across the desk from me, looked up and said, maybe as a joke, I never had the nerve to ask, but anyway she said, 'Raphael can't stay late, he's in love!' And I turned beet red and they all knew it was true. 'Who's the little woman?' my boss said, and I lit out for the train.

"That was the first time ever in my life that I let myself believe that love was something that could happen to me. Always before I'd thought, 'Oh, I'm just too cold, I'm too wrapped up in myself,' or whatever. There were people who could love other people and people who couldn't, and I was one of the latter. And I thought what a shallow and empty-hearted person I must be, who could never be moved by another human being, who could never love somebody except at arm's length.

"And then my officemate said, 'Oh, Raphael's in love,' and it was like her saying it gave me permission to think it might be true, that it could happen to me—that I was a human being instead of a rock.

"And then a few months later we broke up. I couldn't take that fear, you know, meeting at his mother's place and her about to show up any time, it made it ugly and wrong, something to be ashamed of. We were so hot for each other—we'd go into the park at night and make love in the middle of the poison oak, just because we didn't have anyplace else to go. One time a cop came upon us kissing—he was mounted on a horse and he came around this bush and there we were, our clothes on and everything, just kissing, but he pulled out his nightstick and said, 'This park is for decent people.' So then we talked about moving in with each other but every time one of us brought the subject up the other used it as an excuse for a fight. We couldn't face anything like that—it would have been too much like admitting this is it, this is happening, we're two men in love. And so we broke up." Raphael's shoulders seized up, a chill in the midst of the dying day's lingering heat. "A year or two later and both of us had figured out who we were and what was what and we tried to get back together, but that's not how it works, we'd lost something, it was over. I mean, we were still good friends, but we'd let something break and it was gone, it was history."

Tee Junior found them out then. "I *see* you," he sang out triumphantly. "You're hiding."

Raphael knelt in front of his nephew while Nick stubbed the joint against a gnarled apple trunk. "How come you're not watching tapes of the party?" Raphael asked.

Tee Junior shrugged. "Tapes are boring."

"Careful, little boy," Raphael said. "Listen to your uncle. People have been exiled for lesser sins." He smoothed twigs and early-fallen apples from the earth. "You can stay with us."

"But it's getting *dark*."

"That way nobody will see us. We'll be OK. We'll stay here with you." Raphael tousled his nephew's hair. "We'll all hang out together out here. We'll stay out all night and sleep right here in the orchard."

"Really?"

"Sure." Raphael lay down on a bed of crabgrass and lamb's quarter. "Lie here next to me. You look up through the apple trees long enough, you'll see a shooting star. And then you can make the wish you never got to make awhile ago."

Tee Junior studied the ground. "Are there bugs?"

Raphael laughed. "There are bugs." He propped himself on his elbows, pulled some change from his pocket, slid it into Tee Junior's surprised palm. He pointed his nephew toward the house. "You tell them Uncle Rafe and his friend Nick took a walk to get some cigarettes. A long walk. Go on."

Tee Junior disappeared into the darkening yard. After a minute Nick lay down next to Raphael. "Frances will think I've gone off and left her. Not that she would mind. She would just as soon left me home. But your mother made a big deal about my coming. So I came." Nick tucked his marijuana box in his back pocket. "Frances's meetings with Eusebius aren't usually so official. But you didn't hear me say that."

They lay next to each other, their shoulders touching lightly. To the west the bombs and tracer flares of Fort Knox lit the night sky with bursts of light. It was August, the time of the Perseids, and as they watched first one star, then another slid down the sky's violet chute.

"You still see him?" Nick asked.

"Who?"

"The guy whose undershirts you tore off."

"Oh." Raphael folded his arms across his chest. "Well, he's dead. He died a little over a year ago."

For a long while they lay silent, until Nick cleared his throat. "You know guys that have died."

"Oh, sure. Everybody does in San Francisco," Raphael said, and the casualness in his voice shocked himself.

Fenton Johnson

Someone switched off the stereo. *My dog has fleas*—on the far side of the garden, Joe Ray had persuaded Tice Flaherty to take up his ukulele. "Some kickass bluegrass!" Joe Ray bawled. "'Fox on the Run!'" They were gathering to sing— Raphael knew the timing; he'd seen enough of these parties.

"I think of you sometimes, out in San Francisco," Nick said.

"Me? Why would you think about me?"

"I don't know," Nick said. "This is a small town. You got a reputation."

"I can imagine."

Nick was that close—Raphael might reach out a hand and touch him. His hand reached out, a mind of its own. Raphael stuck it in his pocket.

"Everybody used to talk about you all the time, they still do," Nick said. "How you'd made the big break and how much nerve that took and all the things you were probably doing."

"Such as?"

"Oh, I don't know. Surfing, and hanging out at rock concerts, and smoking pot."

"Well, one out of three," Raphael said. "The great bands had all broken up by the time I got there. And the ocean at San Francisco is about the temperature of your refrigerator."

"Even in the summer?"

"Especially in the summer."

"So what have you been doing all these years?"

Raphael thought for a moment, then shrugged. "Never mind. I like your version better."

"I thought then maybe I could do all that, someday."

"Maybe you will."

"You were in love," Nick said, and the longing in his voice penetrated the denseness of Raphael's heart.

166

Around them the first, early-fallen apples were decaying into the moist dark earth. Surrounded by their faint, cloying scent, Raphael felt, as if it were under his hand, the flat hardness of Nick's chest. In another time and place Raphael would have taken Nick's hand in his own, he would have covered Nick's mouth with his own and they would make love right here in the apple orchard of his childhood backyard. He was the city boy; he was the man with experience; it was his place to make the move. Except that he was the man with HIV.

How to explain this to Nick? Strictly speaking Raphael had no need to explain, so long as he was careful, and yet it was there—a third person; no, a phantom, lying here with the two of them.

Through the apple trees came Tice Flaherty's thin voice, quavering a little—he was eighty if he was a day—singing with Rose Ella, high and thin above the ukulele's hollow plink:

Sometimes I live in the country
Sometimes I live in the town
Sometimes I have a great notion
To jump into the river and drown.

And then Nick was kneeling above Raphael, straddling him and taking his head between his hands—his horn-hardened hands scraped Raphael's cheeks—and kissing him, an awkward brush of his lips, and Raphael felt Nick hard against him and he opened his mouth and took Nick's tongue between his lips and they kissed in the orchard with the incandescent stars falling down, the stars under which they'd grown up, under which they had lived, under which they would die falling to earth.

And so they make love. This horn-hard, rope-muscled

farmer (plower of fields, sower of seed) and this gym-toned city boy, lover of books. Their hands are everywhere at once until finally Raphael (man of experience, man of books, city man) says, "Slow, baby, slower, slow," and Nick has known enough of the scarcity of love to understand what he means and so there is the astoundingly erotic pain of flirtation and restraint. They spend unmeasured time on details (the sharp line of Nick's sun-reddened neck is visible even in this near-dark; the strawberry birthmark that rides above Raphael's waist), but slower as they go, however they hold back the moment arrives when their bare chests show pale in the tree-filtered dark. Their shirts are open to the summer air, humid and soft about its edges (no California nights like this, which enforces desire on bodies caught in its embrace).

This is what Raphael wants to do, it is what he once did again and again with his dead lover. For two years and more grief has banked his desire, ash over coals, but now it has burst into flame and he is nothing in front of this wanting, larger and harder than anything he has known—before it he is nothing. He would take Nick in his mouth and love who he is in the here and now until he comes, blood without iron or color, tasting of life that he would carry in his mouth to plant his lips over Nick's.

This is what he would do and more, but Raphael forces himself to think of such things, there is too much to remember: he is the carrier, the potential disburser of disease and he must be gentle, this is what he wants but in the end he must yield to the facts of things, he must be satisfied with less, always with less, but it must be enough.

He accepts what he is given. He would be tempting fate to ask questions of a gift so perfect.

✣ ✣ ✣

Nick was the farmer—he was the man with a bandanna. After they cleaned themselves up Raphael lay back and gave himself up to joy, laughed out loud at the thought of that many-pointed star of his childhood still turning, still pricking in his heart.

Nick knelt over him and again took Raphael's head in his hands. Raphael opened his lips as if to kiss, but Nick was only looking—in the dark Raphael felt his straight-on look. "You don't have to worry, from what we did," Raphael said.

"I wasn't worrying. I'd do it again, right now, even if I did have to worry."

"You can't think that way."

"It's not thinking I'm talking about."

"Then you can't feel that way," Raphael said, and set about explaining: This is what it's OK to do. This is what it's OK to do, maybe. This is what—

Nick laid his hand over Raphael's mouth. "So you're telling me you're dying."

"We're all dying, if it comes to that," Raphael said. A phrase from some writer—Whitman?—welled from memory, from some lesson taught by Miss Camilla, who—he remembered this now—had loved Whitman so very much. "Life is the little that is left over from dying," Raphael said.

Their hands were clasped, Nick was clutching and unclutching Raphael's hand until he clutched it so tight Raphael sat up and pulled it free. "Easy, boy," Raphael said. "Listen to a certified San Francisco diva." He threw out his arms. "*La morte e nulla*," he sang, sotto voce and off-key, but Nick was up and gone like a startled deer, across the yard and into the dusk.

Raphael thought first to leap up and call to him. Then he lay back, looking up through the orchard's tangling black branches. Nick's warmth lingered still on Raphael's skin—his skin still shuddering, electric, exalted from desire—this was enough for the here and now, the only place he wanted to be. Raphael closed his eyes against the stars.

To remove himself to the previous summer, to the church of Saint-Sulpice in Paris, where he has taken refuge from the heat and the crowds of the Jardins de Luxembourg. The church is cool and dark, a relief after the diesel fumes and grime and grit of Europe in a hot, dry summer. Raphael has taken this journey to reward himself, no, to comfort himself, after his old lover's death, after learning that he himself is infected. He bundled his airline bonus miles into a package and paid for an upgrade into a first-class seat, and now he is here among the polite, indifferent French, who pass through polyglot hordes of tourists as if they aren't there, as if they are wraiths.

He himself is not a wraith, not yet, but the thought has dogged him in a way that later in this trip he will manage to lose, and that he will keep more or less at bay for the next year or so, until his blood counts drop and his hair loses its luster and his cheekbones emerge and he cannot avoid the knowledge that something is wrong. But here in France, amid the Germans and Japanese and Italians (not so many Americans; the dollar is weak and the only Americans he sees are honeymooners or exchange students or those like himself, on necessary pilgrimages), here in Paris his mortality dogs him. He has seen his death in the face of his lover, in the faces of his friends, and soon enough he will see it in his own.

Long ago he left behind the Catholicism of his childhood, he sets foot in churches only in foreign countries, but he is in a foreign country now and in a church, and when he enters any church he lights a candle. He has convinced himself that he is leaving this trail of candles not in homage to the patrons of these particular churches (Geneviève, Etienne du Mont,

Eustache, Sulpice—saints that have no place in the American canon, and for all he knows no interest in the affairs of American gay men), but because of the gesture: In memory of his dead lover, in memory of his brother Clark, in memory of those gone before, a leaving of light and beauty for those who follow into these vast and cool spaces; *memento mori* for himself, with the hope that someone will do the same for him when he is gone.

And so past Delacroix's Jacob struggling with his angel, forward to the apse where Raphael takes a candle, passing over the smaller, cheaper tapers for the longest, tallest, most potent ten-franc version. As always he says a prayer—"makes a wish" is how he thinks of it. And as always he remembers from childhood that one is never permitted (by whom? he wonders) to wish for oneself, that this is the surest way to jinx a wish. One must always wish for something for someone else. So he wishes for . . .

But wishes for himself crowd his heart *(for a miracle, for a cure; barring that, a death with my San Francisco friends at hand, for a speedy death, a painless death unlike those I have witnessed)*, and it is awhile before he can set these wishes aside—the image comes to mind of the *pâtisseries* that earlier today he purchased and that the cheerful *pâtissière* wrapped in a small neat packet tied with a ribbon. These wishes for himself he boxes up and sets aside, to wish finally for—"World peace," he whispers aloud. Such a stupid and naive thought, but these are go-for-broke days and why not? Is one so very much more impossible to imagine than the other—a miracle cure, a quick and painless death among friends, world peace?

So he lights the taper and goes about fixing it in place. The candles have small holes bored in their bases, he faces racks of dangerous-looking spikes. All he has to do is jam the candle onto the spike of his choice.

Fenton Johnson

But the wax breaks at the candle's bottom and the candle refuses to stay fixed. He tries again, the wax breaks again, the candle clatters to the stone-paved floor, sharp and sacrilegiously loud. Such is the fate of unbelievers. In America he would return the candle with its blackened wick to the rack and pick a new one, but he would never be doing this in America, where insurance companies have eliminated candles from churches, where he never sets foot in a church anyway.

Three elderly French women are standing behind him now, their two-franc candles lit and poised to be mounted. The immense pregnant globe of the world that fills the church's apse swells before him, splashed by the digitalis blue of glass-stained light and crowned by the Virgin crushing beneath her delicate heel the snake, an enormous conger eel of evil, and here Raphael stands before her unable to accomplish this simple act. Caught between the widows behind, the Virgin before, he suddenly sees his gesture as the height and sum of futility, and he is overcome with anger, bitterness, grief at this useless question: had he and his lover been allowed love—had they had the courage to seize love—might his lover still be alive? Might Raphael himself be whole, clean, free?

He stumbles to the nearest straw-bottomed chair, where he sits with his shoulders heaving hot, choking sobs that echo in the apse, his grief made more unbearable by the sympathetic stares of the elderly women. After some time they fix their candles in place and withdraw (in America they would have scattered instantly, or sat and offered Kleenex, but these widows are accustomed to displays of grief in churches, this is why people come to churches, this is why there are churches) and he is left alone. Furtively he wipes his eyes. He picks up his ten-franc candle with its broken stub of a base and takes it to the votive shrine. He heats its base in the flames of the widows' candles, then jams it onto a spike, where it holds its place.

Lying in the apple orchard of his childhood home, the image of the Virgin of Saint-Sulpice fixed in mind, Raphael tells himself this:

You see: This is where you are. As a young man you were a vessel of desire—the dreams you had, the men you wanted! Across a lifetime you would have transformed yourself into a vessel of memory. You began life filled with what you hoped to be; with time and luck you would have crossed that river, earned a place where you were filled with what you had been.

And this is the fact of things: You have all but crossed that river, you are nearing the other side, you are not much desire and mostly memory, and facing at every moment the terror of the here and now. "You will see worse," the prediction rises through time and memory from Willy, his red-haired German hitchhiker; if not his first love, at least his first lust. Willy—where is he now, Willy of the blackened eye, enamored of cowboys? Alive, dying, dead?

At the thought Raphael was seized by fear so vast and sudden it caught his breath. He saw himself as if in a mirror— a little paunchy at the waist, a little thinning at the crown, a librarian; cataloguer of acts, repository of memory, a man whose forays into an indifferent world fell a little short, came a little late, and still, as surely as if he had fought Contras in Nicaragua, crack dealers in the Tenderloin, chained himself to bureaucrats' doors, they'd brought him to this: him alone, facing his death. Here in the orchard of his memory's backyard, Raphael spread-eagled his arms to clutch at the weedy earth but it fell away beneath him all the same, and he was left alone, with nothing but himself and the impossible thought of the world without him. Surely this demanded the greatest leap of faith—to conceive of the starry universe without his living, breathing self.

In liquid notes a whippoorwill began numbering his ancestors, one, two-three; four, five-six; lost count, began again, lost count, began again. With the whippoorwill's permission the night sounds rose up from the ravine, a high-pitched chorus of peepers underscored by the bullfrog's contrabass. Raphael raised himself to his elbows to look over the creekbed. A long, drawn-out cackle—a solitary rain crow flapped across the last dull light from the west. In the cooling night more fireflies ventured forth, their winking lights spreading up the slope from the ravine, and it was as if a great wave of life were rising to fill the valley, to catch them up in its embrace.

Raphael was brushing leaves from his jeans when he heard a scrabbling in the wisteria. "Nick?"

"Sorry. I can be a lot of things to a lot of people, but I can't be Nick for nobody." It was Catherine. She pulled out a pack of cigarettes, slid one out, tapped it against her wrist. "Promise you won't breathe a word to Joe Ray. He'd have a fit if he knew I was smoking."

"The pot calling the kettle black, if you ask me."

"Isn't that how it usually works?" Catherine lit her cigarette and inhaled deeply. "I like having a secret vice. It gives me something I can call mine."

"Have several. I have nothing against secret vices. I'm a Californian, or hadn't you heard?"

Catherine smoked in silence for a minute. "Raphael. I'm sorry about your friend." She held up her hand. "You don't have to say anything. I just wanted to say I know what he meant to you, and I'm sorry I didn't say that when he died. I know it's been a long time—"

"You might say that."

"—but better late than never. Or so I like to think."

Raphael squatted to the earth, picked up a twig to dig at the dirt.

"You shouldn't let us get away with it, you know," she said. "I don't see why you just don't break out and let the shit hit the fan. But who am I to talk." She laughed, short and harsh. "You owe it to yourself."

"I owe it to him, is who I owe it to." Raphael dug a little hole in the ground, covered it back, dug it again. "So how did you figure out he was my boyfriend?"

"How does anybody ever figure out what's going on in the world? You open your ears and listen to what people aren't talking about. I'm coming to believe the only things you can be sure *do* happen are the things people *don't* talk about. Is that so different in California?"

"Yeah. A little, anyway. If only because it's so goddamn big. Nobody cares what anybody else does."

"Oh, brave new world." Catherine crossed her arms and stared up through the apple trees. "Besides, I haven't lived with Joe Ray for twenty years without learning to recognize pain when I see it."

"So why do you stick with him?"

She inhaled a long drag. "The pleasures of petty vice," she said, letting the smoke filter from her lips in a slow, luxurious cloud. "You think about it, and when you've figured it out you let me know."

"Can you imagine how it would hurt Rose Ella, if I let the shit hit the fan?" Raphael asked. "That's what I worry about. And if I talked to her I'd have to talk to Tom Hardin, and I can't imagine that. It's just not within the realm of what can be imagined."

Catherine sighed. "You think Rose Ella couldn't handle that? Honey, that's what keeps her alive. That's what keeps her strong. You tell her what's really going on—that means you need her. And when somebody needs you like that, you don't have a choice—you've got to be strong for them. And in being strong for somebody else you find out you're being strong for yourself. A man sees that kind of strength as weighing him down, holding him back. For a woman it's who she is."

"And that's why you stay with Joe Ray."

She took the twig from Raphael and crouched to the earth, where she dug a little hole and buried her cigarette butt. "I think your heart fills up with pain until either you drown in all that or you let it break, like a dam, you know, and there's some kind of freedom in that breaking. You let it all flow out, to water whatever living thing is in the way, carrying some part of you along with it wherever it goes. And you think it's all gone, you're dried up, there's nothing left and you think you can give up, you want more than anything to give up, and then you find out for better and for worse that the heart's like a river. There's always more coming." She stood, tucked her cigarettes into her waistband, smoothed her slacks with a pat so they showed no sign of the pack beneath, smoothed over the earth with her shoe. "That is what I think." She pulled out a package of mints and popped one in her mouth, then held them out as if to forestall his speaking. "Have a mint. You want to head back up there together? That will set Joe Ray wondering."

By the time they reached the patio the last of the hospital staff had left, along with some of the brothers and sisters and grandchildren. Out in the yard the remaining grandsons and Dwight Flaherty had switched from poker to buck pitch. They'd pulled a flat-topped cooler beside Michael's chair so he could lay out his cards where only he could see them—he couldn't hold his cards in a regular fan. The monks sat on the patio, their chairs circled around Tom Hardin and Rose Ella, Tice Flaherty and Miss Camilla. Joe Ray was asleep, his head rolling back on the splayed slats of an Adirondack.

"It had to happen," Tom Hardin was saying. "He was a dog with style. There's some dogs you can sit down and teach about the world and they'll take your word for it, and others that's got to go and find out for themselves, and Patch was one of the latters. He was bound and determined to see the other side of that river. It was in his blood. I only regret that I never got my hands on one of the pups he fathered on the other side."

"Now that is not true," Rose Ella said. "That is not how it happened at all."

"The way Rose Ella tells that story, Patch sank like a rock. Never even found," Samuel said.

Tom Hardin folded both hands across the top of his cane. "I never knew a fact that couldn't be improved with a little exaggeration."

The family was gathering its scattered belongings. Catherine bundled Tee Junior into the car. Then she stood before her sleeping husband. "The older boys can stay the night here with you," she said to Rose Ella. "Tell Joe Ray I checked into the motel and I'll come back to pick them up tomorrow. When he wakes up. If he wakes up." She climbed into the car and backed from the drive, throwing gravel with her tires.

"Rafe, I don't know what you did to that poor Handley boy," Rose Ella said, "but he came up here looking like he'd just seen a ghost. He couldn't find Frances, said to tell her he'd walk home. And I guess he did."

"Speaking of the disappeared," Hippolytus said. "Is Eusebius pulling his vanishing act again?"

"Out looking at the black-eyed Susans, I expect," Miss

Camilla said. She leaned over to poke Tice Flaherty in the ribs. "What about it, old man? When's the last time you showed somebody a black-eyed Susan?"

"There's not a single black-eyed Susan within a damned half-mile," Tom Hardin said.

"Oh, yes, there are," Miss Camilla said. "There's a big patch just inside the cemetery gate, right around that little stone bench that Ittybit Muhlenberg put in so people could sit and admire her tombstone. Where kids go to court."

"Sounds like you know the place pretty damned good," Tom Hardin said.

"*Well*, I know it pretty damned well," Miss Camilla said. "Not as damned well as I'd like, maybe, but not for lack of damned men who tried to show it to me." She rose, smoothing wrinkles from her skirt. "I believe it's past my bedtime."

Tice Flaherty stood. "I'll walk you across the yard, Miss Camilla."

Miss Camilla laughed. "I think I know the way. God bless all the Hardins for your kindness, and I hope I hear you out here whooping it up till dawn." She retrieved her cane and set out across the dew-slick grass.

"Tom Hardin, I don't think she's ever forgiven you for getting her that job at the elementary," Rose Ella said. "You know how some people are—you do them a favor and you're their enemy for life."

Tom Hardin heaved himself to his feet. Blinded by the light from the kitchen windows, he walked into Raphael, who seized his father's shoulders to hold him upright. For a moment they tangled themselves in an embrace, and in that closeness Raphael felt the thinness of his father's arms beneath his shirt, and his swollen stomach, and he understood this: that Tom Hardin was going, would soon enough be gone.

Then Tom Hardin shook his son's hands free, stepped around him and inside.

"I think I'll go start the truck," Samuel said. "I think it's past our bedtimes."

The monks were piled into the truck by the time Eusebius ducked from behind the corner of the house. He jumped over the tailgate to sit in the truckbed. There was much chatter and hoopla—Rose Ella gave advice on avoiding the town policeman, Cyril and Hippolytus argued over the best way to get past the gatehouse. They were gone before Frances rounded the far side of the house, yawning. "Stop on up, Rafe," she said. "We'd love to see you out at the farm," and then she was bound for home.

"You'd think she'd at least ask what happened to Nick," Raphael said, as her truck pulled from the drive.

"I expect she's used to him taking off on his own," Rose Ella said. "He's a odd bird, Nick."

"Artistic," Raphael said. "In a word."

From the dark corner behind the spruce there came a climbing strum of metallic notes. "Why, Mr. Flaherty," Rose Ella said. "I thought you'd gone home."

"I just happened to come across my banjo," he said. He winked at Rose Ella. "Turns out somehow it was right there all along."

He played a simple tune, old-style—clawhammer. As he sang the wattle at his throat swung back and forth like an old turkey hen's, and his voice was just as cracked and parched. Raphael recognized the tune, and Rose Ella sang a few words, her voice warbling on the high notes:

She walked through the corn leading down to the river,
Her hair shone like gold in the hot morning sun.

She took all the love that a poor man could give her
And left him to die like a fox on the run.
Like a fox, like a fox, like a fox
   On the run.

When Tice Flaherty was finished, Rose Ella and Raphael clapped, and he stood to take a grave bow. "Encore!" Raphael said, but Tice Flaherty shook his head. "It's a poor dog that don't know when the day is over, and this dog's day is done," he said. "I thank you for the hospitality." He packed his banjo away, stored it on the porch—"Tell Dwight to bring it when he comes"—and walked home.

Through the kitchen windows they could hear the distant clink and clatter of dishes—Elizabeth was at the sink. Out in the yard, under the sugar maple, the murmur and laugh of the card-playing grandsons rose and fell in a stream—an occasional curse stood out like a rock. Rose Ella made the rounds of the picnic tables, the bar, the chairs, the card players, picking up plates, scraping leftovers into a bag for the dogs, stacking plastic cups for washing, unpinning Clark's flag from the dogwood limb. With everything piled neatly on the carriage rock she tossed one end of the flag to Raphael.

They stretched it out between them, Raphael folding from the stripes, one horizontal fold, then another, then one triangle, followed by another—his hands remembered the routine his head had forgotten long ago.

Joe Ray, still asleep, shifted his weight with a grunt. "I thought I asked you to talk to your oldest brother about his drinking," Rose Ella said.

"I thought you asked me just the opposite."

"Well, I didn't mean for you to come right out and say it to his face. Lord! What a thought." Rose Ella's lips drew thin at the notion. "That's the problem with you Californians—you think everything has to be tackled head-on. Like everything under the sun that people do has got an explanation and if you talk long enough you'll find out what it is, when the only thing you can really do is give things a little nudge and then hope for the best." Rose Ella kicked Joe Ray's foot with her toe. His head lolled to one side. "Like with your brother. You can talk about something without saying it. You can talk to him about his drinking. Just be careful not to mention it."

"Joe Ray is right," Raphael said. "I *have* been in California too long."

"Well, maybe it's for the best, who am I to say," Rose Ella said with a sigh. "All your cards thrown right down, faceup on the table. Problem is, what good does it do for people to put all their cards faceup on the table when none of us is ever playing with a full deck? And I don't except nobody from that." She raised an eyebrow and tilted her chin at Raphael. "Not nobody. He's a lot like you," Rose Ella said. "Nick Handley, that is. Artistic."

"For God's sake, Mother, he runs a tobacco farm."

"That's not to say he couldn't sell it off. If I was as young as you that's what I'd do. Sell it off, and then head to California."

"I'm not so young, Mother."

"Why, thirty-four!" Rose Ella said gaily. "At thirty-four I was carting you around in diapers and I still trapped the best fox in Jessup County." Her hands shaped the length and heft of that fox. "Not that I'm so old now." She sat with a heave in one of the empty Adirondacks, the folded flag in her lap. She threw her head back and looked up at the stars. "Stop everything right here, please," she said.

Raphael sat down. "Once, when I was a kid. It was summer, I remember wearing shorts, and that hot light that bounces off the patio into the kitchen. I was standing in the kitchen and you were crying at the table. You had your head down and your shoulders were shaking, you were crying that hard."

Rose Ella made a little church with her hands—they were remembering Tee Junior, with whom she'd been playing hand games just before Catherine took him to the motel. "Raphael. I know how it is when you get all drunked up and you go out and do some things you just might not otherwise do. I just want you to be careful, is all." She turned open the church doors to let out the people. "Promise me you're being careful, out there in San Francisco."

"Why in the hell didn't you tell me that twenty years ago?"

"Because I didn't know the words," Rose Ella snapped.

"You couldn't *say* the words. A different thing entirely."

"So you're young, you live in California. You tell me the words," Rose Ella said quietly. "I'm no fool, even if I do watch TV. I know what's going on out there. What are the words for all that? What words do you use?"

The grind of the katydids grew louder in the silence that followed. Out in the yard one of the card players let out a whoop. "Shoot the goddamn moon!" he cried.

"Are you sick already?" Rose Ella asked. "Is that what you're trying to tell me?"

He told her then: he wasn't sick. Not yet. It would be awhile before he got sick. Awhile? she wondered. Twenty years? Ten years? Nobody knows, he said. Three years? she asked. More likely three years, he said. Or maybe four. And then it would be maybe another year where he would have it under control, like diabetes. And who knows, they might have a cure, or a way to put it off still more, things were changing fast . . . Or he might come back here, that was possible, though it would mean dealing with the local doctors who would be ignorant at best and probably worse than that. He saw himself as having one kind of family here, another in San Francisco; it was hard to say which he'd choose, if it came to that. His friends in San Francisco had experience with this illness; there was a lot to be said for experience. He could speak to that.

All this he said as if it were just news, the latest at his job or the latest book he'd read. It came from some quiet and distant place, the place of the facts of things, which could neither be disputed nor changed but only acknowledged.

They sat for a long while in the Adirondack chairs, adrift on the sea of sounds from the night insects and tree frogs, and over all the whippoorwill's calling. Finally Rose Ella spoke. "Something about the oldest and the youngest—I know a mother's not allowed to have favorites but there's something about the first and last—you can't help but see them as start and finish. Begin-all and end-all. Punctuation," she whispered. "Don't tell me a baby learns everything while he's growing up. I knew every one of my babies before they were born. You were the quiet one, you just laid there listening until your time come and then you got up and left so quiet you were gone before I knew it." She picked her words one by one, as if by saying them carefully enough she might get them to mean what she wanted. "Would it have made a difference if you could have told somebody, talked to somebody, back then?"

"What words could I have used? I'd never heard them. *You'd* never heard them. And even if I'd had the words—who would I have talked to?" This Raphael said not as accusation but as fact, spoken with a dispassion and certitude that silenced them both.

The eastern sky grew light; a gibbous moon had risen, a ruddy egg born from the hollows into rolling clouds. When it rose above the treetops Rose Ella spoke. "What if I had asked, when you got old enough? What if I had sat you down and made up words, if it had come to that? What if I had said, 'Rafe, how can I help?' Could I have helped?"

"Could I have helped?" Raphael asked. "That day I found you crying in the kitchen? Could we have helped each other?"

They sat awhile longer. From the ravine rose the churning chorus of the frogs and the voice of the whippoorwill, calling, calling, calling.

Then Elizabeth came to the door. "Last chance for dirty dishes," she said brightly.

Raphael spoke. "That was the day I learned what it meant to be helpless."

Rose Ella stood heavily, clutching the flag to her breast. "Raphael, the best thing about memory is that it forgets. I just plain don't remember."

"You won't remember."

"I just plain won't remember," she said dully. She gave the flag to Elizabeth, bent to plant an awkward kiss on his head, then stacked cups and plates and carried them in, her arms burdened like a waitress's.

These nights Raphael slept in the guest room, in what Rose Ella called her holy bed, where she stowed the religious who were forsaking their vows to reenter the secular world. She'd entertained a steady stream: monks and an occasional priest who in the sixties had tasted the fruit of the tree of knowledge when the abbot, innocent as Raphael if forty years older, had thought that exposure to worldly ways would weed out the weak of heart and enrich the contemplative experience of those who remained. By the seventies the abbot realized the error of this thinking and ordered the doors to the abbey enclosure sealed, but like the farmer with his famous horses, too late: The monks who in Raphael's childhood had sneaked from the enclosure across the knobs to the Hardin house to bum cigarettes and drink beer and watch football on television, those same monks now showed up at Rose Ella's doorstep at odd hours of the day or night, sometimes smelling of whiskey and always looking for a place to stay for a few days or weeks until they emerged, blinking and shorn of their vows, fearful of and fired by their vision of a new life.

Raphael lay awake (jet lag? it was still evening in San Francisco). His window faced the backyard, where he could still hear the rattle of shuffling cards and the murmur of the boys, interrupted every once in a while with a laugh or a curse. "The cops cut the goddamned buds off before they burned it all." Dwight Flaherty raised his voice in outrage. "Nobody asks where *they* went."

Here in the holy bed Raphael was dogged more than usual by the certainty that he was among those in transit, but not to a new life. Once he had contemplated the prospect that, youngest of his family, he would outlive his generation—attending the funerals, one by one, of his parents, his older brothers and sisters, his in-laws, to be left alone as in her generation his grandmother, youngest of her siblings, had been left alone, outliving all who had known the world as she had. Now he faced instead the likelihood that he would die with witnesses, the numbers of his family in attendance and at the top of the genealogical pyramid Rose Ella and Tom Hardin, dying themselves as he lay dying.

And who would remember him? Who would remember the artistic sons, gone to distant cities to die of euphemisms? Would they—*we*, he forced himself to think it—be remembered better by our blood families? Or by the families we'd formed in distant cities, families that came and remained together, if and when they remained together, out of love? Was love strong enough to make a family? Or did it take that unbreakable, bloody tie, the generational tie that bound people together above and beyond any single person's choice?

He thought of Rose Ella singing from the carriage rock, and he understood for the first time that these parties had been hers as much or more than Tom Hardin's. How much of life would you have to accept, how much grief would you have to know before you could climb on the table and lift your skirts to the world? It was as if a shutter slid open, or a curtain raised to reveal dangling within his grasp the stuff, if not of heroism at least of history, a chance to crash and burn in one glorious public moment. Lying in bed on this hot August evening Raphael was granted a vision of himself as social kamikaze, with the great silence as his target. This was the great and terrible gift of his illness. Years later, long after his death, they'd recall him on cold evenings. "Pneumonia," they'd name it to anyone indelicate enough to ask, or "heart failure"—wagging their heads at the mysteries of life, in which a disease of the old might claim someone so young. And then the children and the refined would go to bed, and the kind that had to find out for themselves would remain around the table, drinking whiskey and asking their questions; the women whose task it was to preserve memory and those men, not the marrying kind (long before their birth, Raphael knew them more intimately than he knew his living brothers), impelled to seek out this skeleton reserved for the strong and inveterately curious of heart.

They were dying—*we* are dying, even now Raphael had to remind himself again that he was among those men who'd had passion and heart and a curious cock, who were passing into that dim world of those gone before, leaving behind nothing more nor less tangible than the courses of their lives. Raphael thought how the meandering paths of his own life had been shaped and directed by unremembered men and women acting not from highfalutin charity but in simple consonance with their generous selves. "Raphael's in love," his co-worker had announced so many years ago, and in her exuberance and joy Raphael had seen the possibility that it could be true even for, especially for, a man such as himself: a man outside of men, a man apart. "You were in love," Nick had said, and in the longing in his voice Raphael understood that there were many who would never know love, not the love he'd known. Life had not denied him this. Raphael lay still, his hands fingering his undershirt, remembering the tearing, the thin-meshed cotton giving way before that surge of joy and love and lust; ten, eleven years gone by since those days when the low-pitched moan of the balky Southern Pacific was enough to fire his blood, well over a year since his lover's death and still his blood remembered that love, that lust, and that was something; the remembering was all there was, it was all there could be, it would have to be enough, it was enough.

He rose and pulled on his pants, tiptoed past Rose Ella's door, past the small room where these days Tom Hardin spent his nights (light still leaked from around his doorframe), out into the yard.

Against the turbulent sky the treetops were beginning to sway; the wind was picking up. The card players were stacking their decks and gathering their winnings. The party was over. Raphael crossed the yard to stand half-hidden by the sugar maple's trunk, watching his nephews and their friends. He stood tongue-tied before the weight of history, a coward still before the speaking aloud of his fate.

Heart like a river, Catherine had said.

In San Francisco Raphael had heard the following, no doubt from one of his friends who was wearing crystals and attending self-healing seminars: that the Hopi believe that at death the breath from one's last words rises to become the clouds, from which rain falls to nourish the corn that in turn nourishes the generations that follow; so that at meals one is eating the gifts of one's ancestors, who have by their speaking made one's own life possible. Raphael stood quietly, thinking of tonight's meal, tonight's clouds, of his unnamed ancestors whose small acts of generosity and courage had made possible the best parts of his life; thinking of Brother Samuel, and of Nick Handley, living in the Hardins' midst, abiding their thoughtlessness and ignorance because they loved them so much. This they did for the Hardins, sorriest of lovers; and Raphael was humbled by the boundlessness of their love.

He stepped forward, dropped his jaw, spoke to his nephews words that breached a dam in his heart, to tap the lake stored there of bitterness and anger and love: all that death, his own death, his love for men, his love for them, his nephews, his love for himself and for his memory as it lived in these children, his children, his blood.

"I'm filled with anger and rage that no one will acknowledge that my friends are dying, and that they're dying of AIDS." The words spoke themselves—he had nothing to do with forming them; they came from some deep and necessary place where they had been waiting until the moment when he gave them permission to be heard. On them followed a silence as big as his life until now, but the words that demanded to be spoken had not yet finished themselves out, and he spoke again. "And I have the virus. I've had it for years."

The silence that followed now was too large to comprehend or speak into. Raphael spread his hands but could not say more, his lips moved to form words that remained stuck in his throat.

Finally Michael spoke. "So at last somebody is letting us in on the big secret."

In the conversation that followed, it was Michael who asked the difficult questions, who filled the awkward silences. With each of his nephew's questions Raphael came to understand what for so long he had not allowed himself to see because he was afraid of the pain of seeing it: Michael's own burden of pain, which the family had agreed to ignore because they found it too large and threatening to comprehend.

They talked into the night. Raphael told them what he knew, a reservoir of information gleaned by simple fact of living with and amid the illness. They told him what they had heard, a mixture of myth and rumor and lies. Little of this they believed—"scare tactics," Michael said wiltingly. But what were they to believe? They plied Raphael with questions until his head thickened. In their questions, in their ignorance he understood how out of fear he had evaded his responsibility to them. He, after all, knew more than anyone here. Any number of times he might have chosen to speak; instead he had held his tongue and contributed another brick to the great wall of silence.

Tonight he released to the clouds the breath of his stories.

Much later, back in the holy bed. The measure of their curiosity had been exceeded only by the magnitude of their ignorance. Where had they gotten these notions? Raphael was exhausted, discouraged by the size of the battle, the shortness of time to fight.

"If AIDS is such a big deal," Dwight Flaherty had said, "somebody would be telling us about it."

"I'm telling you about it," Raphael said.

"Well, yeah, but you're gay."

Raphael consoled himself: That, at least, was some-thing—the ease with which, once given permission, they used words that for Rose Ella and for him had been forbidden. In the remembering and speaking aloud of words lay, not salva-tion—Rose Ella was right about that—but at least knowledge. And what was that? Some chance for life itself. Speaking to his nephews, he understood love's most difficult and necessary of tasks—holding in the heart these contradictions: forgive, and remember; accept, and never shut up.

And then there was his father. On his way to bed Raphael had stopped before Tom Hardin's door—his father's light was still on. This is what all that death and dying had led him to, Raphael thought: the gradual burning away of the layers that he had constructed to protect himself from the great and terri-ble facts of the world. But how much more courage could he be expected to muster? Was there a limit to what love required? Raphael continued down the hall.

Lying in the holy bed, Raphael saw against the ceiling the splayed fingers of the clothes tree, thrown there by a dis-tant flash of lightning. The whippoorwill stopped his calling. Raphael counted, one-and-two-and-three . . . at ten he gave up. Sometime later the thunder came, a distant grumbling.

In the stillness of the dark Raphael felt every farmer, every human being tied in any way to the land, every wild creature awake and lying in stillness hoping, afraid to move from fear that any movement would break the spell, would cause the rain to pass over to some other, more grateful place.

"I think of you sometimes, out in San Francisco," Nick had said. Never before tonight had it occurred to Raphael that a life as humble and unexceptional as his own, as ordinary as Nick's, as quiet as Brother Samuel's might so deeply touch another's life without that person's knowing. It was the most forceful argument he knew for virtue: this symbiosis of interlocking lives, the ecology of love.

"You were in love," Nick had said, and the longing in his voice spoke for itself. Raphael thought on Nick's vision of who Raphael was and what he had done. What Nick held in his heart was a kind of love, Raphael knew this now.

In his twenties when his lover had called him these words—"kind," "handsome," "generous"—Raphael had dismissed him with a mocking, deprecating wave of his hand. "Oh, you're just in love," he'd said in his pretentious, macho, pseudo-worldwise way.

And now Nick was in love, in a way, and though Raphael told himself firmly and instantly there was no future in that— maybe there was some future in that. He owed it to Nick to call—he owed it to himself to call—he would call tomorrow, and ask Nick for what he'd have to call a date.

In Raphael's mind they grew confused, the family and his lover and Nick and his nephews and the monks, so many of whom had passed through this bed on their way from one world to another. He saw them leaping, cowled and cinctured, over the old gatehouse *(Pax Intrantibus)*, over the enclosure walls, up the crucifix-crowned hill, where with a last bound they sailed into the fleecy heavens: Brothers Anselm, Alfred, Asaph, Benedict, Chrysogonus, Chrysostom, Cyril and Darian, Paul, Polycarp, Raphael, his namesake . . . He lay watching the ceiling, waiting for the flash and rumble, waiting for rain.

Rose Ella lay awake, alone. Tom Hardin, who slept fitfully these days, had taken to spending his nights in one of the chil-

dren's empty bedrooms, so as not to disturb her with his tossing and turning. Rose Ella lay and stared at the sheet lightning
flicker and dance across the ceiling.

Why me? Why us? People thought they were so smart these
days, going to the moon and making all this money, but that's
what it came down to, that's what it always came down to and
always would come down to: questions with no answers.

Now she was alone; now she could cry, and she bit her lip
to keep from crying. What had she done wrong? A big, country family, deep enough in the hills to avoid city influences but
with enough flat land to live decent. "The family that prays together stays together," the priest had said. Well, they'd prayed
together, at first anyway, a rosary a night on their knees, then
every other night, then every third night or once a week. Had
they abandoned God? "More like the other way around," she
said this aloud, then muttered a quick Act of Contrition.

All those children in something like a decade, and that
wasn't counting the miscarriages. These no one remembered
except her, who remembered them as clearly as if each of those
babies had been born squalling and whole.

There'd been too many children, off in a million direc-
tions—cheerleading practice, football, homecoming parades,
graduations, births, births, births, and always the cows to
milk. Rose Ella had done her part, had stuck with the church.
She had raised her kids to be good Catholics. Was it her fault
they'd left the church? (At least Clark had escaped that fate.)
What had she done wrong? That was no question worth lying
awake over. If she was old enough to know anything she was
old enough to know that, and still she'd spent a life hiding from
questions that came upon her. Watching Tom Hardin's bald-
ing, jaundiced scalp, his thick silver hair lost to chemotherapy;
staying busy for a lifetime around Raphael because she was

afraid of what he had to say, of letting herself know what she already knew.

She and her husband, she and her daughters, she and her sons—of all of them this was true: They had been less than honest with each other because they had not wanted to speak of these matters, because none had wanted to hear what the others were unwilling to say. But wasn't this true of everyone? What were words worth, when confronted with the mute intuition of things unseen: the infinitude of grief, the high pinnacles of joy, the profundity of love, the omnipotence of desire? How could grief, joy, love, or desire be spoken of, when they weren't comprehended by words themselves? Words; as necessary and shapeless as water.

A summer afternoon. Rafe had talked about the hot light from the patio—that would make it the new house—sometime around 1960? Rafe would have been six or seven. And she had been so upset as to flat-out cry, right in the kitchen where one of the kids was sure to come upon her.

1960. She and Tom Hardin had been married seventeen, no, eighteen years. They hadn't fought in a long while—not since around the time of Rafe's birth. Now when things got tense Tom Hardin hid out in the woodshop. She had her sewing and cooking and cleaning, and one hour a week in the Sacred Heart Sodality when she napped while pretending to pray. When would she have had time to cry? Merciful memory: nothing.

Then something: One of the monks (Brother Edward? Asaph? Benedict? Romuald? he had long since flown north, back where he'd come from) had brought flowers. The monastery had a greenhouse in those days, where they'd grown flowers for the altar (none of that frivolousness now, under the new regime—the greenhouse had been dismantled years ago, the monks had brought her cuttings from the flowers they'd thrown away. These she'd rooted and planted and tended still.) This monk had brought succulents for Rose Ella's cactus garden, and a single stalk of a cymbidium orchid from which there hung eight or ten blooms. In those delicate throaty blossoms she remembered Camp Junior, only son of a rich farming family who rode her around in his father's car and took her to movies and, yes, bought her flowers. At the movies she'd realized how many of the stars were just country girls who had taken themselves to California with a little gumption and talent, and she had plenty of both. Oh, she had plans! The rich boyfriend (well, rich to her) took her out and they parked on the courthouse square and looked at maps. They would drive his new car (to be bought with the money he was sure to inherit) across Route 66 to Pasadena, to Hollywood, where he would go to law school (they must have law schools in California) and she would try her luck in the movies.

Then high school ended and Camp Junior went to the state university. She wrote him letters and waited, until the day when she met Tom Hardin on the courthouse square and she had waited long enough. Tom Hardin was flirtatious, he had no money at all but he had a truck; even if it was an old one it got them where they needed to go. By the time Camp Junior returned (in fact his father had died, in fact he had inherited the farm and a good deal more, in fact he was on his way to Vanderbilt Law), Rose Ella was married. She had her children and named them for movie stars and put all that foolishness behind her, until the day when that monk (Tobias? Brendan?) brought orchids and Rafe found her crying. Typical, she told herself sternly, that in a life with plenty of good reasons to cry Rafe should have come upon her crying over nothing.

California—the place where their children went. She

imagined herself there now, standing at the middle of the Golden Gate Bridge—this was easy to do; on her only visit to San Francisco, Rafe had walked her halfway across, and she returned here often when she had trouble falling asleep. She felt the bridge tremble and sway beneath her feet—"It's nothing but a plain old swinging bridge," was what she'd said to Rafe on that first visit, "just like the bridge Tom Hardin built across the creek behind the old house, only bigger." And Tom Hardin had the good sense to put a high chain-link fence on *his* bridge, she might have added, but this was California and there was between her and giddy air only a metal banister not much higher than her waist. To look over and look down was to be sucked in—you might fall off such a bridge just by looking down too long; she thought this then, standing next to Rafe, and now in her imagination she yields to temptation. She leans over and looks straight down, until the scalloping waves mesmerize her and she falls.

At first she tumbles head over heels, but then she spreads her arms like the Olympic divers she's seen on television, thrusting her ample breasts before her, pointing her toes to the retreating sky. A flock of mud swallows attacks her with sharp beaks and beating wings, but she falls through them and they bank and wheel back to their nests, built on the underpinnings of the bridge. She falls past screaming gulls, toward the billowing sails of the boats on the bay, past the crenellated turrets and gun emplacements and astonished tourists' faces crowding the Civil War fort, into the sea, splashless as a pelican. The cold waters of the Golden Gate close over her; she runs her tongue over her lips and tastes salt.

The tide is withdrawing—she floats sideways, west toward the sun, toward the foreign places of her imagination, until pressure from the water above overcomes her buoyancy and she sinks. Rafe, who knows such things, has told her that the channel here is very deep—three hundred? four hundred feet? A shark swims by, the great white shark that breeds in the bay. It bares its teeth; she faces it down, smiling. She has not failed her scattered children, her dying husband, her youngest son.

Above the waves, the sun spreads itself across the Pacific. Tongues of livid scarlet yield to rose, then muted yellow, then the deepening violets of dusk. On the rocks of the Farallons, elephant seals slide into the water. Tens of thousands of birds— murres, puffins, petrels, cormorants—sink to darkness, finding nests and niches, tucking bills into their breasts, ruffling feathers about their young. Sinking below the waters Rose Ella remembers: Alfred, bringer of the orchids, and she sleeps.

Some Kind of Family

[1990]

Elizabeth is standing at a San Francisco dockside, clutching the jar of Raphael's ashes she has carried from Kentucky. At her side Andrew cranes his neck to study a herd of sea lions sprawling on nearby boat slips, sunning in lazy contentment except for a few young males who butt heads and hump each other with half-hearted grunts of pleasure. Elizabeth watches what her lover watches, as the mourner's question, old as grief, presents itself to her: Why should these animals have life, when her brother is dead? Weak-kneed, she sits on the closest bench, next to a group of tourists from Texas (*you don't know they're from Texas*, she admonishes herself as she sits) who are complaining loudly about how hard it is to find parking in San Francisco.

She is haunted now, as surely as any house, and memory is her ghost. As a child she'd been plugged into the continuity of things without even knowing it was there. Every other Saturday morning she'd tooled through the cemetery with a basket of flowers arranged by Rose Ella for distribution among the Hardin and Perlite family graves. Among her vast sea of relatives someone was always slipping over the horizon even as someone else was being born. And then of course there'd been her brother Clark, killed in Vietnam; after his death the graveyard visits became more frequent, the flower arrangements more elaborate, as if Rose Ella were using them to vent some passion for which she had no other outlet.

But then Elizabeth moved to California, time passed, not a single death in her life until Rose Ella died in an instant; one moment there, another gone. On an ordinary Los Angeles day ("Morning low clouds, followed by clearing inland . . .") Elizabeth had picked up the portable telephone to hear through its crackle and static her oldest brother, Joe Ray, weeping that their mother was dead.

However many funerals she'd attended, before Rose Ella's death Elizabeth had not given a thought to what now seemed so obvious: the unanswering deafness of this door, the finality of its closing. Then Rose Ella was gone, so quickly that Elizabeth was left with almost nothing to remember her by.

As she'd aged Rose Ella had shed the things she owned, giving away first her old treadle sewing machine, next her grandmother clock, next her hurricane lamps. These she gave to the married children, those with heirs. Elizabeth told herself she wasn't hurt—how would she wrestle a two-hundred-pound sewing machine to California? Where would she fit it in her postage-stamp apartment? But she knew the answer to that question—had Rose Ella given her something, she would have figured out how to get it there and a place to put it.

Instead she was left with an old red coat with a real mink collar. A nice coat—a perfectly preserved period piece that would be the talk of any L.A. party, except that it never got cold enough in L.A. to wear a coat that heavy. Rose Ella herself had never worn it—not that Elizabeth remembered—but there it was in her mother's closet, carefully wrapped in tissue paper and mothballs and labeled FOR BETTE C. In the heat of late summer Elizabeth wore it to Rose Ella's funeral.

And then her father's death, and Raphael's, both dying in the intensive-care ward of the Jessup County Hospital. Elizabeth had known they were sick, but she'd known this in the way that she knew the names of most of the state capitals or the number of ounces in a cup. She'd known that they were sick with diseases that allowed for no recovery and yet she said nothing.

Until she'd called Raphael and invited him for a drive, the first and last journey they'd take together; unless, of course, she counted the plane trip with his ashes. Thin as winter light, his dark eyes spectral and round like twin moons, his skin all but translucent, parched and spotted—when she saw him Elizabeth thought of gentian violet, the medicine that Rose Ella had painted on their summer scratches. For the duration of their childhood summers they'd carried spots like those on Raphael's arms and neck, big blotches of purple.

She drove him along the coast north of San Francisco, in what they knew without acknowledgment was his last journey in this world. Highway 1: plunging, bucking, twisting road of postcard dreams, nothing between them and that other world but the flimsiest of guardrails. One miscalculation, a slip of the steering wheel or a failure of brakes and they'd be floating through blue space to the lovely jagged rocks below and the vast, seductive Pacific; a better end for him, no doubt, than that which was waiting.

And she drove caught up in the busyness of living, she drove to get somewhere, she was caught up in that number—miles ticked off, highways covered, scenery seen—in shame she remembers this now, watching the crew prepare the boat that is to take them out on the bay, under the Golden Gate Bridge for the scattering of the ashes. She remembers approaching an intersection, Raphael's last-minute direction to turn *here*, her slamming the brakes, her small sense of triumph at managing the turn without having to pass up the intersection, turn around, backtrack. A few seconds saved; but what could that have meant to him?

Fenton Johnson

She busied herself with chatter—avoiding names for what he was approaching, searching for cheerful talk. When his silence grew too large to ignore she asked the only words she could bring herself to say that didn't beg that void, question that hole. "Are you in pain?"

He reached across the seat and held a finger to her lips. "I'm happy being quiet here with you," he said.

They finished their drive in silence. Under pungent eucalyptus, past fleecy sheep scattered over sheer golden hillsides, the sun staining the cliffs burnt-orange and still no words. Her head filled with words, none adequate to the cause and so she said nothing but drove on.

At a high cliff overlook they stopped and she saw on his right arm a dark bruise, where in swerving to make the turn she'd thrown him against the car door—he bruised so easily these days! She was racked with shame and terror and rage. How could he do this to her? He was her younger brother, the baby of the family. How could he bring upon her this sadness and pain, how could he leave her alone in California?

Back on the road she'd thought this: they could continue driving, in her heart she longed to continue north on Highway 1 through Jenner and Salt Point and Mendocino, north past Fort Bragg and Crescent City into Oregon and beyond, through Washington and into Canada, far enough north and the sun might never set, this day might never end. They would present a moving target, ten steps, two steps, one step but always ahead of this thing, this death. Ever her father's daughter, she could not bring herself to say this and so she said nothing but drove on.

And now not much more than a few months later and he is dead, and there is no more saying to be said. She should be grateful for the memory of that Highway 1 journey—she is old

200

enough and familiar enough with the workings of time to know that in a few years she will be grateful. But now, waiting to board the chartered boat that will carry her and Andrew and some of Raphael's friends under the Golden Gate Bridge to scatter his ashes—now she can remember only with humility and shame her unswerving fixation with the world to come, the scenery down the road and around the bend and on the other side of the mountain; even as Raphael himself was living in the here and now, past and future fallen away. *I'm happy being quiet here with you.* The necessity, the sufficiency of that state of being . . .

She steps to Andrew's side and makes this pact with herself: when they return to L.A. she will live more fully in the here and now. She will ease herself out of real estate and back into acting. She will love Andrew as he deserves. She will risk her heart in a way that she has never allowed herself to do.

She looks about: Raphael's friends are arriving in small groups, men and women exchanging kisses and hugs. The tourists with whom she has been sharing her bench stand and gather their belongings. "You won't see *that* in Dallas," one says as they walk away.

"Family," Raphael had called his friends on their journey up Highway 1, and again as he lay dying in the Jessup County Hospital. He had far too many friends for the boat—not knowing who among them was closer, who was more distant, Elizabeth had taken Raphael's address book and telephoned the names from A through P, explaining that there wasn't enough room and asking them to stay home (she hopes no one will notice that the mourners' last names all begin with letters after Q). A few faces Elizabeth recognizes—the two men upstairs who'd fixed him meals and did his laundry and enabled him to stay in San Francisco where he'd wanted to stay, where he'd wanted to die until his trip to Kentucky for Tom Hardin's funeral, during which Raphael became too ill to return. She recognizes the woman who'd adopted his cat, and an ex-boyfriend with whom she will sit down tomorrow to sort through belongings.

His friends spoke so matter-of-factly of it all—the IVs, the medications, the names of obscure infections, death. It was as if they spoke a resurrected tongue, the language of dying and death whose grammar and syntax and vocabulary she'd learned as a child but had forgotten. They took her in as a foreigner, a well-meaning anthropologist exploring their culture. The night before, several of Raphael's friends stopped by his apartment, where she and Andrew were staying. "Take our word for it. You don't want to sit around here," they'd said. "We know that number." Over her mild protests they'd taken the two of them to a bar where men wearing Stetsons and cowboy boots danced two-steps and waltzes and the Cotton-eyed Joe. From some childhood county fair her feet remembered the San Antonio Stroll, and she found herself out on the floor doing its funny little kickstep, and, yes, enjoying herself. Elizabeth thought of the times in her childhood when she'd accompanied Rose Ella to a house where someone had recently died; of the excuses Rose Ella concocted to get the mourners out and about. Raphael's friends were speaking that language—they'd rediscovered it, or maybe reinvented it on their own here in San Francisco; a language that she recognized and remembered and welcomed in the way of returning to any foreign tongue once learned, then neglected and forgotten. *We know that number.*

Unlike her own friends in Los Angeles. They'd been sympathetic at the news of her father's death and then, so soon on its heels, her brother's death. But in their voices she detected a suspicion that she was somehow responsible for so much death in such quick succession. "Right now you're into loss. You'll work through it, and then things will turn around."

"Give us a call if you need us," her friends said. "Stop by any time," leaving to her the burden of calling. There were plenty of times when she *had* needed them, had gone to the phone only to argue with herself: *They'll be busy. I'll interrupt their work, their dinner, their plans for a pleasant evening.* Once when Andrew was out of town and she was desperate she'd made that call, to hear "no" in her friends' voices even as they said "yes." She'd stopped by their house, to sit amid strained conversation *(have I caught them in the middle of a fight? Of making love?)* until after an awkward pause the host cleared his throat. A contract deadline—an entirely new software package due yesterday—he was sure she understood, and of course she did.

Was this distanced sympathy better, or worse, or just different from the scene at Tom Hardin's death, when such a stream of relatives and friends stopped by bearing food and flowers and condolences that she hid herself in the bathroom when the doorbell rang? It had been her choice, finally, to live in the city, the place where people go to be alone.

The crew lowers the gangplank. She and Andrew and Raphael's friends crowd aboard. Someone has brought a feast of the delicacies that Raphael once told her were the real reason to live in northern California: tarts from La Nouvelle Pâtisserie, melons and berries from the Mission District Farmer's Market, bread from Fran Gage. Someone else has brought bottles of Veuve Clicquot, a linen tablecloth, crystal champagne flutes. These they lay out in the boat's small cabin—a California version of the corn puddings and country ham, green beans and mashed potatoes and Kentucky bourbon that fed and watered the crowd at Tom Hardin's funeral.

Around her she hears small talk, a little strained, but different from Raphael's memorial mass at Our Lady of the Hills, back under Strang Knob. There she'd seen the dark side of the warm womb of rural affection: Much of the town, some of the family had refused to attend, from fear (she supposed) that their names might be associated with AIDS; or maybe (she tried to think generously) from simple uncertainty as to how to name this unspeakable death. Because Raphael was to be cremated and returned to San Francisco, the pastor at first refused to conduct the mass that Raphael probably hadn't wanted in any case—when the priest brought last rites to Raphael's hospital room he'd mustered the strength to turn his back. Of Raphael's high school friends, only Nick Handley came; when she'd approached him to say thanks, he all but turned and ran. None of her high school friends attended except Dennis, her old boyfriend, who hung around afterward long enough to give her a hug and a kiss on the cheek. He hadn't mentioned Raphael.

The boat heads into the open bay. The current grows stronger; a cold, damp, penetrating wind picks up. The boat bucks and rocks, people clutch at each other and the railings. No one eats. A heavy fog hangs over the water—within minutes the shore is no more than a dark gray mass against the paler gray fog, and it is as if they are riding some roller coaster through a cold, wet, featureless hell. Scattering his ashes outside the Golden Gate—it seems like another of those romantic but hideously misguided ideas of which Raphael was so fond. Why did he want this done here, thousands of miles from the place both of them still called home? "They're my family."

Only they are *her* family now, for the duration of this brief journey anyway. Families come in two kinds—she had talked about this with Raphael, on that drive north: families given by chance, and families taken on by choice. She has her blood family that she can never escape, because it's in her blood *(in every sense of the word,* she thinks). Then there's adopted family. The first chose her, and binds her to it—no small part of its comfort and meaning comes from the involuntary nature of that binding. The second family she'd chosen and might hold to herself, if she was strong enough to accept all that would come with it. Because sooner or later both families placed the same demands—sometime or another somebody got jealous, somebody wanted more than she might comfortably give, somebody got sick, somebody died.

Andrew is at her side, not touching but close at hand, and in the comfort of his presence she understands that in the end family must come down to who is close: close in that they knew Raphael and loved him and helped when he was sick; but close as well in the simple proximity of their living selves, down the block or up a hill. She could only do so much—she was fooling herself if she thought it was very much—from four hundred miles away. "A phone call is fine, but it's no substitute for chicken soup"—she recalls Joe Ray saying this at the last gathering, maybe the last ever gathering, of her blood family.

Standing amid Raphael's adopted family, Elizabeth realizes that her own family has no fixed boundaries but is eternally changing, a river whose banks are formed by all those to whom she chooses to bind herself with the joys and burdens of love. *Raphael had found some kind of family in San Francisco,* she thinks. *Have I found a family? And who are they?*

The boat lurches. Andrew, who has visited the buffet, returns clutching two *tartes aux framboises* and a flute of champagne. She frowns, shakes her head. "Somebody's got to eat this stuff," he mutters. With a guilty sideways glance he wolfs it down.

The boat stops, as much as stopping is possible, just past the graceful arc of the bridge. She overhears the captain murmur to a passenger. A friend has brought flowers—another detail that happens without Elizabeth's having lifted a finger. She takes a rose—someone has carefully clipped its thorns. A friend (has she met him before? she has met so many people) rises to speak.

"I will not talk of sadness here," he says in a voice strong enough to overcome the rush of the wind and the slap of water against the boat. "To die loved, amid relatives and friends— this is no small miracle. This is a gift that we cannot question but can only accept, in gratefulness and humility."

Very lovely, very moving—around Elizabeth people are wiping their eyes. But this is what Elizabeth thinks, as she lifts the top of the ceramic urn and pours his ashes into the sea: *I will continue growing old, while my memory preserves him ever more perfect.*

One dies, the other lives and ages, she thinks, dry-eyed, numbed from herself. *If there is a heaven, will he recognize me in it?*

They toss the flowers after the ashes. *This is the scattering of my family,* she thinks as she watches the surging palette of colors disburse and sink into the gray-green water. *This is the scattering of my blood.*

Mercifully they turn to head back. The boat still pitches but as they pass under the bridge the morning fog lifts, and they are granted a vision of the city's towers and spires rising from the mica-flecked bay and silhouetted against a pearling sky. The houses stack themselves up the hills, their windows mirror the sun. Pelicans wheel and turn and slice the waters; one emerges with a fish flapping in its bill. The foghorns moan (alto, basso profundo, soprano), their chorus evoking Raphael's passion for this city of dreams.

She searches for Andrew's hand, but he has left her side to hang his head over the stern. A horde of gulls gathers, spoiling his attempt at discretion. With each buck and heave of his broad shoulders they drop greedily to the water. At first Elizabeth feels a disrespectful urge to laugh; instead she finds herself weeping.

Back on shore Raphael's friends store the leftover food and champagne in the trunk of her rented car, and she is too distracted and polite to refuse. Andrew is too green about the gills to drive, so she takes the wheel and heads into unfamiliar streets. She drives up and over some ridiculously steep hill—at one point she comes to a stop sign on an incline so sharp she cannot see over the hood of the car; she must accept on faith that the street continues over and down the other side of the intersection.

She is lost. She is driving aimlessly, with no notion of where she is going or why, when she finds herself on a flatter street lined with flirty-eyed young men—boys, really—wearing T-shirts sliced across their midriff to reveal flat, shaved stomachs. They chat and mingle with women of all ages and races, dressed on this chilly morning in net stockings and miniskirts and sequined tops with plunging necklines. Here and there a man or a woman pushes a rusting shopping cart filled with rags and recyclable bottles.

Elizabeth pulls into a bus zone in front of a porn video palace (LIVE SEX ACTS! BONDAGE ON STAGE!). Before Andrew can ask questions she opens the trunk and carries the food and champagne to the curb. A small crowd clusters about. "Wedding reception leftovers," she explains, blushing at her small lie, but it makes the food seem more festive.

The children of paradise do not ask questions. Within minutes the food and drink are gone, all that lovely, expensive gourmet fare. She climbs back in the car. Andrew rests his hand on her leg. "I liked you for that," he says, but her mind and heart are still out on the bay, sinking with Raphael's ashes and the nine family flowers: Rose Ella, Tom Hardin, her brothers, her sister, herself. *Life,* she thinks. *Is there no end to it?*

Where Do We Come From, What Are We, Where Are We Going?

[1990]

His choices are these: breathe and cough, or don't breathe. So he breathes, and coughs, and with each cough catapults himself into an altered state of being. The pain transports him beyond pain, into some parallel universe where the knowledge of pain is impossible because pain itself forms the substance and being of existence. His consciousness shrinks to a white dwarf of a star, concentrate of pain, brilliant pointed star turning in the darkness of his chest. The clarity and purity of this feeling he has never before known—it is the closest he has come to ecstasy.

Only anger is keeping him alive. In his family's faces he sees his agony, reflected as their wholly comprehensible wish that he hang it up, turn it in, kick the bucket, call it quits. What they don't understand is that he hangs on so as to see their pain. Partly from love—how can he let go this dearness, earned so dearly?—partly from sheer orneriness. They are distressed, sorrowful, they pity his incontinence and pain, but they are not *here*, they are in that other world, the world of the not-sick, whose horizons extend beyond the here and now.

He is hanging on, and hanging on, and then he sees Miss Camilla, who totters in one afternoon. She is dressed in white, and at first he mistakes her for Frances Handley, who visits him on her every shift at the hospital. He is barely conscious as she goes through the routine ("It's Camilla, Camilla Perkins—can you hear me—squeeze my hand"). He retreats into his private universe of pain.

He drifts there until he hears her voice from some far and cavernous place. "Forgive," he hears her saying, more than once, a pesky breathing at his ear. He would raise his hand to brush it away—*forgive what? what can it matter now?*—but he cannot control his hand, it drifts off the bed and he is following it to where it is going until he is called back to consciousness by her sour old breath. Smell! His nose is as sharp, maybe sharper than ever.

She is leaning over him, her eyes bulging, her eyebrows forming half-moon arcs above his own. "Let go," she whispers. "You have earned your death."

Who could have imagined this happening to him, to anybody? He has seen many deaths and still this is true. He shakes his head as best he can. *No, no.*

She holds up a small brass-cornered chest, its leather straps dangling. "I've come to take your heart," she says. He raises his eyebrows. "I'm taking your heart," she repeats.

"Take my heart," he says aloud. "Crazy old maid, friend and lover, mother of sorrows, angel of death." As he speaks he breathes, as he breathes he coughs, as he coughs his lungs rack and swell until his chest bursts and his breastbone splits cleanly down the middle—he is splitting wood, plunging an ax into a thick straight poplar log that divides neatly into halves, a few splinters, a gush of blood from the wood's pale yellow heart—he is gutting deer, the swift sharp stroke he learned from his father and that his father learned from the father before him and on back to whenever there were knives to wield, whenever there were fathers to teach, and the quick spurt of blood, and his thought when first he made this cut, years ago: *Who might have imagined that a single animal, any animal holds this much blood?* He is covered with his own blood, until he smells his flesh burning and the blood stops and his chest opens wider of its own accord and lifting itself from his chest his heart, ringed with thorns and encircled in flame and rising to hover above his dissected chest, until Miss Camilla holds out her strongbox and he yields his heart into her quavery hands, that guide it into this casket of gold, ciborium of leather and brass.

His chest knits itself together. The pain is as transcendent as ever, but he breathes easier now that his swollen heart is not crowding his fluid-filled lungs, now that his heart is in safekeeping, away from these doctors, this hospital, away even from his blood family. He knows what she will do: She will take his heart and place it in the woodshop stove, which she will fire using the badly glued block of wood from which he was to learn, or teach, and all of him that is of any count will rise to the clouds to join all that has gone before, and when the stove has cooled she will shovel the ashes into her strongbox and drop the whole from the Perlite Ford Bridge, so that they may join all that remains behind. This is right and just, a fitting and proper end for the joy and grief, evanescence and futility of human endeavor.

Miss Camilla Speaks

[1992]

In my mother's time only traveling photographers brought picture taking to the countryside. Once a year they'd come through, take their pictures, and leave, not to return until a year later. Sitting for one of them, placing money in his hands was like teaching or farming, making art or having children, a gesture of faith in the continuity of things—in this case, that the pictureman would return the following spring with the developed prints.

But the pictureman who worked Strang Knob in the fall and winter of 1913 did not return. He came through once, stayed long enough to photograph the town and all its men, women, and children, and to lure my mother to Chicago, where they were engaged, then married, then had me, their single child.

In the absence of any better story, this has had to do.

For Rose Ella and Tom Hardin there was this: They bound themselves to each other and it was a hurtful binding, hurtful at times for them and hurtful at times to live next door to. In my years as their neighbor I never heard them raise their voices at each other but there were times when I felt the strain—times when that house wanted to break apart and send its lives flying to the cardinal corners of the earth. Love like a slip knot—the harder they strained at it, the tighter it bound them one to another, until at the end there was no more or less than this, the knowing that in the face of all that trial and trouble they had been loyal to each other, and from that loyalty the next generation took its footing.

Surely a lifetime of loyalty is as good as any other human virtue—I tell myself this often.

And this is what my self asks in return: Should I have yielded to myself—should I have yielded to Tom Hardin on that High Bridge, the first time he made love to me, the second time he made love to me? For love is what it was, however it might not have been what I pictured in my dreams. Now I understand that, too late. Which is better, to keep one's self-respect or to act? In the end I was left with only pride, the devil's virtue.

I knew, of course, what Tom Hardin wanted, on our first drive to High Bridge. On that drive I thought of nothing else. I was a plowed field waiting for seed; he was a better man to plant it than most. It was easy for Tom Hardin, it would have been easy for me on that bridge, to forget about Strang Knob—a half-day's hard drive distant in a time when people stayed close to home.

On that first drive I refused him because of fear—mostly for my job, a little for my soul. I understood then, standing on High Bridge, that he was looking elsewhere for love because being a man, he had elsewhere to look. I had nowhere to look, and so it was easy for me to see the love this man was overlooking.

And I knew my place—I felt it on my skin like dirt, I tasted it bitter as dirt. We would return to Strang Knob and Tom Hardin would be forgiven by the women, envied by the men, and I would have done what they knew I was going to do before they laid eyes on me, before they'd even heard of me. The city woman, come to the country with her city airs, and not here a year before she's in the pants of her next-door neighbor's husband.

After that first trip to High Bridge I closed off, once and for all, any possibility of desire. In this I saw no choice—this was a matter of survival, if I were to stay in this small town, and I had nowhere else to go and no wish to go anywhere else. To permit desire in my life when it had no way of coming to fruition was to court scandal and disaster.

So I willed some part of myself to desiccation, watched and listened, smelled and tasted (no touch—this I had willed into submission) as it curled and dried and withered into a bitter kernel I mistook for dead.

Then Raphael Hardin arrived and changed, or at least fractured, all that. I was a ray of light traveling toward darkness, and high time, or so I thought; he was a prism that I struck along the way, a young man dying.

And then came my second trip to High Bridge with Tom Hardin, and my second refusal. Why did I say no then?

A young man dying; his father dying; an old maid schoolteacher who lives next door, dying. The two men who have brought this woman as close to love as she will come in this life; the woman who tried, in her pale way, to bring these men together.

The winter after Rose Ella died, Raphael Hardin came to stay with his father. He came from the airport straight to my house, his ticket still jutting from his pocket, his suitcase in the backseat of a rented car. He looked older than when I'd seen him last—his hair had lost its sheen, his skin was dry, stretched across his cheeks, translucent—in the sharp winter light I could see veins branching under the thin flesh of his temple. His hand was cool to the touch. He was thinner—thin.

He'd come to me to ask this favor. He would be visiting

Tom Hardin for the winter, maybe longer. He wanted a place to come daily to take his medicine, where he would not disturb his father.

—Of course.

—This medicine is complicated—needles, tubes, an hour or more each day.

—The kitchen door is never locked.

—You won't mention this to Tom Hardin.

—Whatever you wish.

I have heard all the stories of their parents' and grandparents' picture takings. They have taken care that I, the pictureman's daughter, should know them.

This is Rose Ella's story, which she told me for the first time when Tom Hardin went to hunt deer in upstate Wisconsin and left her pregnant with Raphael and through her own foolishness stuck without money for food, when she came to me in that ridiculous red coat and I fed her and her family for two weeks without once asking why.

She told me this story when Tom Hardin was hunting in Wisconsin; she told it many times later. Women are not supposed to need or want to get away from their husbands or their children. Women are not supposed to be left by their husbands—women who are left by their husbands (for however short a time) must be doing something wrong. And so at such times, like most Strang Knob wives, like most wives, Rose Ella went looking for someone to put down by way of saving herself, and I, the pictureman's old-maid daughter, was the easiest of targets; easier even than the dead.

She carried this story framed and matted in her heart, to trot out for display for my benefit on those days when Tom Hardin disappeared, or Tom Hardin got drunk, or when she was just plain worn out by so many children and their incessant needs and wants.

—My folks rode a half day down from the hills for no reason other than to sit for your father's camera. They dressed up and rode down from the hills and then turned around and rode back—couldn't afford a hotel, they'd put all their money into your father's stretched-out hand.

(It's that stretched-out hand that got to her—every time she said those words she'd give her head an angry little shake.)

—Mother wanted no part of her wedding day but the forgetting. They'd got married in pouring rain in some half-built log church with a half-drunk priest they never saw again. It was the picture she wanted, for remembering. She searched out the best dress you could come by in these parts to wear for that picture, ordered it from a catalogue, come all the way from Chicago. Watered silk—green to match her eyes—handmade lace at the throat and sleeves. She carried it down all the way from the hills and fixed her hair and pinned a magnolia blossom at her ear, to hear my mother talk about it you'd think she'd done all this yesterday.

Somewhere around the watered silk dress my patience always wore thin.

—My father never talked much about his life before he came to take pictures under Strang Knob, I'd say, taking care to sound casual, not to show too much interest. —What did your mother have to say about him?

But Rose Ella waved away my question—she was not interested in the pictureman except to visit his sins on me, his child.

—You should have seen my mother's eyes when she talked about that lace! (Or the petticoat imported from New Orleans, or the dark green leather boots with the buttons up the side, or the carnelian brooch at the throat.)—To buy a dress like that would have been no different than taking bread from her child's mouth, she with one child in hand and another loaf of bread in the oven, and already all the family money gone. So she ordered that dress on installment and wore it that day and mailed it back soon as your father took the picture. Didn't even carry it back up the hill, what was the point of taking the chance she'd give it a tear or a spot? She told me she still carried a little shame for ordering that dress knowing she was going to send it back two seconds after the shutter's click. "The only lie I ever told," my mother said to me more than once, "for the sake of a picture neither you nor I nor anybody else ever got to see."

By this point she'd have vented her pique, and with timing and luck I could intercept her before she launched into speculation on the shiftlessness of a photographer who would take money in his stretched-out hand and then flat-out disappear.

—More coffee? I'd ask.—Or something with a little more kick?

This is the story that I have told the women of Strang Knob:

My mother followed her pictureman to Chicago, where he acknowledged his mistake in leaving her behind and took her as his lawful wife. A year later my birth cemented their union. An only child, I devoted myself to my parents, who devoted themselves to each other. As I was approaching my forties each passed to a quiet death, my mother dying a few months after my father, as befitted a woman so deeply in love. "Photographs?" I ask, when the women of Strang Knob asked after their parents' or grandparents' pictures. "My father never took a photograph after he married, that I know of. And any pictures he took beforehand—why, they must have been destroyed, or lost."

Fenton Johnson

As for me, I returned to Strang Knob (if "return" may be used to describe moving to a place where I had never lived, that I knew only through my mother's memories). "The city is not a pleasant place to live these days for a single woman," I said when I came back, and they nodded. "I wanted to bury my mother in her hometown," I said, and they nodded, happy to believe the evidence I offered that things are better here than anywhere else on earth.

This is the secret of charm: helping others believe the stories they tell about themselves and their world.

Before anything else children see the holes in things. My father was the hole in my mother's life, the thing not talked about, that I took early on as my own. A time came, lost to memory but preserved in the heart, when I noticed that other children had fathers—and they, of course, noticed that I had none.

I asked after him. "Your father left our lives when he was still young," my mother said. "I barely had time to get to know him myself. That's all you need to know." And I, overwhelmed by the thought of such loss, asked no more questions until she was dead and I found the strongbox in her bedroom.

To imagine my father I look in the mirror, subtract my mother, and guess at what's left. Those high eyebrows—that arching hairline—surely these are his. My mother was quite beautiful, as she saw fit to remind me; she'd hardly have fallen for any but a handsome man. I can suppose that it must have been the combination of their features that was unfortunate.

I never saw him. I own no photographs of him, nor of him and my mother together. If my mother had wanted a picture of them together there was no one in Strang Knob to take it—no doubt he kept the secrets of his equipment to himself (he was

218

a man, after all). Anyway, which of her neighbors might she have asked to trip the shutter without revealing her own secret? After some time (a month? two months? time took longer in those days) he took the train west with his equipment and his negatives and his customers' money, leaving my mother with a stack of receipts and me in her belly. A few months later she took herself to Chicago, his hometown, where she hoped, I can suppose, to find him.

And then what?

She had a single photograph taken of herself, which I have framed in silver plate and mounted on the end table where anyone sitting on my couch might see it. In it she wears a wedding dress of a style that arrived on the scene somewhat later than one might want for the sake of verisimilitude—floor-length, with a train, veils, pearls, all in white like some John Singer Sargent painting.

She is not the only woman I have known who has fabricated a fairy tale wedding.

The women of Strang Knob have admired the picture—if anyone notices the anachronism they're too polite to say so. But they ask with studied casualness:

—Where is your father?

—Why, behind the camera. It must have been the last photograph he took.

—Why, of course.

Carefully as I have listened, I hear no shape nor color in their response.

In her lifetime my mother never showed me the strongbox. In one- and two-room apartments she concealed it from me for all my life. Then she died, and I returned from the Little Sisters to find it sitting at the foot of her bed.

Until then I never allowed the thought that I might have family—blood ancestry—except at those times (Father's Day, Christmas) when the world at large forced the thought to mind. At such times I thought of myself as having sprung from my mother alone. "Parthenogenesis," I read in a high school biology textbook. "Reproduction, especially among lower animals, in which an unfertilized egg develops into a new individual." *Yes*, I thought. *I am the drone bee.*

Then I found these photographs—a slap in the face; as if an archaeologist were to offer conclusive evidence (a handprint in stone; Adam's fossilized rib) of the existence of God. A father whom I had known only in fantasy became a man, a human being in whose hand my mother had once rested her own.

In the strongbox: photographs, taken by my father on his one trip to Strang Knob. How did they arrive in her possession? How did he locate her so as to send them? Why send these and nothing else? Would a man who would abandon a woman pregnant with his child later mail her the photographs of her townspeople, from whose outstretched hands he'd taken money? Probably. Confession *(mea culpa)*, absolution, penance in a single gesture—a man might see it this way. Perhaps he, a lifelong wanderer, had no understanding of what these photographs must have represented to her and would come to represent for me. In my more generous moments I think this of him. At darker times I think of him as taunting from afar.

The box is compact, a small trunk bound with leather hinges and with brass-plated corners, now tarnished. It's dated on the outside, a few months before my birth: STRANG KNOB, KENTUCKY, AUGUST 1913–JANUARY 1914. I have examined the photographs carefully, of course; by now, almost forty years under Strang Knob, I can name many of the subjects. I look at a photograph, then I look at the townspeople; I find the bloodlines. Here one family's unmistakable nasal slope, there another family's knitted eyebrows. Some faces I know, some I can guess. Most names are simply lost, forgotten even as they stare into the camera's eye with this calm certainty: *I am remembered.*

There are one hundred and fifty-six photographs, none marred by so much as a fingerprint. Some of the pictures include more than one person (two, or five, or ten persons frozen in history for the price of one. I wonder how they paid my father—a dime, a quarter collected from every person in the picture? Or did he take these for the sake of his pictureman's art?). Taken as a whole the box is a sculpture of memory: unlabeled, jumbled willy-nilly, disordered, haunting.

Here is a photograph of Tice Flaherty, who has told me often of his holy parents, the only people in town who thought more of music than of booze and more of God than of either. In the photograph Tice scowls in miniature overalls and sharp-toed cowboy boots, wearing a one-gallon Stetson and with a small wiener of a dog at his side. He is surrounded by older, bearded men; behind them whiskey barrels are stacked at the Strang Knob railroad landing. The men are carrying sledge-hammers and axes. It is the first day of local prohibition, and Tice was brought here (so he says, when he tells his particular memory of the pictureman's visit) by his father to witness and learn from this act of moral fervor.

But look at the photograph more carefully, and there are buckets—large buckets, two for each man, and the bearded father carries three and a sign: A SAD DAY FOR THIRSTY BOYS. Little Tice holds in one hand a string attached to the dog's collar and in the other an already filled bottle. Why buckets? Why a sad day?

Or the wedding photograph of Rose Ella's parents. Rose

Ella's mother sits, her husband stands stiff as death for the camera's slow exposure—my father's subjects had to sit *still;* or maybe they were scared, or remembering the hard-won money they'd just placed in my father's outstretched hand. Rose Ella's parents are wearing the homeliest of homespun. Her father's trousers reveal a long stretch of ankle; her mother's dress, quilted from a patchwork of cast-off materials, is losing its hem.

There is no lace, no watered silk, no obsidian buttons. As for the magnolia blossom at her ear—a tree in the background is bare as teeth; no magnolias will be blooming for months.

At the bottom of the box: one photograph of my mother. She is in a small room built of unfinished lumber (a cottage? a shack?). Behind her chintz curtains billow from a half-open window filled with a light so blinding that it presents itself only as a white square—it's broad daylight, but my mother is wearing a nightgown. She is huddled on a rough cot, rumpled bedclothes at her feet. Dark half-moons of sleeplessness under her eyes—I imagine her blushing (it was 1913) at the thought of this moment recorded for someone, anyone. She ducks her chin in modesty, but her eyes are bold with desire.

On first encountering it, I set aside this last photograph. For some unmeasured time I lay on my side on the floor of my mother's apartment, curled into a ball and searching for the strength to rise, in the face of this strongbox evidence of one person's cruelty to another.

How the course of a life is changed by each act, the reverberation of our smallest gesture into the lives of all those by whom we are surrounded: That photograph held the burden of my mother's dreams, which she had so long concealed from me. Never having seen it, I would have stayed in Chicago; seeing it, I was drawn back to a place where I might live, if not amid blood relatives, at least among those connecting events that had made my mother who she was, and so had made me.

I brought the two of us back to Strang Knob to be buried, one of us dead, the other alive. I told the town priest that my mother's deceased husband—my father—was buried in Chicago, but that my mother had wanted to come back for a proper burial in her hometown, and I, the good daughter, was honoring her wishes. He balked for a bit—no doubt he had heard rumors—but it was a warm day in spring, the coffin carried its own implications, I bought the plot with cash. They dug the hole quickly enough.

What was I to do with these pictures? They did not belong to me, I had no right to keep them, but to have handed them out on my arrival would have led to questions that for many years I was not prepared to answer, until what at first might have been explained as simple oversight ("Oh, by the way, when I moved from Chicago I came across these old photographs. Do you recognize them?") took on the dimensions of a lie, which, like all lies, perpetrated itself into a life of its own.

I exaggerate only a little when I write that the photographs in the box constitute, for some several hundred people under Strang Knob, the difference between the world that they have created and need to believe in—a world in which they can have faith—and the world as it is, or was. As for me, I have heard their stories so often repeated and embellished that they have taken on the authority of truth, until it is the photographs that I begin to doubt.

This mystery deepens with time.

It is possible, of course, that I have deceived myself. Perhaps, in fact, my mother met my father in Chicago, lived with him long enough to realize her mistake, then left him, taking the strongbox with her as sustenance for forty years of memories.

But of all horrors the acknowledgment that we have deceived ourselves in love (whether of parents, or family, or friends, or partners) is the most painful, which we will go to ever-greater lengths to avoid; even so far as to spend half a lifetime under Strang Knob.

Which is better, the world as it is or the world as we need and want it to be? How much reality can we accept and still keep going? I close and lock the strongbox lid.

I had decided to leave the photographs to be found after my death—I liked the notion of this small cruelty visited on the people of Strang Knob: the camera's inarguable comeuppance. Then Raphael Hardin returned to stay that winter and spring with his father.

This was how it worked:

Each morning he rose, a little later each day, but as early as his strength allowed. He made coffee for Tom Hardin, took it to his shop, sat with him in silence. Then he crossed the yard to my house to administer his IV treatment.

I served him a cup of tea, or coffee, or a glass of water. Then he'd stand and roll his IV pole from the closet. On the first day I asked if I might help.

—If I need help I'll ask, he said brusquely. Then, a little more kindly, —The day I need help to do something as simple as this, that day will be some kind of watershed, some kind of frontier I'll have passed and there'll be no turning back. Besides.

—Besides?

—If you stuck yourself—there's a risk. A small risk. But a risk.

What could risk mean, at my age? How much I wanted someone for whom to take risks! But after that I was careful to keep an excuse at hand, some errand that took me to another room until I judged enough time had passed for Raphael to hook up his IV and get his medicine flowing.

Then I sat and we talked about books, or the weather, or his job as a librarian, or my years as a teacher. For an hour and more he told stories of himself as a child, stories of the town that Rose Ella and Tom Hardin had created from their memories for his memory, stories of his life and his friends in San Francisco—all the stories of his life, with a needle in his arm and the slow drip of the IV.

Then he'd glance at the IV bag.

—Almost empty, he'd say, and I'd find an excuse to leave the room.

Not long before he returned to San Francisco a day came when I asked some trivial question. Raphael did not respond. I gave him a sharp glance—there had been more of this recently, his passing in and out of attention.

He glanced up at the IV bag. —Almost empty.

But before I could rise to go he pulled on a fresh pair of latex gloves and slipped the needle from his arm. This he had never done before while I was present.

—Do you suppose, he said, that if we made our dead welcome they would visit us more often? People in other places talk about their dead as if they are still alive. Is it possible that the dead visit them more freely and comfortably? I know a Oaxacan woman in San Francisco whose brother died of AIDS. She built an altar to him in a corner of her apartment—a *recuerdo*, she calls it, where she put all the artifacts from his life, everything from photographs to his favorite coffee cup to a half-empty bottle of tequila he was the last person to drink from. And his toothbrush. She lights a candle there every night, and once a week or so she sits down and talks to him, tells him about her life, even asks him questions. Superstition, or so I thought until all these people who made up my life died. Then I realized how my boundaries didn't stop at my skin— how my life was a sum of the lives I have touched and who have touched me. Take away all my family, all my friends, all my loves and there'd not be much left. Is this superstition?

—I don't know. When I kneel to pray I think on my father.

He inserted a first, then a second hypodermic into the catheter buried under his skin. It was the first time he had performed this intimate act, this sacrament in front of me.

—I feel them with me even now, all of them. I wear their clothes—my closet is filled with clothes from six or seven men, all snappy dressers in very different ways, and when I put on a coat or a shirt that belonged to one of them I feel his body wrapped around mine. I hear them in my voice—I think and say things that I learned from them without knowing I was learning. Or maybe they learned them from me, but I didn't realize I said things that way until I heard them from some other person's mouth. Where do they end? Where do I begin? We had this symbiotic life, this *love*, I don't know another word for it. How can they be dead, when I feel them with me still?

He was bundling together tubing and needles, for disposal in a hideously red plastic garbage bin. He spoke without meeting my eyes.

—What is this life? he asked, and in his voice I heard only bewilderment. —You tell me. How is it possible to lose all and go on? Crucifixion—piece of cake, compared to what I've seen my friends endure. Jesus had the satisfaction of being a martyr, right in front of the masses. People compare all this dying with the Holocaust. That's fatuous. It's not like the

Holocaust at all except in this one single way: You watch this happening to a world you thought you knew and you wonder: How can this be?

—This is a great and terrible gift. The understanding that we understand nothing.

— Great. Illness as blessing.

—You have a better response?

—For a long while I was enraged—in rage. Now I am trying to accept.

—Why aren't you saying this to Tom Hardin?

—I wouldn't do him the favor.

—Which is why you've come across a continent to spend time with him.

To this Raphael gave no answer.

When he finished disposing of equipment I spoke a command—a teacher knows how to get what she wants.

—Name them.

—Name them?

—Your friends. Tell me their names.

Raphael swabbed his arm with orange disinfectant.

—Well, there was Salvador, with the sleek black hair. Bill, who liked politics. Curt, who made movies. Robert, who showed them. James, with the leopard-skin tights and violet blouses. Greg, who wanted to write; Michael, who did. Arturo, who taught. Fred, who fought for human rights. Alain, who made pastries; Larry, who ate them, and who taught me how to love.

He spread his hands. The IV pole fell clanking to the floor.

—They were my family. Now who will remember me?

I mirrored his gesture.

—Who will remember me?

❈   ❈   ❈

We fall in love not with the real person but with an ideal of that person as we want them to be. If our love endures, with the passage of time it comes gradually to spring from our knowledge of the real person, the beloved as they are rather than as we would have them be. What is love but the intersection of memory and desire, past and future, the beloved we have known and the beloved in our hopes and expectations?

But in love something miraculous happens. In loving someone we give them an ideal against which to measure themselves. Living in the presence of that ideal, the beloved strives to fulfill the lover's expectations. In this way love makes of us the bravest and best persons that we are capable of being.

A photographer may take a dozen or a hundred pictures of a human being and he'll look ordinary as pancakes, and then she gets the right one, she and her subject and the light are all in the same place at the same time and there's a kind of magic that transpires, the picture that floats up out of those chemicals is larger than any of the people who had a hand in it.

That was the way it was between Tom Hardin and myself. I would see him a hundred times and he was ordinary as dirt, as plain as any man, and then he'd get his hands on a dog or pick up a block of wood and be transfigured. This is what I would call love, I don't know what else to call what I saw in his hands, the way they brought out the best in an animal, or the grain and contour of that wood, and transformed it when everything was right into something larger than himself or the dog or the block of wood—something as large as life itself. Under his hands a hunting dog or a block of wood became its best self, the best thing it could possibly be. And if it was too bad he didn't have that talent (the way only a few people do) with his wife or his children or with me, it's better that he had it for animals, or wood, than not to have had it at all.

As for me—was it love for me? Was it the thing that transforms?

One day Raphael said this during his IV treatment:

—We're among the last to remember.

—What do you mean?

—You're among the oldest of your generation still alive. There are only a few left who remember the world as you came to it. That's true for me among a certain group of friends—of eight or ten people I once did everything with, shared every memory, I'm one of two still alive.

The sun, which when he first came to my house had slanted low through my windows, had climbed enough into spring that it shone full in our faces. I rose to pull the blinds, but Raphael continued talking as if I were still sitting across from him.

—Can you imagine what it would be like to have a son die of this disease, of any disease, and no one to whom to speak your grief? Then you turn on the television and some nationally prominent figure is being treated with respect, or at least deference, while he talks about how your son, and by extension *you*, are somehow to blame.

I sat then, and took his hand—the hand whose arm was hooked to its IV.

—Does anyone in your family know?

He told me of speaking to Rose Ella, and to his nephews, on the night of the last great Hardin family gathering.

—Once I told my nephews, I figured everybody would find out sooner or later. You know how my family grapevine works. There are no secrets.

—Except from Tom Hardin. Did Rose Ella tell Tom Hardin?

—No. Mother would have taken her time—if she could bring herself to tell him at all—and she wasn't given time. But it's no secret from him, if he'd let himself open his eyes and see.

—But he won't open his eyes unless you open them for him. None of us wants to see the world as it really is unless we're shocked into it. You can do that for him.

Raphael's lips tightened—I know that thin line; I have felt it on myself.

—Let him ask first. I'm the one who's sick. *(He is too much like you to speak first,* I recalled my words, spoken in the woodshop to Tom Hardin. Surely this would be the act of greatest courage—as much as or more than speaking before a crowd: sitting down and speaking something hard and true face-to-face with someone you love.)

—You're both sick.

—He can come to me. He asks, I'll tell him. All he has to do is ask.

Remembering this person or that person, Tom Hardin or Raphael or me—this matters only in the short run, however it might be a good way to spend a rainy afternoon. It's the accumulation of remembering that counts. The land remembers—the place remembers—people remember, if they give themselves the time and place. The tree remembers the forest that has come before. The earth remembers the people who have lived on it. People remember without knowing they are remembering. Have we left our place in history in better shape than when it was given to us? This is the big memory, the memory that matters, the sum of all our stories rendered into one big story, one big truth. What are we, finally, but accumulations of memory? The heart remembers, the body remembers what has been done to it, what has come out of all that's gone before and what, with devotion and skill, may be given to those who follow. Memory is a gift. It does not belong to us; it's not part of us. It's ours to enjoy and replenish while we're alive and to pass on, augmented, at our deaths.

On his last visit, the day before he returned to San Francisco, Raphael finished his "drip," as he called it, and packed away his medical paraphernalia in a large duffel bag.

I poured us each a finger of whiskey. Raphael raised his glass in a toast.

—To life. *L'chaim,* as the Jews say.

I raised my glass and drank. Raphael drained his glass, then set it by his medical paraphernalia and asked this question, his father's famous question that echoed in my memory.

—How about going for a drive?

I gave the answer which it was my place to give.

—What do we have but time?

We went outside to the car. Sitting at the steering wheel, I paused before turning the key.

—Inside.

—Ma'am?

—There's a small box next to my desk. An old-fashioned box—it has leather hinges and a big combination lock. Would you mind going in and getting it?

I drove through the countryside to the Perlite Ford Bridge. A cold front had passed through the day before—high winds, tornado watches, spring. On this day the trees pierced an impossibly blue sky with livid shards of green. Raphael gestured at the sky.

—In San Francisco there's never this landlocked light. There when the weather blows through you get these brilliant days of marine light—all that light reflected from clouds and water and the pastel buildings and the sky is filled with light, but always it's refracted light, with water in it or behind it. But here this dry light comes sweeping down from the north and brings a kind of polar clarity. It's as if the cold air brings the arctic light along with it.

In the distance the light—this polar light, as Raphael called it—greened the branches that lined the riverbank. Over moist, dark furrows barn swallows swooped and dipped, caught up in the exuberance of spring. The sky's electric blue suffused every visible thing with its presence and color.

We crested the backbone of a ridge and dropped into Perlite Hollow. Farms fanned out to either side, a patched quilt of plowed and fallow fields alternating with woodlands where brands of lavender redbud showed among the pale green limbs. On the north-facing slopes the trees were still gray and barren. Here and there in the fields long rectangles of white muslin billowed over fledgling tobacco shoots.

I parked at a graveled turnabout. A few years back the highway department had replaced the old cable-and-girder bridge, built in Tom Hardin's prime, with a new bridge, a stark two-lane concrete structure. We took a few steps onto it. I walked to the railing and tried to look over.

—I can't see the river. The railings are too high.

—Progress. Must be safer to build it that way.

—Or cheaper.

We returned to the car. I drove us down a side road, a gravel road that led to the old cable-and-girder bridge. We climbed from the car. I took my cane from the trunk.

—You'll help me with this box.

He picked it up, then searched the brush until he found a long branch to use as a walking stick—his step had taken on a gimp in the last week or so. He tried to break the stick over his thigh, but the wood was too thick, or perhaps he had lost his strength. In the end he broke it by smacking it against the ground. We struck off, Raphael humming a tune, whose words we'd both learned from Tice Flaherty.

She walked through the corn leading down to the river,
Her hair shone like gold in the hot morning sun.
She took all the love that a poor man could give her
And left him to die like a fox on the run.

We walked a slow quarter of a mile, past the rotting stumps of two huge white oaks, until we came to the old bridge. The highway department had removed the planking from the middle of the bridge, leaving a framework of rusted cables and girders. A sycamore sapling shot through gaps in the bridge flooring. The riverbank was strewn with household trash—a bent and dented galvanized tub, broken bottles, a refrigerator door, the tube (somehow unbroken) from a television set, watching from the mud like the eye of God.

We walked a few steps onto the old bridge, until we could look down at this flowing green, the living artery of the land. I leaned on my cane. Raphael set the strongbox on the planks, leaned on one of the rusting bridge supports. I pointed to a mossy wall downstream.

—That's what's left of the foundation of what they called the Perlite mill. When I first came to Strang Knob there were still some buildings here, but those are all gone now.

—Mother never much liked coming here. I think it reminded her too much of what her family had lost.

—Well, the Perlites never had as much as they claimed or thought.

233

—Mother always talked about a whole town they owned and ran out here.

—So she saw fit to tell me.

We stood for a long while without talking. The water slurped and gurgled around the bridge pilings. Downstream a flash of red slipped through the brush lining the banks. Raphael pointed with his stick, but the fox was gone.

—Tom Hardin told me long ago that the fields around Perlite Ford had the best fox trapping in the county. But then they built this bridge and the foxes disappeared.

—With the new concrete bridge farther upstream maybe the foxes are coming back.

I bent and worked the combination lock, to open the strongbox.

—What's in there?

I lifted the box, retrieved one photograph, then held the box out and turned it over. The silver-framed photograph of my mother in her rented wedding dress dropped and sank like a stone, but the other one hundred and fifty-four unframed pictures fluttered like leaves, caught in the breeze that blows just above the river's surface. It bore them a few feet aloft before settling them on the eddying water. They floated along, circling like paper boats, following the living current as it traversed the river from left to right and back. I watched them round the bend, out of sight, bound for the Ohio, the Mississippi, the Caribbean, the Atlantic, the Gulf Stream, Europe.

—What was that about?

I handed him the photograph I'd held back.

—I want you to have this one.

He looked it over carefully.

—I ought to know these people.

—You ought. They're your grandparents—Rose Ella's

parents. This is their wedding picture, taken by my father, if Rose Ella is to be believed. I see no reason to doubt her.

—But they're not dressed for a wedding.

—They're dressed in the best they own, if that's what you're wondering.

He peered at it a second longer, then laughed.

—You mean—

—It's your picture now. It means what you want it to mean.

He studied it awhile, holding it to the spring sunlight.

—What about the fancy green dress from the Chicago mail-order house?

I shrugged.

He looked at it long and hard, then closed his eyes and dropped it through the bridge planks. It fluttered to the river and followed its companions downstream.

—Now why did you do that?

—Well, you dumped the whole damned box.

—I had my reasons. What I want to know is your reasons.

—I don't know. I like the story of my grandmother ordering that fancy mail-order dress for a single hour's wear, then sending it back.

He took up his walking stick; I took up the strongbox, now empty.

—Your mother and father. Out of their love came you and all your brothers and sisters. This is the chain of being, that breaks and reforms and continues itself in ways of its own devising. I am a dead end—I have no issue; I have nothing to pass on.

—*We* have nothing to pass on.

—Except our love.

—How can you know this?

—Because I have been loved, and in love.

—My father loves you. You know that.

—What makes you think that?

—Do you know how many women he's ever allowed in his shop? Much less invited in.

—I've never been one to wait for an engraved invitation.

—Well, sure. But you should hear the jealousy in his voice when he asks me about you. There's no other word for it.

—Jealousy?

—"What do you *do* over there anyway?" He asked me that one day.

I turned and walked toward the car, into the field. —None of your damned business, is what I hope you said.

—Have you told him that you love him?

With a child's accuracy he let fly that arrow; and I twisted and broke it off in place, by saying nothing.

Foolish old woman! What was there to say? A few words, and I said none of them.

We worked our way back to the road. I took his arm and pointed with my cane. A fox (the fox we'd seen at the bridge?) was slipping along the ditch, not more than a few yards in front of us. The moment I pointed she broke from a curious amble (how long had she been watching us?) into a full run across the fields.

And Raphael took out after, throwing his walking stick into the ditch and breaking into a headlong, heedless run across the sassafras shoots already taking root among the stubble of last year's corn—at this distance I smelled the pungence of their bent and broken twigs. I saw the fox pause, look back, laugh (but they always look as if they're laughing), and disappear down a hole. Raphael threw his hands in the air and gave an exultant cry. I heard his cry, and saw him fall to the earth.

I poled to his side as fast as I could. Death, I know it's

coming soon, and I tell myself I'm not afraid, I've seen it all and what I haven't seen, what difference can it make to me? I wanted nothing more for Raphael and for me than that we might die suddenly, out there in the blinding polar light. I told myself all this and yet I crossed that field afraid. And then I was at his side and he was lying facedown, laughing into the dirt. He raised himself on his arms and tried to pull his legs under him to stand but fell once, then a second time. I held out my hand. He brushed it away, tried to stand again. Watching, I remembered my mother, Tom Hardin, all these people acting brave in the face of our collective bewilderment, whistling in the dark, and it struck me that it is surely as hard—a different kind of hard, but just as hard—to watch the dying of someone you love as it is to come yourself to death.

Raphael fell a third time. I stuck out my hand.

—I don't want—

—Shut up, dear child, and take my hand, or we'll be here until we're buzzard meat.

I braced myself and helped him struggle to his feet, then I brushed his face and pants and scraped mud and manure from his shoes with a twig. He watched all this in the bemused and distant way that had come upon him in that last week.

—So you tell me, he said. I asked you first. Why did you throw those pictures away?

—It was my way of forgiving. I am forgiving the town, by allowing it to keep its stories.

We started back to the car, the two of us helping each other. Raphael spoke through his shortness of breath.

—I liked those stories. I liked listening to them change and grow. I heard them for almost forty years and at first I liked them better than the truth and then I realized that they *were* the truth.

He bent to kiss my cheek. His lips were warm and moist against my skin—not at all like my own lips, cool and cracked with age. For all his dying, he was a young man.

—Raphael. Have you forgiven your father?

His reply came from some historical place, out of time and intuition. —Have you forgiven him?

I gave no answer.

Should I have sent Raphael then and there to Tom Hardin? Probably. But I, a woman with secrets, was pleased to be entrusted with his. I took him in as a mother might take in a prodigal son, or as a woman might take in an old lover, with whom there was no heat but only afterglow. Sitting with Raphael while he opened his veins to hope—surely this was more familiar than lovemaking; this was as intimate as love itself.

But not love itself, because it came too easily for me. This is what I'd been searching for across those years: love without pain, or risk, or loss. Now that my lovers are gone, now that Tom Hardin and Raphael are dead, I understand this. It was not love I'd been searching for; it was power—the power to make him, them, the world ask to be forgiven, ask me for my forgiveness. Which I would then deny. Only now do I understand this—that forgiveness must come from within.

On our way home Raphael asked that we drive down the side roads and lanes of his childhood: along the river, past the red-brick church where Tom Hardin and Rose Ella had married, past the distillery (now closed) where so many Hardins had worked, past the empty lot where once had stood the peeling clapboard house where his parents had first lived, where Raphael himself had been born.

Raphael cleared his throat to speak.

—I never knew what I had until they were gone, all my friends, my mother, even Clark. But that's an old story.

—They aren't gone. They're here with you.

We rode in silence. We touched, then drew back—the nearness of our deaths could not change this. But unspeaking, we acknowledged the ways in which we were bound to each other by ties that were strong as blood: student and teacher, neighbor and friend; not bloody ties, but ties of love. Looking back at that afternoon drive through springtime, I understand it as a moment of grace, the third of three such moments in my life: my first trip to High Bridge; my second trip to High Bridge; my last drive with Raphael. In one way all these moments were alike—each was partly seized and mostly lost. Now, after father and son are dead, I am torn—between remorse that these moments were so short, and gratefulness that they happened at all.

And what is a moment of grace? I lived by guarding my heart— I saw no other choice—but in every long life moments come when our guard is lowered and what we are given is a moment of grace, a chance to forgive.

The first time Tom Hardin kissed me on High Bridge, it was easier to turn him away. He was a married man, I was a woman protecting a secret, marinating in a bitterness of my own making. A plain woman with no means about me but my wits and precious little chance to use those, I had plenty of reasons to be bitter, and my creating the bitterness on which I thrived gave me a reason to live, a way to stay alive. Then almost forty years passed and I saw what became of a block of wood under his hands—I had dreamed of myself as that block of wood, stiff and sharp-cornered, taken under his lathe and transformed into something supple and smooth and round.

"My God, Camilla, why are you saying no now?" At night, when the house is quiet and there is nothing to drown the ghosts' voices, I hear Tom Hardin pleading, on our second visit to High Bridge. Both times I refused, so as to send him back, first to Rose Ella, later to Raphael—or so I hoped. And on that second trip I said no to punish him—to teach him about all my years spent alone; there was that. But mostly I said no out of fear.

What would it have meant, after all this loveless time, to love a dying man?

This is what it would have meant: forgiveness, learning to forgive. To forgive Tom Hardin for turning away from the love his wife freely offered him, to assume it instead from the woman nearest at hand; to forgive him for being himself. To forgive my own self, for nursing this bitterness in my heart, for seizing my chance after so many years to punish him; for being myself.

"Do you think she forgave me?" This was his question on that second trip to High Bridge. I knew the answer—I had known Rose Ella, had heard her stories across those long summer afternoons and winter evenings when Tom Hardin was running away from love. I had seen Rose Ella do what she had to do—set this aside and move on. An imperfect forgiveness, surely, but forgiveness all the same. An imperfect love, but love nonetheless, of a kind that I (who have held out for perfect love) have never known.

"Do you think she forgave me?" he asked, possibly the first real question of his life, the first time he had opened his heart to the possibility of an answer, and I in my bitterness could not refrain from thrusting in the knife that he'd placed in my hand. "No," I said. "No, I don't think she ever did."

History is memory's skin, under which pulses the blood and guts of our real lives. Our stories are our way of fashioning a surface with which we can live, that we may present to our neighbors, our friends, our family, our children (especially these last). The truth lies not in the facts of the stories but in the longings that set them in motion. Truth lies in Tice Flaherty's story of his tee-totaling father, in Rose Ella's story of her mother's dress, in my story of my mother's married life, though it lies not in the facts. Which is more true: The strongbox photograph of my mother in a nightgown on a disheveled bed? Or my end table photograph of her in her rented wedding dress?

What matters are not the facts (disputable at best) but the stories they inspire, and our hearts' need for creating and preserving these stories to pass on: to me, to them, to you. This is our true act of perfect love. No single person may give to another any part of what she or he believes to be true without also giving love. In this way our stories become our way of lovemaking, our way of creating love.

In the end this will be all that remains. If we are born lucky, it is what we are given to build on; it is all that we may legitimately create. Buildings, roads, fortunes, gravestones disappear, even as our stories accumulate, the humus of human life, to become part of those who follow ten and ten thousand years later, just as some infinitesimally small part of last century's composting heap returns to nourish today's garden.

"Maybe this is the definition of death." This is what Raphael Hardin said to me on that last day, when he was pulling the catheter from his veins. "No single moment—now you see us, now you don't—but the lifelong slipping from the territories of desire into the territories of memory."

This is what I learned from those days in Tom Hardin's workshop, from sitting with Raphael Hardin as we remembered our stories. And now they are both gone, and I live beyond hope and desire; now I live only in memory. It is this, more than the passage of time, that has made me old.

I write now from the stone bench in front of Ittybit Muhlenberg's tombstone. I am surrounded by black-eyed Susans. The Hardin tombstone stands across the alley, a pointy-headed hunk of Italy set down in this Kentucky country cemetery.

I visited them both, first Tom Hardin, then Raphael, as each lay dying in the county hospital, and to each of them I spoke the same words:

—Forgive me.

I said this to each, when each could no longer respond.

—Help me forgive myself.

I think of the last of the great Hardin family gatherings, and of Raphael's question, nearer to his death than either of us might have known. Will anyone remember him? Will anyone remember me?

Will anyone visit my grave? A former student, maybe, on her way to her mother's grave. She'll pass by and happen to look in the right direction at the right time. "I didn't know old Camilla Perkins had died," she'll say. "High time," her husband will say. "The old bird outstayed her welcome for more years than you'd care to count."

And how long will the longest of such remembering continue? A few years. As I sit here writing I look up at the procession of faceless names on the tombstones that surround me. What are a few years of remembering?

"Never write anything down that you want to keep secret." My mother is a lifetime distant and still I hear her voice. She was fond of giving bad advice, but I have lived long enough now to learn that on this point she was right. Over more than eighty years I have seen the ways hidden things come to light, often by means of some letter or note or diary. The writer thinks she is writing only for herself, but this is a nosy world and there are plenty of people who, like cats, have nothing better to do with their time than to concern themselves with others' affairs. The web of concealment the writer takes an hour to devise they spend weeks considering how to unravel, and in the end they succeed.

And then the writer dies, and her life is considered an open book, through which anyone with time and patience may paw at leisure. I have seen this happen; I have participated in it. I am as nosy as you.

And so you are the discoverer of what I have left behind: my letter to the world that did not write to me, and this badly glued block of wood. And out of the one hundred and fifty-six photographs my father took (if I'm to be believed!) under Strang Knob, the single photograph that I have kept: the portrait of my mother amid disheveled bedclothes, caught at her most beautiful, at the moment when she was more alive than at any other time in her life; caught in the truest moment of her life, that all-at-once moment when desire becomes act, act becomes memory.

At one time I had decided to leave those photographs to be found, to let them tell the story of the woman who had carried them with her for much of her life. Then I spent days with Raphael remembering his friends, and evenings with Tom Hardin in his woodshop, and I came to understand that I might leave behind something better than photographs. I came to understand that I, Miss Camilla Perkins of the plain countenance and unlived life, had a story worth telling, embellishing, debating, distorting, denying, leaving behind. "The Old Maid's Version of What Happened to Her Randy

Old Man's Pictures"—I should like to hear it told, ten years after I am dead, layered over the multiple stories surrounding those photographed lives. "I never knew a fact that couldn't be improved with a little exaggeration"—I hear Tom Hardin speaking across time.

So I have destroyed all the pictures but this one. In destroying them I began, so late, to forgive my mother and father. I began to forgive myself. In place of photographs I am leaving behind my story of learning too late to forgive Tom Hardin, the world, myself.

Remember me, remember me—this is my story, that I am writing down for you. "Life is the little that is left over from dying"—is it Mr. Whitman who writes this? In my writing it he lives anew, and in my teaching it to my children, for that is how I think of all those students over all those years.

I taught this to all the Hardin children: Joe Ray, Barbara, Leslie, Robert, Clark, Bette C., Raphael. They may, perhaps, remember what I taught from love. Through love—the way that has been given to me—I will have entered the chain of being.

I taught these words, and though I have taken too long and known too much death before I learned them, I have learned them, learned this much. I write as someone who for too many years has lived very carefully indeed; I know whereof I speak. Given that it is impossible to live a life carefully enough, surely the best course is not to live it carefully at all.

Writing here amid the dead, I am struck by the memory of some remembered fairy tale, in which a parade of barbers saw the emperor's goat's ears and spoke aloud their curious questions and promptly lost their heads. Then a barber arrived, more clever than his unfortunate predecessors. He saw the emperor's hairy ears as clearly as anyone but held his tongue. He cut the emperor's hair, received his fee, and was invited to cut the emperor's hair another day and another. He was established in the capital in luxury.

After some years the burden of knowing became too great, and the barber went to the country, where he dug a hole, spoke his secret aloud to the earth, and relieved his conscience. Freed from his burden, he returned to the city to cut the emperor's hair again, to drink more wine, make love to more women (or maybe men—I think of Raphael here).

The following spring a reed grew from the hole the barber had dug. A shepherd cut the reed and shaped it into a pipe, which when played spoke aloud to the town the secret that all had known but no one had dared acknowledge—"The emperor has goat's ears!" With the secret spoken aloud, the town rose up, deposed the tyrannical emperor, and replaced him with the benevolent barber.

You are the dark and fertile earth, into whom I have whispered these stories.

Afterword

Scissors deepens and amplifies my engagement, begun in my first novel, *Crossing the River*, with the nature of families—the families we are given by fate and the families we choose. Dennis, the responsible parent, says to childless Andrew, "You might like your friends, but you don't have kids you're taking care of." In response to this observation Raphael Hardin, the gay HIV-positive son, snaps, "Instead I'm taking care of friends who are dying. A lot of them a thousand miles from parents or brothers or sisters who could care less." Which family is of greater consequence: the blood relations or the affinities of the heart?

In the mid-1980s, midway through writing *Scissors, Paper, Rock*, I realized that no gay character living in San Francisco in the 1980s could occupy the page without engaging the catastrophe of AIDS. I thought then—and I think now—that the greatest separation between persons arises not from race, gender, sexual identity, or even economic class but from the gulf that separates the healthy and the sick. I agonized as to whether I, an HIV-negative man, could conscionably write from the point of view of a character—Raphael Hardin—who knew in the most intimate way what it was to live with foreknowledge of an especially prolonged and brutal death, as the immune system deteriorated one T-cell at a time until the body became a petri dish for opportunistic infections. In the end I gave the manuscript to my partner, already ill, and asked for his frank opinion: Had I successfully imagined his life, his world? With his endorsement, I published the book you hold.

Afterword

It was the last book he read in its entirety. Four months later he was dead.

Astute readers have noted that the family tombstone includes the names of children whose stories are not told. Those stories live in my heart but are still, decades later, too intimate to see print. Those same readers have asked for the story of Nick, the tobacco farmer who appears at the family gathering and with whom Raphael makes love in the ancient apple orchard. Nick is the central character of a published story titled "Bad Habits," but in *Scissors* I wanted to focus on the immediate members of the Hardin family and Miss Camilla, their next-door neighbor. No matter where I placed Nick's story it felt like a digression—an outsider's intrusion into the family—and I did not want him to be a digression. The interested reader can find the published version of "Bad Habits" on my web page.

Scissors broke ground in subtle but notable ways. To my knowledge it is the first work of literary consequence to portray the intrusion of AIDS into a rural landscape. I have the remarkable Sisters of Loretto to thank for this inspiration. In the mid-1980s, when people spoke of AIDS in hushed voices, the Sisters constructed an AIDS memorial on the grounds of their motherhouse in rural Kentucky, honoring local men who had died of the disease. If they can do it, I can do it, I thought, and resolved to follow their courageous footsteps.

Published in 1993, *Scissors* was also among the first books in a late-twentieth-century revival of a tradition as ancient as the Gospels or Boccaccio and as American as Sherwood Anderson's *Winesburg, Ohio,* even if at the time it was seen as carving new territory: a novel composed of interconnected and interdependent stories, unified not by a dominant narrative line but by tones and themes. The form has never entirely disappeared, but Louise Erdrich's superb *Love Medicine* (1983) paved the way for its revitalization and served as my inspiration.

I light a candle of homage at the altar of the early James Joyce. I make no claims to be other than a devotee, but for anyone seeking to teach herself or himself how to write, I note that in writing the long central chapter of *Scissors*, I taught myself the intricate choreography of crowd scenes by propping open Joyce's *Dubliners* to its greatest story, "The Dead," and studying sentence by sentence how Joyce accomplished in fiction what choreographer George Balanchine accomplished on stage: the art of keeping attention focused on central characters and actions while secondary characters/dancers swirl about them and occasionally sweep them up.

The Hardin family picnic's setting is divided—as our mythologies divide the afterlife, as Joyce divides "The Dead"—into three distinct worlds: upper, middle, and lower. Joyce sets his primary action in the middle world, with the other worlds suggested mostly through sound—by the noise of dancing (upstairs) or the clink of cutlery (from the kitchen below). In *Scissors*, the music emanates from the outer reaches of the yard, the cooking noises from the kitchen inside the house. Joyce's Irish holiday spread is more lavish than the summer fare of the Hardins—Joyce grew up in a culture that better appreciated food—but his description is, well, mouth-watering and worthy of imitation. And in writing as in life, we learn through imitation, the sincerest form of flattery.

Scissors taught me—is this not why we write, why we read?—that the writing is wiser than I. My characters, and at times my narrative voice, made observations that had never occurred to me before their writing. In the opening chapter, "High Bridge,"

Tom Hardin chooses to remain holed up in his woodworking shop rather than apologize to his wife for leaving her alone and pregnant while he goes hunting. After he returns, Miss Camilla violates his sanctuary to tell him, "One way to know evil is that those who do it hide from what they have done. You are hiding, here, from what you have done." Across the years I have perceived the truth of her observation over and over (consider American foreign policy!), though when I wrote those lines of dialogue I was only searching, as every fiction writer searches, for the right words at the right time from the right character's mouth. When Joe Ray identifies memory as "the third agony" and says that the "best thing about memory is that it forgets," he gives voice to a profound truth that I have quoted many times since; though it is important to note that I am quoting not Fenton Johnson but Joe Ray Hardin, who like all children are of their parents even as they have lives and minds and memories of their own.

I have imagined that, for family and friends, reading *Scissors* is like entering a fun house of mirrors—they see something or someone they think they recognize, only noticing the broken shards and distortions on closer inspection. But from the first, Miss Camilla insisted on speaking in the first person. I tried squeezing her round peg into the square hole of third person, since every other chapter was in third person and that seemed consistent and appropriate, but she was having none of it. Finally I let her have her moment at center stage, as she had so richly earned: the spinster, the outsider, the watcher next door. She is the book's only genuinely autobiographical character: always and everywhere I have been the outsider, watching from the corner of the room or from next door.

As I write this afterword, more than two decades after the

book's first publication, I am seized with an uneasy sense of déjà vu—an epidemic virus that causes cancer, spread through means that include but may not be limited to sex? I might have written that sentence in 1984 about what later came to be called HIV—human immunodeficiency virus—except that this is 2015 and the acronym has changed its central letter—it's now HPV, and the angel who passed over my door in the 1980s has chosen to knock.

I write with a picc ("peripherally inserted central catheter") line in my right arm, used for delivering chemotherapy and saline fluids during the course of treatment for cancer caused by HPV, human papilloma virus, now understood to be the cause of most cancers of the body's openings—mouth, throat, cervix, anus. The treatments have been brutal, their outcome uncertain—success in 50, 66, or 80 percent of cases, depending on which doctor I listen to. I find myself not exactly in the position of Raphael, the HIV-positive son: at the time of the writing of *Scissors*, a diagnosis of AIDS was a death sentence, whereas I have odds to play. All the same, I am living with doctor visits, infusions, painful and debilitating side effects, violations of the body to uncertain ends, and the moment-by-moment understanding of mortality.

In the 1980s we had a cohort of vocal, angry activists who demanded the nation's attention and got results. Far from condemning those who shouted down Health and Human Services secretary Louis Sullivan when he spoke at San Francisco's Moscone Center, or those who blocked the Golden Gate Bridge, or who interrupted mass at St. Patrick's Cathedral, we should be issuing commemorative stamps and assembling those leaders still alive to receive Congressional Medals of Honor. They drew attention to a worldwide plague that was well established even as it was assiduously ignored by mainstream institutions. AIDS would inarguably have claimed millions more lives worldwide—straight and gay, women, men, and children of all races and creeds and nationalities—had those brave souls not acted up, had they not fought back.

I did not sit with those activists at the Moscone Convention Center. I did not help block the Golden Gate Bridge, though I was living in San Francisco at the time and could have joined either action. Instead I was at home, writing about the dying and the dead, about community and how we build it, about the families that we are given and the families we choose; instead I was writing *Scissors, Paper, Rock*. I leave to you the assessment of that choice.

We are all mortal on this fierce and fearsome Earth. How merciful are the ways and means of life, including most especially death! The writing of *Scissors*, and the suffering and deaths of many friends and family, taught me that death is the mother of beauty, to invoke Wallace Stevens's most memorable line, and that if we open our hearts to its lessons, suffering will teach us how to love.

I thank the members of my family who have so patiently accepted my occasional cadging of details from their lives and borne readers' assumptions, however mistaken, that I modeled the Hardin brothers and sisters on them, when in fact each is a fictionalized version of me. I thank the University Press of Kentucky for bringing this novel and its predecessor back into print. Like all my books, it represents an effort to teach myself how to love and, through writing, to convey what I have learned to others; for teaching and learning are the most erotic of acts.

Fenton Johnson

Acknowledgments

I wrote these stories and chapters with the generous support of the following fellowships and awards:

A Wallace Stegner Fellowship in fiction from the Stanford University Program in Creative Writing; a fellowship in fiction from the National Endowment for the Arts; the Joseph Henry Jackson Award, given to a California writer by the San Francisco Foundation; the *Transatlantic Review*/Henfield Prize, given by the Henfield Foundation; and a Nelson Algren Fiction Competition award, given by the *Chicago Tribune*.

For providing me quiet time in which to work, I thank the MacDowell Colony and its astoundingly wonderful staff, as well as Villa Montalvo Center for the Arts.

I thank Professor John L'Heureux for his invaluable guidance on earlier drafts of several of these stories and for his years of support and encouragement. Heartfelt thanks for their advice and patient listening to Larry Rose, Haney Armstrong, Bill Bradley, Melanie Beene, and Doug Foster; for their love and generosity, my patrons and friends Fred and Kathy Rose; for their hard work and suggestions, my agent Malaga Baldi and my editor Jane Rosenman; and for his long-standing hospitality Dr. J. Michael O'Neal.

No book is written in a vacuum, and it would be impossible to name the writers and people, past and present, whose intelligence has informed what is good in this work. But I take pleasure in acknowledging my debts to Wendell Berry, Anton Chekhov, Paul Gauguin, and James Joyce.

The Land We Dreamed: Poems
Joe Survant

Sue Mundy: A Novel of the Civil War
Richard Taylor

At The Breakers: A Novel
Mary Ann Taylor-Hall

Come and Go, Molly Snow: A Novel
Mary Ann Taylor-Hall

Nothing Like an Ocean: Stories
Jim Tomlinson

Buffalo Dance: The Journey of York
Frank X Walker

When Winter Come: The Ascension of York
Frank X Walker

The Cave
Robert Penn Warren

The Birds of Opulence
Crystal Wilkinson

CPSIA information can be obtained at www.ICGtesting.com
Printed in the USA
BVOW08s0030090116

432064BV00003B/3/P

9 780813 166568